HIGH PRAISE FOR CHARLES ATKINS AND
THE CADAVER'S BALL!

"A very skillful chiller."
—*Booklist*

"Intense and immensely entertaining."
—*Kirkus Reviews*

"Its chilling suspense all but shackled me to my chair."
—F. Paul Wilson, Author of
The Keep

"A savagely entertaining journey into the human mind and
heart from an author who knows the territory."
—Paul Levine, Author of
Solomon vs. Lord

"*The Cadaver's Ball*, a revenge novel par excellence with
surprises and tension enough for even the most exacting
reader of thrillers."
—Charles L. P. Silet for
Mystery Scene Review

"Fast scary fun!"
—Sarah Graves, Author of
Home Repair is Homicide

"A work of art in science."
—David Hodo, MD, *Journal of the
American Medical Association*

"A psychological thriller of the first order, this one
shouldn't be missed."
—Stephen Padilla for
New Mystery Reader

ANOTHER ONE

I glanced at the clock; it was five thirty. The television was still on with the sound turned down. I grabbed the remote and turned to the local news, which was just coming on with the early morning edition.

A woman reporter was running through the morning headlines. One in particular stopped me cold.

> This morning police discovered the body of a local nurse in the fens. The woman's identity is known but has not yet been released, pending notification of the family. This case is being treated as a homicide, although police are not yet willing to comment on the motive.

Perhaps it was the hour or my lack of sleep, but I had a sickening premonition that the nurse would turn out to be someone I knew.

Other *Leisure* books by Charles Atkins:

THE PORTRAIT
THE CADAVER'S BALL

RISK
FACTOR

CHARLES
ATKINS

LEISURE BOOKS NEW YORK CITY

To Harvey and Cynthia Atkins.
And to Laurie Duncan and Mary Ann Berube.

A LEISURE BOOK®

January 2009

Published by

Dorchester Publishing Co., Inc.
200 Madison Avenue
New York, NY 10016

Risk Factor is a work of fiction. Any resemblance to persons living or dead is purely coincidental.

ISBN 10: 0-8439-6085-X
ISBN 13: 978-0-8439-6085-3

Visit us on the web at www.dorchesterpub.com.

ACKNOWLEDGMENTS

The author wishes to thank the following for their support, guidance, and expertise: Gary Jayson, Ida Marls, Barbara Jayson, Sarah Colwell, John Porter, Lisa Hoffman, Marika Rohn, Ruth Cavin, Doreen Elnitsky, Ellen Ebbs, Donna Hanson, Donna Ford, Lydia Capuano, Steven Schneider, Lucille Janatka, Sandra Watt, Patricia Hacket, Stacey Rubin, Stacey Asip, Teri Leyh, Carol Cestaro, Sandy Bacon, Malcolm Bowers, John Karle, Larry Wight, Jane Odin, Irma Ross, Tony Leonardi, Sue Kociszewski, David Lowell, John Strauss, and the Thursday night writer's group—Alex Demac, Julia Knerr, Raina Sotsky, Jeffrey Boyd, Dolores Aguirre, Margaret and Colin Munro, Elizabeth Atkins, Robert Cassidy, Carmen Lopez, Rick Johnson, and Claire Hall.

RISK
FACTOR

PROLOGUE

"Double code!" Sheila Gray shrieked down the hall of the mostly sleeping inpatient psychiatric ward. "Call a double code! Somebody call a double code!" She backed away from the scene that confronted her. It couldn't be true, not here, not now, not Helen. Waves of nausea and fear threatened to overtake her and send her tumbling down on knees that trembled with surges of adrenaline. She mouthed the words, "No no no," like an incantation that might magically clear the horror that she faced.

It seemed like ages for help to arrive; in reality it was less than a minute before Hamilton 5, the inpatient adolescent unit of Boston's Commonwealth Hospital filled with excited interns, aides, security guards, medical students, and nurses. A double code was a rare event; it signaled that both a medical and a behavioral emergency were taking place. Clearly, this qualified.

There, by the locked door that led to the back stairwell, a young man who had been admitted with his first episode of what would likely turn into schizophrenia sat poised like some blood-soaked

1

Buddha over the motionless body of nurse Helen Weir.

"He has a knife," a white-coated intern observed.

A murmur went through the group, none of whom was prepared to move closer to the gory tableau.

"Garret," a nurse cooed, hoping to attract the motionless boy with her soothing tone, "put down the knife."

There was no response, and eyes shifted to the four security officers.

With more force than was necessary the blue blazer–clad guards swarmed over Garret Jacobs. They twisted the black-handled baker's knife from his grip and pulled him back and down to the floor. There was no struggle, but the boy's limbs were stiff as pipes.

Two nurses and an aide wheeled out a bed with leather restraints coiled at each of the corners. The guards hoisted the boy onto the bed. He lay unmoving, his clear blue eyes staring motionless into space. The nurses quickly fastened the restraints, tightened the straps, checked to make sure there was the proper amount of give, and then locked them down.

As they worked to restrain the boy, the collective attention shifted to the still-warm body of Helen Weir. A senior resident kneeled at the nurse's head and checked for a pulse or for some sign that life still beat within the crumpled body.

"I have no pulse," he said, and he pointed to a nurse. "Begin compressions. I need a crash cart, oxygen, and blood gases."

Taking refuge in the routine of a late-night code, no matter how futile, helped. A bed was ordered in the intensive care unit, and the residents, medical students, and nurses started IVs, checked blood gases, injected powerful drugs, and three times defibrillated using large jolts of electricity in an attempt to restart a stilled heart. The nurse who performed chest compression tried hard to focus on her task, to ignore the fact that Helen and she had worked together for over ten years. Tears streamed down her face as she pumped up and down on the lifeless body. Just last week they had gone out for afterwork drinks, they had laughed and reminisced about birthday parties that their now-grown children had shared. She tried to ignore the blood that clung to her gloves and drenched Helen's sweater. There was too much of it and it had already begun to thicken and gel like homemade preserves as they set.

The code continued for forty-five minutes, about fifteen longer than is usual. In the end, they were defeated, but they would always be able to say that everything that could have been done to save their colleague had been done.

The chief resident pronounced her dead at 3:00 A.M. He then proceeded to call the police, his attending, the medical examiner, and the hospital attorney.

Chapter One

The psychiatric emergency room of Boston's Commonwealth Hospital buzzed around me. It was 11:00 P.M. and I was wondering, not for the first time, why in God's name I had done this to myself. You would think that by now I would have learned to resist my more grandiose urges—guess I hadn't. So there I was, slogging through the paperwork for my fifth admission that evening. I briefly calculated the time that remained on my shift—nine hours, and then set up a fraction in my head to see how much was over and how much remained. It was a mental game that I played when I was on call. I don't know why, but knowing that I was two-fifths done with the night's entertainment was comforting.

A knock came at the door, followed by a head that popped in unbidden. "Dr. Katz." Billy the aide's tone was apologetic.

"You don't have to tell me," I answered, "another evaluation waiting to be seen?"

"You got it."

"Give me three minutes to finish this and I'll be out."

I reapplied myself to the task of completing the four-page preprinted admission form, and then I booted up the computer to enter the patient's orders. In some ways it was probably best that it was busy. Nights on call go much faster if you're seeing patients.

I signed my name to the triplicate form, left the relative calm of the tiny physician's office, and headed into the open area of the psychiatric assessment and triage unit, or PATU.

The PATU consisted of seven small observation rooms that faced out onto a common area. The staff, a psychiatric nurse and aide, lived behind a Plexiglas nursing station that included a split-screen monitor so that we could watch the activity in each of the rooms. Before me lay the efforts of my evening's work.

In cubicle one, huddled under her sheet, was Marisa Thomas, a frequent flyer who was crashing from her most recent crack cocaine and heroin binge. She had come to the emergency room threatening to kill herself and pleading to be admitted to a rehabilitation program. Unfortunately the state had limited drug rehabilitation beds and the few that existed were reserved for high-risk cases, such as pregnant women. At present, Marisa was fast asleep curled up in a ball beneath the flimsy breakaway sheets. In the morning she would be told there were no beds, but by then she would have had a chance to sleep, would no longer feel suicidal and would begin to feel the searing pangs of heroin withdrawal. She would be given a phone number for the methadone clinic and maybe a brief round of "We know you can do it." Then she would leave, get back out to the street, and hunt down her next fix.

Cubicle two contained Eddie Wauslausky, a forty-three-year-old man with a long history of chronic schizophrenia. He had been brought in by his caseworker and the police after they tracked him down. Eddie had stopped his antipsychotic medication two weeks ago and had been drinking steadily since. He became paranoid and barricaded himself inside his room at the residential motel where he had lived for the past twelve years. When they broke the door down, they found Eddie with no weapons surrounded by empty liquor bottles and ravaged boxes of Girl Scout Cookies. All the lights had been turned off and the sockets had been ripped from the walls. A point of concern was his single kerosene lantern and five gallons of fuel.

When I asked him why he had the lantern he told me, "I was camping. Is that a crime?"

"Why did you tear out the sockets?" I had persisted.

"They were leaking."

"Leaking what?"

"God, don't they teach you anything? Electricity, they leak all over the place. It pours out of the wires and into my brain. I don't want to be electrocuted. I didn't kill anybody."

Nestled in bed three was a bearded man the police had picked up walking on the highway in his bare feet. He had no identification, refused to give us a name, and sat on his bed mouthing words and gently rocking. His clothes were filthy and reeked of stale sweat and cigarettes, his blood alcohol level and urine drug screen had both come back negative. Whatever craziness he experienced was organic. When I had reviewed his case by telephone with my supervisor, Dr. Adams, he had said, "Sounds like a wanderer."

"Which is?" I had asked.

"There's a breed of schizophrenic who seems to wander from town to town. Although sometimes they stay in one place for years and you see them along the road walking and walking for hours on end. They resist treatment, and the minute they're out of the hospital they stop medication and get back to walking. A lot of them have religious or quasi-religious delusions."

"Like they're Jesus?"

"Exactly. There's a lot of John the Baptists running around too."

"So what should I do?"

"He's not talking about killing anyone or himself?"

"No, but his feet are in pretty bad shape. He's got an infected toe that should be treated before he loses it," I added.

"Think he's gravely disabled?" he asked, intoning one of the three catchphrases that can get you admitted against your will.

"He is."

"Then go ahead and admit him."

"I don't even know his name."

"Do it as a John Doe, and in the morning we can call around to see if anyone at the mental health center knows him."

Bed four was Colleen Finch, a platinum blonde

who had a profound urge to hurt herself as a way of psychic release. She came in after having overdosed on her antidepressant. She carried a diagnosis of borderline personality disorder—which basically meant that she was trapped between overwhelming emotions and a profound sense of emptiness. I had seen her before in the emergency room. The last time it had been after she had cut herself too deeply in the stomach with a kitchen knife. I remembered how she had argued with me, saying that she didn't want to be admitted to the hospital. "I do it all the time, what's the big deal? If you make me go into the hospital it will only make things worse."

She was probably right, but at the time I didn't see what choice I had. She had been in and out of the emergency room with an increasing frequency and an increasing severity of self-mutilatory acts. Something was brewing within her, and I didn't want to be the one to send her home to kill herself.

My fifth evaluation, Fred Granger, had already come and gone. Fred was a longtime patient at the local mental health center who frequently visited the emergency room when he needed somebody to talk to and couldn't get in touch with his therapist. He came in, spoke to the nurse for five minutes, had her fill out his paperwork to get his telephone reconnected and then he went on his way.

From the relative sanity of the nursing station I watched as my next evaluation was brought through the outer locked door. My heart sank as the triage nurse led a young girl back to the locked unit.

"Face of an angel," Carla Williams the psychiatric nurse stated, breaking into my reverie.

"What did she do?" I asked.

"Let me look." She ferreted through the triage paperwork. "Here it is. Jennifer Ryan, age thirteen, brought by police to E.D. after she attacked her mother. Mother stated, 'She's out of control.'"

I let out a sigh. This was no place for a child.

I went over to introduce myself. "Hi, Jennifer, I'm Molly Katz, Dr. Katz."

Her clear blue eyes sized me up. Her face was free of blemishes, but not of makeup. I tried to remember what my own daughter had looked like at thirteen. This girl should have been frightened, yet she appeared poised and out of place. Her clothes were clean and her red hair was tied back into a shiny ponytail. "I shouldn't be here," she stated simply.

"Let's see what we can do about that." And I led her back into the small interview office.

She looked around, taking in the avalanche of paperwork that spilled over the desk and the half-dissected Styrofoam cup that I had shredded while on the phone with an insurance reviewer earlier in the evening.

"So why are you here?" I started.

"My mother thinks I'm crazy or something."

"Why would she think that?"

"I have no idea." She made direct eye contact.

"Did the two of you fight?"

"All the time."

It was like pulling teeth. "What do you fight about?"

"Everything."

I tried to let a silence build, hoping that she would fill the space. Apparently she was fine with quiet and if I wanted the details I was going to have to dig for them. "Give me a for instance of a fight."

"She doesn't want me to do anything. I can't go out with my friends, she gets mad with what I wear, who I see, she doesn't like my boyfriend. I can't do anything."

"Did something happen tonight?"

"What do you mean?"

"Why would she bring you into an emergency room? Has she done that before?"

"She sent me to Riverton last year."

My ears perked up at the name of the private psychiatric hospital. "How long were you there?"

"Four, five days."

"Why did you go?"

"It's my mom, she thinks I'm this horrible person. She just wants me out of the way so she can . . ." She shook her head. "I don't know."

"What about your dad?"

"Long gone."

"Dead?"

"No, he's in Jersey. I tried to stay with him, but it didn't work out."

I tried to reconcile the normalcy of Jennifer's baggy jeans façade with the story that emerged in bits and starts. She looked older than thirteen, almost as if her sexuality had developed before her body had reached its full height. Her breasts were those of a woman, and I could imagine the effect that would have on the boys her age and older.

"Have there been other times in the hospital?" I continued, trying to flesh out any past psychiatric history.

"Just the one time. I was supposed to go to a day program, but it was a joke."

"Where was that?"

"Same place."

"Have you ever been on medication?"

Before she could answer, the phone rang. I picked up.

"Molly, it's Carla. I've got your evaluation's mother out here wanting to talk with you."

"Tell here I'll see her in another five minutes. Anything else out there?"

"Not yet, but the night's still young."

"Yes, and I'm getting older by the minute." I turned back to Jennifer, trying to regain my train of thought.

"That was my mom, wasn't it?" she broke in.

"Yes."

"I don't want to go into a hospital. You have no idea what those places are like."

"We'll see how things go. So what grade are you in?"

"Seventh."

"You like school?"

"It's okay."

"How are your grades?"

"Don't ask."

"That bad?"

She winced. "Not good. They're going to make me repeat."

"Has that ever happened before?"

"No, they came close last year. All that time in

the hospital really set me back. That's just what's going to happen now if you send me to a hospital. You'll just make it worse. You should see what it's like at school. Everyone goes to those places and they come back more screwed up than when they left."

"You have friends who've gone into psychiatric hospitals?"

"Yeah, it's weird; they, like, brag about it."

"Why do they go?"

"Stupid stuff, like, one girl tried to cut her wrists and they sent her away for two days, like that's supposed to make her better or something?"

"Doesn't seem like much, does it? What about you, do you ever feel so bad that you wished you weren't alive?"

"Sometimes."

"Have you ever tried to kill yourself?"

"Not serious. I tried to take some pills once, but nothing happened."

"How long ago was that?"

"Before I went to Riverton; that's why they sent me there."

"What kind of pills did you take?"

"Like, my mother's stuff. It was, like, Valiums or something."

"Did they pump your stomach?"

"Yeah, and there was that gross black stuff."

"It sounds serious," I commented, realizing that someone had thought her overdose dangerous enough to warrant gastric lavage followed by charcoal.

"I don't know."

"What about now? Do you sometimes think about killing yourself?"

"Sometimes."

"Do you think about ways of doing it?"

"Like taking pills or something?"

"How often do you think about stuff like that?"

"I don't know, every day maybe."

"Does it get worse when you and your mom fight?"

"Yeah, I just wish she'd mind her own business. I know she's going to try and send me away. It's like she just holds that over my head."

"I'm going to need to talk to her," I admitted, wondering how that would sit with Jennifer.

"Yeah, whatever."

"What I'd like to do is meet with her alone, just as we did and then the three of us will sit down and try to figure out what comes next."

She gave me a look that seemed resigned and too old for her face. "She's going to tell you that I do all sorts of stuff; none of it's true. She lies about me all the time."

"I'll keep that in mind." And I led her out to the row of bolted chairs in the common area. Her mother, who I judged to be around the same age as myself, was sitting tightly clutching her pocketbook.

"Are you the doctor?" she asked, getting to her feet and avoiding her daughter's gaze.

"Yes, I'm Dr. Katz, Molly Katz."

"I need to talk to you." Her eyes were red rimmed and I noted that a crumpled bit of tissue was caught in the latch of her worn black handbag.

Most striking was an angry red bruise that had blossomed on her right cheek.

"What are you going to tell her?" Jennifer asked, an accusatory edge coloring her words.

Mrs. Ryan looked straight at me. "I need to talk to you."

"Let's go into the office."

"I have a right to know what you're going to say. It's not fair. You can't believe—"

"Jennifer," I said, not wanting her to escalate in the emergency room, "it's like I said, I have to talk with your mother and then the three of us will sit down. I need to get all sides of the story."

"It's not fair." She gently stamped her sneaker-clad foot. "I want to hear what she says."

I shot the nurse, who watched the interaction from behind the Plexiglas wall, a warning look. "Carla, maybe you could sit with Jennifer and fill out the paperwork. At least we could get that out of the way."

"What kind of paperwork?" the teen demanded. "Is that to put me away?"

"No, we do it with everyone, it's just a bunch of forms."

Before she could argue or get more upset, I ushered her mother back into the interview office.

"She seems pretty angry," I offered, taking the chair opposite Mrs. Ryan.

"That's nothing, wait till she gets going . . ." She looked at me, sizing me up. "Do you have children?" she asked.

"Two."

She thought that over, was about to say something, and then changed her mind.

"So what's been going on?" I prompted.

She laughed; it sounded forced and a bit too hard. "What hasn't been going on?"

"What happened tonight? It must have been something serious to call the police."

"It's just too much. I can't handle her. Everything I say is wrong and she won't listen. She swears at me all the time, but that's nothing. It's when she starts throwing things and hitting . . . I can't handle her."

"Did something happen tonight?" I persisted.

"Yeah, I came home from work to find her and her seventeen-year-old boyfriend in my bed." She put her hand to her bruised cheek and pushed a stray lock of brittle blonde hair back behind her ear. "She's thirteen; she refuses to use birth control. I know she's using drugs. When she went into the hospital last year, they said she had been smoking pot, and God only knows what else she's using. I get calls from her teachers every week. They call me at work and tell me I have to go in for conferences, but how am I supposed to do that? I work as a teller; it's all I can do to hold on to my job and then I come home to *that*. They were naked in my bed. I couldn't believe what I was seeing. When I told him to leave she started to yell at me, like I was the one who was doing something wrong."

"How long has this been going on?"

"She hasn't done a thing I've said since she was ten, and God only knows how long she's been sleeping around. It just keeps getting worse. I'm scared to go to work in the morning because I have no idea what I'll find when I come home. She sneaks out at night; I have no idea where she is. I think she's at school and then I get a call to tell me that she never showed. Department of Social Services has been to the house, and they threaten to take away custody. Frankly, I wish they would. I'm sorry if this makes me a horrible person, but I wish someone else would take over. I can't handle her . . ." She looked down at her hands now twisted in the strap of her bag. "I can't take her home."

"Why did you call the police?" I asked, knowing that there had to be more.

"I didn't know what else to do. She wouldn't let the boy leave, she kept pulling him back, so I had to threaten statutory rape to get him out of there. At least I think he's her boyfriend. She's only thirteen; I don't know how many boys she's slept with. When she was eleven she had gonorrhea. I had taken her to see my gynecologist because she had just started to get her period and he told me that she had gonorrhea. When I asked her how she got it, she lied. 'I don't know how I got it. No, I've never had sex. He must be mistaken.' So like an idiot I believed her. That's the other thing, she lies constantly, to me, to her teachers, to her father. You never know what to believe. I can't trust a single thing out of her mouth. She even accused one of my boyfriends of touching her. He wasn't even around when she said it happened. If she makes a promise, she won't keep it. What am I supposed to do? Someone has to be with her twenty-four hours a day. And I have to work."

"So the boyfriend left and then you called the police?"

"She was out of control. I admit that I wasn't in the calmest of states. I told her to go to her room and she wouldn't. It's like she becomes an animal when she doesn't get her way. She started to come after me with a lamp and I got that away from her and then she just started hitting me. If she could have killed me, she would have. I dialed 911. I couldn't think what else to do."

"That was the right thing to do."

"I can't take her home." She pleaded, "You've got to admit her somewhere. I just can't do this anymore."

A vein throbbed on her forehead, and the lines in her face were taut and underlined with harsh dark shadows. For a brief moment I caught the image of her skeleton trying to leap out from under her skin. I wanted to tell her that it was going to be okay, but in my heart I knew that was a difficult statement to make. "Do you feel ready for me to get your daughter?"

"If we have to, but I won't take her back."

On one level I wanted to shake her and say, "You can't just abandon your child in the emergency room." On the other hand, if this had been my daughter and she had done these things . . . "I'll be right back."

Jennifer looked up as I came out of the interview room. "Can I go?" she asked.

"I'd like you to come in so that the three of us can talk."

"You're not going to let me go home, are you?"

"I think we should sit down and come to some decisions about what the plan will be."

I watched as the teen struggled to maintain

self-control. "What did she tell you?" Her voice crept up in pitch and tone. The crack- and heroin-addicted woman in bed number one responded by closing her door.

I said nothing and held the door to the interview room. As I waited for Jennifer to enter I looked around at the too-small space. Mother and daughter would be sitting almost touching each other. I felt the tension rise and rethought the strategy. "You know what," I said, "why don't we sit in one of the holding rooms." And I motioned for Beth Ryan and her daughter to follow me into cubicle number six.

The two of them sat at opposite ends of the cot while I stood against the wall by the door. Jennifer looked at the floor and her mother stared straight at me. None of us wanted to be there.

"We need to pull together some sort of plan," I started. "It's clear that things have gotten out of hand at home."

"What are you talking about?" Jennifer shot back. "What did she tell you?"

"The truth," her mother stated. "I just told her the truth."

"Like you even know what that is. You're just mad because I can get a boyfriend and you can't."

"You see," Beth said, looking at me for confirmation. "This is how a thirteen-year-old talks to her mother. Beautiful, isn't it?"

I felt myself sinking into quicksand. "Look, it's clear that the two of you have a lot of things to work out, but right now we have to figure out a plan that will be safe."

"Let me go home," Jennifer stated. "That's the only plan I want."

"How would you be able to keep yourself in control?" I asked.

"What are you talking about?" the teen shot back.

I looked at the growing bruise on her mother's cheek and I chose my words carefully. "The police report said that you were pretty upset and hit your mother."

"I never touched her. I told you she lies."

"Then how did I get this?" Beth Ryan asked, turning to look at her daughter. "Care to tell the doctor how this happened?"

"How should I know? Maybe you fell, maybe you hit yourself. Don't go blaming your problems on me."

"That's it," Beth Ryan stated, getting to her feet. "I just can't take this right now."

"What are you saying?" I asked.

"You have to put her somewhere."

"You bitch!" Jennifer erupted, and lunged for her mother.

Beth Ryan, apparently used to such a reaction, was on her feet and out the door.

Jennifer followed her into the waiting area. "You fucking bitch!" she shrieked, and hurled curses after her mother.

I looked across the nursing station at Carla, who had already pushed the panic button under the desk. Through the small glass window in the reinforced door that led out to the main emergency room I saw three security officers as they raced to our assistance. Jennifer had cornered her mother and appeared ready to strike. I tried to calm her down, but was prepared to grab her right arm, which was raised in a clenched fist.

"Jennifer, you've got to get under control," I said, as the guards pulled her away from her mother. The minute they touched her she began to thrash and to scream. My heart pounded in my chest as I helped the guards get her onto the restraint bed.

"What are you doing?" she yelled. "Noooo!" She kicked and spit at us as we held onto our assigned limb and proceeded to tie her down. "Help! Mommy, help!"

Once she was secured I turned to Carla. "Get her two milligrams of Ativan, ASAP."

"Coming up."

I turned away from the cursing girl and tried to find her mother. I couldn't imagine what the effect of watching her daughter placed into restraints would have been. "Where did the mother go?" I asked one of the security officers.

"I don't know."

I quickly checked the cubicles, thinking that maybe she had gone into one of them to get out of the way. But she was gone.

As Carla returned with the syringe full of tranquilizer, I told her, "I think the mother left."

Jennifer strained against the restraints and screamed as Carla injected her with the medication. "You bitch! You fucking bitch!"

Carla turned to me once she had given the shot, and in a voice that only I could hear, she whispered, "And who can blame her?"

CHAPTER TWO

"Mom, where are my sweats?" My son's voice bellowed up the stairs and intruded into my cocoon of sleep. I moaned quietly and turned over to look at the red LED readout on my clock radio. It was eleven-thirty on Sunday morning. My shift had ended at eight, and I was trying to give myself a few hours to recuperate. Josh, being seventeen, had figured that I had slept sufficiently, and with a basketball tournament this afternoon, which I was going to try to attend, his concerns were more focused on getting his gear together.

"Check the laundry room," I yelled back through my closed bedroom door.

"They're dirty."

"Then run a load of wash."

"There's no time."

I checked the clock again. "Your game's not till one. You can just make it."

"I know, but it's already after twelve."

"What are you talking about?" I muttered, swinging my bare legs out from under the warmth of my flannel sheets. "It's only eleven."

"You forgot to push your clock ahead."

"Oh." And I felt the vague regret of losing an

21

hour of my most precious Sunday. I stumbled to the bathroom and set about reviving myself. Last night's call in the emergency room clung to me; I half remembered bits and pieces that had re-worked themselves into my two hours of sleep. I kept thinking about the woman who had left her daughter in the emergency room. We had finally reached her by phone around three. We needed her permission to admit her daughter and she had dis-appeared before signing the various forms. There was also some question about her abandoning her daughter, which would trigger a report to the DSS—the Department of Social Services.

I dropped some rewetting solution onto my lenses, which I had forgotten to remove before passing out. I looked at my reflection and saw a thirty-nine-year-old woman with large brown eyes and a thick head of dark curly hair that had been frizzed and made lopsided by my restless sleep. I brushed my teeth and turned on the shower. As the warm water washed over me, I clung to the comfortable familiarity of being in my own home and of knowing that I had a few hours to spend with my kids. As much as possible the three of us tried to get together on Sundays. It was hard, and every week that passed made me realize how little time was left with my children. The face I had seen in the mirror was too young for this. Megan was a freshman at BU, and Josh was starting to field of-fers for basketball scholarships. In one more year, he would be gone as well. And unlike his sister, I suspected his sights were set on schools that were mostly out of state. His only requirement was that they had a top-ranked division-one team.

I toweled off and went in search of a clean pair of jeans, sneakers, and a sweatshirt. As I hunted through a pile of unfolded laundry a knock came at the door.

"Mom, are you up?" Megan asked.

"Come on in."

"Rough night?" she asked, handing me a mug of steaming hot coffee.

"God bless you," I said, marveling at the difference in our relationship now that she had been living away from home for the past eight months. As I drank in my daughter's appearance and the first dark bite of coffee, I couldn't help but make mental comparisons with the thirteen-year-old from last night. Megan was dressed in her usual baggy jeans and knit jersey. She had her father's blue eyes and her hair was a dark reddish brown, similar to the color of mine. In truth our auburn tints came from a bottle. "So how's school?" I asked

"Not bad, and you?" She perched on the edge of my bed with her long legs stretched out in front of her.

"Piece of cake."

"Yeah, right. So, I have to sign up for next year's classes by the end of this week," she offered.

"Do you know what you want to take?"

"There's not a whole lot of choice, if I'm going to stick with premed it's pretty much a done deal. I got the biology out of the way this year and if I don't screw up the midterms I'll be in good shape. So next year I need to do organic chemistry and physics."

"Hopefully your father's genes will serve you better with physics—that was not my subject."

"Yeah, but you made it through."

"Barely," I admitted. "If any one thing was going to keep me out of medical school, it was that."

"You must have done okay. I remembered you really struggling with it . . . so what did you get?" she asked, not for the first time.

"I'm not telling you," I said, not wanting to share my one inglorious C– with my daughter.

"Oh, come on."

"No, because you're going to get a better grade and I'll never hear the end of it."

"Probably," she admitted with a smile, "but I will find out."

"Don't count on it. Of course I did get straight A's in chemistry."

"Yes, I remember you telling me that on several occasions."

"Don't get fresh with your mother; she's ancient and cranky."

Before she could respond, my six-foot-four son bounded into the room. "I have no clean sweats." He was clearly upset.

"What are you going to do when you go away to college?" Megan asked her brother. "You know she's not going to be around to do your laundry."

"Mom," he pleaded, somehow expecting me to magically produce some clean gym gear.

"Sorry, can't you just wear jeans?"

"That'll look stupid."

"What about a pair of dirty ones?" Knowing my son's fastidiousness, I realized that would not be an option—of course where he got that particular trait was a mystery. I half suspected that my mother had initiated him into the strange cult of the anal-retentive while I was struggling through my first two years of medical school.

"They're all disgusting," he complained. "I can't believe there's no clean clothes anywhere in this house."

"Josh, I'm sorry, but you've got to keep track of this for yourself. Your sister's right, what are you going to do next year?"

"You mean they don't have someone to do your laundry?" he asked, looking at his sister.

"You've got to be kidding. There's a great big laundry room in the basement of the dormitory. If you're lucky you can find a machine."

"No way," he responded, not liking the picture she presented.

"Way, and then people leave their disgusting clothes all over the place and someone forgets to take their clothes out of the washing machine for days on end and they get all moldy and skanky."

"Megan, stop scaring your brother."

"She's kidding, right?" he asked in an anxious tone.

"Sorry, dear," I said. I was still not used to the ultrashort buzz cut he had started to sport. But then I reminded myself that some of his teammates had shaved their heads entirely. A few had their team logo picked out in a buzz-cut design. And as I often do being the proud mother of two teenagers, I thanked God for small favors. "Tell you what, Josh, on the way to the game we can stop at Marshall's and pick up a pair of sweats."

"Awesome, how about the Gap?"

"If you're paying?" I countered.

He looked at his sister. "Marshall's it is. But we got to go."

With a tinge of regret for the comforts of my unmade bed, I allowed myself to be drawn downstairs and out to the car. Over the past few years I had developed blinders to some of the key issues that had been central to my life. As a wife and mother (and how long ago that seemed) I had prided myself on a tidy home, tidy gardens, and tidy children. My mother's admonitions were given life in the body of my ten-year marriage. Mary Katz, born Murphy, brought me up with a strong helping of Irish-Catholic ethic, while she herself had committed the one fatal sin that effectively separated her from the rest of her family—she had married my father, a Jewish man from Dorchester.

As I took in the overgrown thicket that had once been my flower beds I reminded myself that it was time to call the lawn service. I knew that Josh could, and probably should, cut the lawn, but his life was focused on basketball and the all-important quest for a full athletic scholarship. I couldn't fault him for his single-mindedness; his accomplishments and sense of direction filled me with pride. But his basketball, like my decision to leave nursing and go back to medical school, were commitments that spread over our lives, leaving little time for housecleaning and mowing lawns. At this point, anything that I could afford to pay someone else to do, I did. And the other stuff . . . well, sometimes you vacuumed and sometimes you didn't.

We piled into my Honda, Megan up front and Josh sprawled across the backseat.

"You sure you wouldn't rather stop at the Gap?" Megan asked, throwing her allegiance in with her brother.

"I thought we were just getting a pair of sweats," I said.

"I wouldn't mind if we stopped at the Gap. You know I do make my own money now," she reminded me.

"How's that going?" I asked, referring to her ten-hour-a-week work-study position in one of the BU research labs.

"It's okay. They're letting me do more and more stuff. We're doing all these experiments on antibiotic sensitivities."

"I hope you're being extremely careful," I cautioned her, remembering how cavalier people could be in the microbiology labs.

"What are you guys talking about?" Josh asked.

"I grow bacteria and then try to kill them with different antibiotics."

"Gee, that sounds like fun," he sniped. "So, like, what happens if you drop something?"

"The world as we know it ends," she shot back. "Sad, perched on the edge of basketball stardom, Josh O'Connell, age sixteen—"

"Almost seventeen," he interjected.

"Almost seventeen, dead of bubonic plague. Tragic."

"All right," I said, having acquiesced and bypassed the discount outlet store for the more expensive, yet apparently de rigueur Gap. "We have eight minutes to buy a pair of sweats. Anyone not complete with their purchases will be left behind."

"Yeah, right," Megan said, already heading out of the car.

I followed behind, realizing what a pushover I was with my kids. At the same time I was incredibly thankful that they were both on track. Megan's last two years of high school had been hell. The two of us had had a series of fights that would leave me shaken for days. There would be doors slamming and her screaming that I just thought about myself and I didn't care about her. She'd accuse me of being a hypocrite and why couldn't she stay out with her friends until two in the morning on a weekend night? I thought it would never end. And then there were the boys. I think she deliberately went out of her way to bring home the most extreme examples of adolescent angst and rebellion. There was Mohawk Boy—which I thought had gone out of style in the eighties. There was the boy with the extensive facial piercings and the one who I found out had been arrested three times. But the episode that most made me want to kill my daughter was when she, without my knowing it, went to New York on a Saturday morning and came back with her tongue pierced. Her father accused me of being an unfit mother, even though it was his weekend to be looking after them. My own mother recited the familiar litany of my sins, if only I was home more and spent more time with my children these things wouldn't happen. Dad was the one constant support. My father is not one for long discourse, rather he cuts to the heart of the issue with an uncanny accuracy. His one comment was, "This will pass." He was right. About three months before she left for college something changed. The fights that blossomed out of casual comments vanished. She and I began to talk about different sorts of things. She asked me about the divorce and about my decision to go back to school. She talked about how scared she was going off to college and wondered about all the changes she would soon make. In hindsight I think we had to go through those two awful years, that it was all normal stuff. But the truth about raising a teenager is that as hard as it is on the kid, it can be worse for the parent.

I stayed outside the store watching my children shop. They both dwarfed the sales help; the Katz clan is a tall one. My ex-husband, James O'Connell, was six foot four and I'm an honest five foot nine.

I watched as Megan studied the discount rack and Josh flirted with one of the salesgirls. In fact, he was paying little attention to any sweatpants. And then I realized . . . I had been had. What was I thinking? Josh rarely used sweats for his warm-up, and when he did they were his team sweats with the AAU logo. I looked closer at the girl, who was blonde, fresh-faced, and possessed an enviable figure that was conveniently displayed in a horizontal striped jersey top and short denim skirt. A thin strip of exposed and impossibly firm abdomen peeked out from below her shirt. I looked at the two of them together, my son and this very pretty girl; he was smitten. Josh had always been something of a goof as far as girls were concerned. Up to this point his attention had been focused on the following: basketball, AAU, and the desire to get into a division-one team on a full scholarship. This was new. Competing emotions swept through me. He's too young, I thought. No he isn't, I countered. I'm too young. No you're not. At least she seemed to be interested in him. Her body language was open, the two of them were laughing about something, and the way she kept pushing her honey-blonde hair off her face were all indicators of attraction.

Megan looked up and caught me peering through the window. She gave me an odd expression and then turned to look at her brother. She smiled back at me and rolled her eyes in the direction of Josh. I realized she was not unaware of his interest in the Gap, and I suspected that I would be able to extract the details during the course of the game.

Megan grabbed a couple of knit shirts similar to the one Josh's salesgirl wore and brought them over to the register. She paid with cash and then pried her brother away from his love interest.

I met them as they exited the store. "So did you find some sweats?" I asked.

I watched as Josh's face turned a deep shade of red.

"She's lovely," I commented, unable to keep my mouth shut. "What's her name?"

"What are you talking about?" he stammered. "We're going to be late."

"The girl in the store," I persisted, as he disappeared into the backseat of the car.

"She's just a girl from school. We were just talking."

"That's nice, dear." And I shot Megan a look that let her know I would require a full account of the details.

"Are Grandma and Grandpa coming?" Megan asked.

"Probably."

"I was thinking of asking Grandpa if I could use him for a subject in the English paper I'm working on," she offered.

"He'd be delighted. What's it on?"

"We're supposed to write a biography and I thought I'd try to use someone I actually knew. Besides, it's a good chance to get a handle on his side of the family. I can never keep them straight. I remember growing up he used to talk about what it was like living in Boston and Dorchester when he was a kid—I think it could make a nice paper."

"He'll be thrilled."

"Can we invite them over after the game?" she asked.

I thought about the dust kittens that lurked in the corners of my home and of the mountainous pile of laundry that towered next to my washer/dryer. As I mentally surveyed the condition of my kitchen, I realized that I was not prepared to have my mother anywhere near my home, particularly on a Sunday. "I don't know about that," I said. "I'm not really up to cooking for anybody other than ourselves."

"What about Chinese?" Josh interjected from the backseat.

Thankful for the out, I rapidly acquiesced. And then I caught the look of collusion between Megan in the front seat and Josh in the back, and for the second time that morning I realized that my children played me like a violin.

CHAPTER THREE

Monday started with a bang. When I reached Hamilton 5, the inpatient psychiatric unit, I was met with the sight of a uniformed officer standing, or rather sitting, guard outside one of the rooms. Within minutes I heard the news that my patient, Garret Jacobs, had stabbed and killed a nurse and was scheduled to be transferred to a forensic facility sometime later today.

My office mate, friend, and fellow resident, Robert Jeffreys, took me aside and pulled me into our too-small office. There amid our paper-strewn desks and mismatched chairs I tried to let the information settle.

"It doesn't seem real," I blurted out. "How could something like that happen?" I looked up at Rob. "Who was the nurse?"

"Helen Weir."

"Oh my God. Her poor family. Jesus, how could we have missed this. He never gave me any indication of violence. He was just *really* psychotic." I felt like I should be doing something. But the harder I thought about what that something might be, the less clear it became. Waves of numbness washed through me. My knees wobbled and I had to sit. My thoughts boiled up fast and disconnected. I must have forgotten something, overlooked something. How could I have missed this? I need to look at the chart. This is the sort of thing that ends in lawsuits and here I'm not even out of residency. A burning guilt settled in my belly.

"It's not your fault," Rob offered, as though reading my thoughts. "It's a fact that the prediction of violence is a guess at best. There's no way you could have known. No one who worked with Garret saw this coming. These things sometimes just happen and we're all left trying to figure out why."

I tried to listen to his words of comfort, so like the ones I had given him last year when one of his patients had committed suicide. "How is he?"

"He's been in restraints since Saturday night."

"Why didn't anybody call me?"

He looked at me and smiled, his large hazel eyes shone with compassion. Not for the first time I noticed how young he looked with his round cheeks and unlined skin. It was a face that incited some of our older women patients, once they were feeling better, to give him pecks on the cheek and tell him how much he reminded them of their grandchildren.

"We're pretty low down on the food chain, Molly. I'm sure they went straight to Felix."

"Right. Have you seen him this morning?" I asked, dreading the thought of having to confront Dr. Felix Winthrop, the unit chief for the service.

"No, and the word is that we're going to be

34

starting rounds half an hour late because he's meeting with the hospital attorney."

"I want to see him," I said, getting to my feet and trying to move myself into some kind of action.

"Winthrop?"

"No, Garret. I can't deal with all of this unknowing. I've got to at least take a look at him."

"You sure that's a good thing?"

"Not at all." And I headed out the door in pursuit of my patient's chart. As I hunted through the racks behind the nurse's station I overheard snippets of conversation, all focused on the tragic event of Saturday night.

"Only a matter of time," one of the nurses commented bitterly. "Something like this was bound to happen. It's a fact, they just don't care about us."

"It's true," her colleague replied, as she counted and arranged pills onto a tray of white paper cups. "After every downsizing there's fewer of us and more of them. I really should have gone into administration."

"Not too late."

"No, I think I'll wait till the nursing shortage makes it to a crisis level and then I'll become a union organizer."

"I'd join."

"We could really use one. This kind of stuff just shows how vulnerable we are, and no one seems to care. Although after this I'm sure there'll be all sorts of wonderful gestures."

"Yeah, right, for about two weeks and then it will be back to business as usual."

I tried to focus on the charts but I couldn't find

Garret's. "Excuse me," I said, "have either one of you seen Garret Jacobs's chart?"

They turned and looked at me. "You're his resident aren't you?"

"Yes." I felt the heat of their scrutiny.

"You're the one who used to be a nurse?" the taller of the two commented.

"Yes."

"What do you think about all of this?"

"It's horrible," I stammered, wishing that I had stayed in the safety of my office. "Have you seen the chart?"

The other nurse spoke up. "They took that away first thing this morning. I'm sure they're poring over it line by line as we speak."

"Who is?"

"The lawyer, Dr. Winthrop, whoever else gets involved in these kinds of things. When this hits the papers the hospital is going to need to do some major damage control."

"You mean it hasn't come out yet?"

"Not yet. But it will. Although I'm sure they would love to keep it all hush-hush."

"Do you think I could go in and see Garret?"

"I don't see why not," the first one said. "You are his doctor."

"Right." I was his doctor, and right now I wished that I wasn't. I turned away from the station and headed toward the room with the uniformed officer. "I'm Dr. Katz," I told him. "I'm Garret Jacobs's resident." I was prepared for some sort of objection, but the officer seemed satisfied with my credentials and allowed me in.

Once inside, I stopped. There before me, manacled in four-point leather restraints, lay a motionless seventeen-year-old boy. His cornflower-blue eyes stared fixedly at the ceiling, and a bit of crusted drool had coagulated in the corners of his mouth.

"Garret," I said, "it's Dr. Katz."

He didn't respond and I moved closer. His stillness was so complete that I caught myself staring at his chest, wanting to reassure myself that he was still breathing.

"Garret, it's Dr. Katz." Nothing, there was no acknowledgment of my presence, no flicker of the eyes, nothing. He was catatonic. How had he gotten to such a state?

When I had admitted Garret to the hospital over a week ago, it was clear that he was having a psychotic decompensation. His mother had come home to find her son, a senior in high school, standing on the roof of their home convinced that he was receiving messages from God. At his evaluation he had rambled incoherently about the face of God and about secret messages that had been implanted in his brain. As I had questioned both him and his mother, it became clear that something had been developing over a period of months, where he was sleeping less and less and acting increasingly bizarrely. His schoolwork had deteriorated and his mother described a series of sessions with the school's guidance counselor and psychologist where they had questioned if Garret might be doing drugs.

Garret's inpatient workup had been fast and aggressive. I thought about my own son and about how devastating this must be for his mother. We checked his blood and urine for drugs—they came back clean. We did a CAT scan of his head—also normal. We ran a full series of bloodwork that provided no clue, no hint of anything other than what we had suspected from the beginning. This was Garret's first psychotic break; chances were that this was the manifestation of schizophrenia or of some variant of manic-depression. That he was so young and so symptomatic were not good prognostic signs. And now this . . .

I walked around the bed to see if he would track me with his eyes. He stared at the ceiling, or perhaps he was focused on some other point either inside his head or in some other dimension that only he could appreciate. With catatonia I was never certain if it was the absence of thought or an overload of thought.

"Garret," I said into the hollowness of the space. "I'm going to touch your hand and try to move it." Gingerly I reached out for his manacled right hand. I first checked his pulse to ensure that the restraints were allowing for adequate circulation and then I attempted to reposition his fingers. There was a steady, leaden resistance to my attempt, but as I applied a bit more pressure the fingers moved and then remained where I had maneuvered them. He had waxy flexibility, a textbook feature of catatonia that I had never witnessed firsthand. I immediately thought of getting Rob, to show him, and then realized that this was neither the time nor the place for such clinical enthusiasm. "Can you hear me at all?" I asked, listening to the sound of my voice as it bounced off the hard white walls. There was no response, but the quiet of the room and of my patient allowed my thoughts to slow. In his present state he looked young and incapable of the horror that he had perpetrated. Still, from what I had gathered there was little doubt as to his guilt; the larger question was why did he do it? What demon had caused him to act in such a way? I wondered if I would ever find out.

As I pondered the mysteries of Garret's disordered thoughts, my pager sounded. The readout showed the number for the nurse's station; it was time for rounds. Reluctantly, I left my patient, and filled with a sense of dread anticipation, I headed down to morning report.

CHAPTER FOUR

The air crackled with unspoken tensions as Dr. Felix Winthrop attempted to move forward with morning rounds. The nurse administrator, Carol Petrullo, clasped her metal clipboard firmly and went through the motions of business as usual. No one was fooled. The usual banter and Monday morning jokes were absent. There was no half-eaten box of donuts, and as I looked around the large group room with its bank of windows and Magic Marker murals that had been drawn by the adolescents, I caught nervous glances and more than a few pair of red-rimmed eyes among the staff.

"It's going to be difficult," Dr. Winthrop admitted. "We've had a tragic occurrence on the unit that has affected everyone in this room. But we also have a ward full of patients who may have been traumatized by the events of Saturday night. We somehow need to take care of one another but still get on with the work that we're all here to do." He paused and looked around at the twenty or so nurses, social workers, aides, house officers, and medical students who sat attentively in their folding chairs. "It might make sense if we started with a moment of silence for Helen Weir."

I felt for him as he struggled for the right tone to help get his shell-shocked staff back on target. I thought about Helen, whom I knew peripherally, in the way that I knew most of the nurses on the unit. When I had applied for residencies I deliberately avoided programs that would have put me in contact with hospitals where I had been employed as a nurse. Still, with all the mergers, downsizings, right-sizings, buyouts, etc., that had swept through the pantheon of Boston hospitals, it was impossible to avoid my past. Not that I was ashamed of it, more that I was trying to have a fresh start. For a time Helen and I had worked for the same visiting nurse association. I'd see her at inservices and meetings; sometimes we would cover for each other's days off. I thought about Garret and tried to imagine what could have possessed him to kill her. Had she turned into someone, or been a part of some delusional fantasy? And there were all the other questions that I hoped would be answered: most important, how had a patient managed to get a knife onto the unit?

Dr. Winthrop looked across at Carol and nodded.

She cleared her throat and began to speak. "The funeral is Thursday morning. I've made arrangements to get nursing coverage from the medical floors so that anyone who wants to attend the service can. The secretaries are collecting for flowers and . . ." She stopped as a surge of emotion choked her. She tried to push down the tears; it didn't work.

Dr. Winthrop picked up. "This is going to be a very hard day. Carol and I have arranged for counselors to be available either by phone or on the unit for any staff who wishes to speak with somebody. It's probably a good idea for people to block out an hour either today or tomorrow to go and talk with a counselor. Again, we will do whatever is necessary to ensure that there's coverage. Also the employee assistance program is aware of the situation, and if people would prefer to go that route, that's another option." His dark eyes scanned the assembly.

"Garret Jacobs will be transferred today," he continued, "hopefully this morning. Are there any questions? There will be significant opportunity to review the incident, so don't feel that we have to get through everything right away."

No one spoke up, and I don't think that it was for lack of questions.

Carol broke the silence by pushing her clipboard forward on the table. She held it tightly in both hands and flipped it open. She took a deep breath. "Let's start with the green team. Who has Ashley?"

There was comfort in moving to the routine of treatment planning. One by one we reviewed the patients on the adolescent unit and then moved on to the adults who occupied the other half of the floor. There was little discussion of the cases; no one had the heart to engage in debates over whether or not to raise a patient's lithium or to try a newer mood stabilizer.

As we approached the end of the stack, a knock came at the door. The nurse closest to the exit opened it to reveal a tall, well-built man in a dark gray suit and Sonja Aaronsen, the hospital's attorney.

Felix excused himself and went out into the hallway with the attorney and her companion.

"Something's up," I commented under my breath to Rob.

"No doubt," he agreed, matching my tone. "This is going to be a very interesting day."

"Old Chinese proverb, 'Pity the man who lives in interesting times.'"

"Very true."

Dr. Winthrop returned closely followed by the thirty-something lawyer and the stranger. We watched as Winthrop returned to his place at the back of the room next to Carol. "I think many of you know the hospital's attorney, Ms. Aaronsen, and this is Lieutenant Harris with the Boston police. They'd like to say a few words."

"Thank you, Dr. Winthrop," Sonja said. "I'm sure this is a very difficult time for everybody, but because of the nature of the incident there will be a police investigation in addition to the hospital's own internal process. Lieutenant Harris is with the Major Crime Squad and will want to talk with members of the staff, as well as with some of the patients. I am hopeful that this will not be a lengthy process and that we can get through it and move on to the work of taking care of our patients."

As I sat listening to this well-groomed woman in her dark-green Saks Fifth Avenue suit and perfectly pressed cream silk blouse, I found myself hearing little criticisms. I looked at the broad-shouldered man behind her and wondered what he made of her comments. His expression was unreadable.

As Sonja stepped back the lieutenant spoke up. "I'd like to echo Ms. Aaronsen's remarks. This has got to be a very painful time for everyone in this room." His voice was deep and calming. "I know what it's like to lose a colleague." His dark blue eyes made contact with each person in the room. When it was my turn I found myself caught in his gaze. I thought I saw the hint of a smile and then he had moved on to Rob. I wondered what he was looking for. Was it just a question of wanting to connect with each person, or was he looking for something?

As he stood there about to speak, letting the silence build, I felt there was a deliberateness to his manner. I also caught myself looking for the telltale wedding band on this tall man with his full head of salt-and-pepper hair and well-groomed mustache.

"I assume that most of you have had little interaction with the police," he continued. "I think I'll refrain from asking for a show of hands as to how many of you have been arrested."

A few titters of nervous laughter.

"My crew and I are very aware that this is a hospital and that you all have important work to do. We'll try to keep our inquiries down to what's absolutely necessary. Already we've taken statements from everyone who worked on the unit Saturday night. Today we want to speak with the rest of the staff. Ms. Aaronsen has kindly agreed to be present for all of those interviews." He paused. "Any questions so far?"

There were none.

"We'll also interview some of the patients who were here over the weekend. I'm aware that individuals on this ward have emotional problems and so we'll do everything in our power to not upset them further. Again, I know this is a hard time and we'll make every effort to keep the disruptions to a minimum."

He stepped back, looked at Sonja, and in a voice that could not be overheard, said something. She leaned across to the seated Dr. Winthrop and whispered in his ear. Satisfied that the message had been communicated, the attorney and the lieutenant left.

As the door closed behind them, a silence settled in the room. The clicking of the head nurse's clipboard finally broke it. "Okay," Carol said, as she tried to decipher the handwriting from last night's charge nurse. "Who's got Billy Keene in 513?"

Rob whispered to me under his breath, "Why do I get all the baby sociopaths?" And then so that Carol could hear, "That would be me."

Chapter Five

"Your turn," Rob said as he exited Dr. Winthrop's office, which was occupied by the police lieutenant and the hospital attorney.

"Great," I said, trying to keep a handle on my competing anxiety and curiosity.

"It's pretty benign," he offered, as he debated whether he would head to the nursing station and start on his notes or take a quick jaunt down to the cafeteria for the coffee and donuts absent from morning rounds.

"Thanks. Am I just supposed to go in?"

"Yup." And he veered toward the back stairwell in pursuit of nourishment and caffeine.

I knocked and a man's voice answered, "Come on in."

It was strange seeing the familiar chaos of Felix's office, with its avalanche of papers, charts, and reprints, now occupied by the immaculately groomed attorney and the police lieutenant.

"Dr. Katz, is it?" the lieutenant asked.

"Yes, Molly Katz." I took the seat closest to the door.

"As I understand it," he said, "you are Garret Jacobs's student physician?"

"Resident physician," I corrected him. "We do have medical students but not on the adolescent side."

"I see. So where does that put you in your training?"

"I have one more year to go."

"I understand you're also a nurse. That must be quite a balancing act."

"I was a nurse," I explained. "I haven't worked as a nurse since my last year of med school."

"How come?"

"(A) I have no time, and (B) I can make more money moonlighting as a doctor than I can picking up per diem work as a visiting nurse."

"That makes sense." A smile broke over his full mustache. "Basically, this is just an information-gathering interview. I'd like you to tell me everything that you can think of about Garret, his admission, anything that might help us understand what happened here."

I looked at Sonja. "Can I do that?"

"In cases like this, it's best."

"What about patient confidentiality? Plus, he's a minor."

"This is a murder investigation," she explained. "You do have a choice, but as the hospital's attorney I think it's in everyone's interest to cooperate fully with the investigation."

I thought about the catatonic boy in his room across the hall and then I thought of Helen Weir. "What would you like to know?" I offered.

"If you could start at the beginning," the lieutenant coached. "How you met Garret, that sort of thing."

I smiled at his use of the word *met.* "I admitted Garret over a week ago. Could I see the chart?" I asked, looking at the blue notebook-style hospital record on the desk behind the attorney. Sonja reached back and handed it to me.

"Thanks." I flipped it open to my admission note dated April 1. I suppressed a comment about April Fool's Day and quickly reviewed what I had written. I summarized the history that I had taken from his mother. I watched as the lieutenant nodded and took an occasional note. As I spoke, I remembered how drawn and anxious Sandra Jacobs had appeared the day her son had been admitted. I couldn't imagine how I would feel in her place.

"Was there a history of violence?" the lieutenant asked.

"Not that I recall. According to his mother, he had always done well at school up until about a year and a half ago. There was no mention of conduct problems. In fact, things seemed to go in the other direction. Garret tended to stay by himself and didn't have a whole lot of friends."

"Any history of fire-setting?" he asked, keying into one of the red flags that might indicate a predisposition toward conduct disorder and sociopathy.

"No, and there were no abnormal developmental issues like protracted bed-wetting or feces smearing. No cruelty to animals or documented learning disorders. In fact, prior to this year he had no contact with anyone in the mental health professions."

"So he just out of the blue became psychotic?"

"Unfortunately, that's how it happens. We see a

fair number of adolescents and young adults who present with their first episode of psychosis."

"Why doesn't it get picked up earlier?"

I tried to explain. "It may not be there earlier. Both schizophrenia and the psychosis that can be associated with manic-depression typically don't appear until the late teens and twenties. There are a lot of theories as to why this is but no one really knows. Some people are making a case for a prodromal syndrome, characterized by odd behaviors and social withdrawal. Maybe that's what Garret was showing over the past year or so."

"So Garret's case was typical?"

"Unfortunately, yes," I commented, while taking note of how very blue the lieutenant's eyes were.

"Now you said in your evaluation that he had"—and he flipped back through his notes— "'Psychosis NOS.' What is that?"

"It means psychosis not otherwise specified. It's a diagnosis you use when someone is clearly psychotic and you don't know why. At the time I admitted Garret there was some question as to whether this could have been drug-induced, or perhaps his presentation was the manifestation of some nonpsychiatric organic process."

"Such as?"

"A variety of possibilities," I replied, feeling like a medical student being pumped on the top ten causes of kidney stones. "Different illnesses can present with psychosis as a symptom, like lupus, or a brain tumor, or various endocrine abnormalities."

"I see, and did he have any of those?"

"No. We ran bloodwork and did a brain scan, but nothing was abnormal."

"So then at this point, what would his diagnosis be?"

"It's likely some form of schizophrenia."

"I see." He sat back in his chair. "Now, since he was admitted it sounds like he's had some pretty bizarre behavior."

"True. When he first came in he was profoundly delusional and was hearing voices."

"What kind of voices?"

"He was hard to understand, his words jumbled out, but there were a lot of religious themes. He talked about God and about secrets that had been dug into his brain. He was pretty intense."

"Were you frightened of him?"

I thought back to my first interview with the wild-eyed Garret. I remembered that I had moved my chair back further than I might usually do and that I had kept the outer door to my office open. "I don't know if it was fear," I hedged, "but a sense that he was very frightened and very psychotic and therefore I didn't know how he would respond. I was *careful* around him."

Lieutenant Harris nodded as I spoke. "At a couple of points in the chart the nurses described him as 'agitated.' What did they mean by that?"

"Let me see." I flipped through the blue progress notes, trying to find the passages. "Here's one." I read the brief entry out loud. " 'Client continues to respond to internal stimuli, needed to be room-restricted after he became agitated in the dayroom. Given prn Haldol 5 mg and Ativan 2 mg with good response.' I'm trying to remember what happened. There were a couple small incidents with Garret. When he first arrived, I think because he was frightened, he picked up a chair in the dayroom and threatened to throw it at another patient. That's probably what the note is referring to."

"What was the other incident?" Lieutenant Harris asked.

"That was less of an incident and more of a behavior. It must have been last Wednesday or Thursday." I searched for the corresponding note in the chart. "He had gotten into this pattern of walking back and forth down the main hallway talking to himself and making these odd gestures. At first no one thought anything about it, but it went on for hours and he kept walking faster and faster and seemed to be more agitated as he went. When we tried to redirect him and get him to stop, he wouldn't. Eventually we had security come and we room-restricted him."

"Would you say that his actions were purposeful?" the lieutenant queried.

"In what way?"

"From what you described it sounds like Garret was capable of a sustained purposeful action."

"I don't want to split hairs," I said, feeling uncomfortable with the direction this was taking. "Oftentimes with schizophrenia you get idiosyncratic behaviors that can be sustained for a very long time. It's not always clear as to what purpose they serve . . . if any. It could be something obsessional or it may just be a way to try and calm down. I think that with Garret's walking it was probably more the latter. Like a small child who rocks back and forth when they're upset."

"You said he was making motions. What kind?"

"He was waving his arms and that's what finally made us decide that it had to stop. We were concerned that he might knock someone over or accidentally hit someone."

"So he was put in his room. How were you able to keep him in?"

"We use a lockable Plexiglas door. That way we can see in and they don't feel quite so isolated."

"I see." He sat back in his chair and looked across at me. I met his gaze and waited. "On Saturday night you were on call?"

"Yes," I admitted, surprised at his level of information.

"So you would have been one of the first to know about the murder?"

"No. I didn't find out until this morning. I was on call in the emergency room. There would have been another resident on call for the floors."

"I see." He looked back in his notepad. "So that would have been Dr. Botwan?"

"Exactly. Raj was covering the floors and I was in the ER. There's about twenty of us that rotate through the two schedules. So basically I'm on call somewhere every tenth night."

"Still," the lieutenant persisted, "don't you find it odd that you weren't called? It seems like a major event and the patient in question was yours."

"I thought about that," I admitted, "but if I

were in Raj's shoes I'm not sure how many people I would have called."

Sonja cleared her throat. "It was no accident," the attorney commented. "When I was called at the time of the incident, I specifically instructed the house staff as to who needed to be informed. That I didn't have Mr. Jacobs's resident called was an oversight on my part."

The lieutenant nodded at that piece of information. "That explains that, but there's still the bigger question of how did a ten-inch knife find its way onto the unit."

"Serrated or nonserrated?" I blurted out.

The lieutenant smiled and the attorney shot me a warning look.

"Why would you ask that?"

Suddenly, I realized that I had stepped into a realm that was potentially risky for the hospital. But having made the comment, I didn't know how I could gracefully back out. "I was just wondering," I backpedaled, wishing that I could have kept my mouth shut.

"Are knives ever kept on the unit?" he persisted.

I looked at the attorney, whose face had hardened into an expressionless mask.

"Yes," I answered simply.

"What are they used for?"

"It's sort of fading away. But they used to do a weekly family meeting on the unit where the patients and the staff would prepare a meal in the dayroom. Since the stays have been getting shorter and shorter and the patients are more acute, we don't do it that often. Usually we just get coffee and pastries from the kitchen when the families come."

"So there are knives just lying around the unit?" he asked incredulously.

"No. They're kept with the other sharps in a locked box."

"Could you show me where that is?" he asked.

I looked at Sonja.

"Go ahead," the attorney said, clearly unhappy with the direction this had taken.

"They're kept in the nurse's station," I said getting to my feet.

As I opened the door of Dr. Winthrop's office I was met by the sight of two police officers and two ambulance attendants wheeling Garret Jacobs down the hall toward the outer door. I looked at my patient as they passed. He was securely re-strained to the ambulance stretcher, his eyes were wide open and fixed on the ceiling. Again, I was struck by how young he looked. I stood there in the doorway and felt sad, and something more, I felt an acute sense of failure.

"Dr. Katz."

I turned at the sound of a woman's breathless voice calling out my name.

It was Garret's mother, Sandra. She looked away from her son as they moved him out through the unit door. She was neatly dressed, but her sandy blonde hair was uncombed and had been hastily tied back. Her face was free of makeup and her eyes were puffy from crying. She stood by the door looking at me and then glancing back at her son as the door closed behind him and he van-ished toward the bank of elevators. She couldn't decide what she was supposed to do, so she stayed rooted to the spot.

"Excuse me," I said to the lieutenant, not offering the opportunity for him to object. I went over to Sandra Jacobs, not certain of what I was supposed to say. "I'm so sorry," I offered.

"He's sick," she stated simply. "Don't they know that?"

"They'll do assessments," I said trying to offer reassurance. "They'll have a psychiatrist examine him."

"But what will happen to him? Look at him. Can you imagine what will happen to him in prison?"

It was a scary thought and one that I had not considered.

"They're going to kill him. Somebody's got to do something," she whispered, with her hand to her mouth. She bit down on the crook of her index finger in an effort to keep herself from crying. "What am I supposed to do?"

I didn't know and I put my hand on her shoulder.

"You've got to talk to them."

"To whom?" I asked.

"Where he's going. You can do that, can't you?"

"Yes," I said, not really certain if that were true or not. I had little experience with forensic psychiatry and didn't know what the rules were around patients at Whitestone Hospital. But then again, it was fairly standard for a doctor from one facility to communicate with a doctor at another about a transferred patient.

"You've got to help him," she pleaded. "He's

not a bad boy." And the tone of her voice let me know that in some ways she still thought of Garret as a child. "He's just sick," she repeated. "He needs help."

I glanced down the corridor at Sonja and Lieutenant Harris, who were waiting for me to show them knives. "I'll try to talk with someone at the forensic hospital. I'll see what I can do."

"Thank you," she said in a disconnected voice as she stared at the floor.

"I have to go now."

"Yes."

And I left her there, against the nursing station, lost in thought. The lieutenant and Sonja met me in the hallway.

"Sad," he commented, while looking in the direction of Sandra Jacobs as she slowly made her way out of the unit.

"It must be horrible." Without knowing why, I asked him, "Do you have children?"

"One." He offered no further information.

"I can only imagine what she's going through. Do you know what will happen when he gets to Whitestone?" I asked him.

"They do an intake," he said. "They'll have at least one psychiatrist and probably a psychologist take a look at him. The judge is going to need to know whether or not he's competent to stand trial."

"That should be pretty obvious," I commented.

"Maybe," he said.

"Garret's catatonic," I replied. "You can't get him to look at you, let alone talk."

"Couldn't that be faked?"

"I don't think so," I said, feeling defensive. "Particularly with the degree of accuracy that he displays. Unless he's been studying psychiatry it's a pretty odd symptom to fake. From what little I know about malingering psychiatric symptoms, people usually try to fake hallucinations and delusions."

"True," he agreed. "But you said Garret has both of those. Isn't it possible that he's just taking things one step further?"

"It's possible. I just don't think so."

"You're probably right," he conceded, "but it's important to keep an open mind . . . you were going to show us the knives?"

"Right." I led them down the hall and back behind the nurse's station. I asked the clerk for the key to the sharps box. She reached under the counter and pulled it out from its hiding place. I then proceeded to unlock the small safe where all of the patient's razors, etc., along with the knives and other kitchen implements for the cooking group were kept. I removed the black metal box that contained the knives, set it on the counter, and opened it. Inside were two small paring knives, a French knife, and a large serrated bread knife. I was about to reach inside when the lieutenant stopped me.

"Don't touch them," he said, and he pulled out a pair of latex-free disposable gloves.

I looked in at the contents and compared them to the inventory list taped to the inside cover of the box. "Nothing's missing," I said.

The attorney let out a relieved sigh. "Good."

The lieutenant looked through the contents of the box. "Hmm," was his only comment as he rechecked the inventory list against the actual items. "Where do these come from?" he finally asked.

"Don't know," I said. "Probably the kitchen."

"Makes sense. So the key is kept under the counter like that?"

"Yeah."

He looked at the attorney. "You might want to do something about that. So basically anyone who knows where the key is kept could get into the box."

"But then they'd have to come behind the counter and open the safe," I explained, feeling as if I had to defend the unit. "And besides, everything is in there."

"But late at night," he said, deep in thought, "there's much fewer staff."

He had me there, and I could picture how a patient who had observed the hiding place could come behind the counter, open the safe, and take whatever he or she wanted.

"But everything's there," I persisted.

"True." But it was clear as he hung onto the metal box and proceeded to write out an evidence tag that something about it wasn't exactly right.

Chapter Six

It was a hard feeling to shake, but this entire wretched Monday had been like a trial where I stood accused. After the morning's interview with Lieutenant Harris and Sonja Aaronsen I was summoned to a noon peer review, my first as a physician. Over the course of my years as a nurse I had participated in several peer reviews, but always as someone who provided information and not as the one who was being investigated for possible negligence or poor judgment.

It was held in the administrative conference room on the eighth floor. Normally Felix would have led the proceedings, but as he was the unit chief for Hamilton 5, that would have been a conflict of interest. In fact, as the unit's attending, he carried the ultimate responsibility for all of the patients. If I had screwed up, he would be blamed. So for one of the few times in my three years as a house officer I actually got to see the department director, Harold Schlessinger.

Dr. Schlessinger was a ghost presence in the department. As a younger man he had done extensive research in the field of behaviorism and had quickly climbed the ranks and become a tenured professor by his fortieth birthday. He had been the department director for over ten years, and as far as any of us could tell, he now did very little. He hadn't published in over a decade and he was rarely seen on the wards or in the clinics. His silver-haired presence at the peer review was not a promising sign.

We were seated around the massive Honduras mahogany coffee table. Copies of Garret's chart were passed around, and attached to them were two additional pieces of paper. One was a disclaimer that included a description of peer review and the more current *sentinel event*; the latter referred to any serious untoward event that befell a patient while in our care. Anything that was considered a sentinel event had to be aggressively investigated and reported to the agency that accredits hospitals. This was indeed serious business. The second attachment was a blank form that included a section for the assembled physicians to vote on the severity of any perceived clinical breach. The categories ranged from "No untoward outcome with no deviation from the accepted standard of care," all the way down to "Major untoward outcome with significant deviation from the accepted standard of care." Below that section was a lined area headed up by the statement "Proposed corrective or disciplinary action."

I looked across the table at my classmate Raj Botwan, who had been the resident on call for the wards Saturday night. He attempted to smile, but the strain showed on his face. Likewise, one of the night nurses who had tried to resuscitate her murdered colleague had been asked to attend.

The rest of the participants were physician members of the faculty.

"Let's get started," Dr. Schlessinger said, peering down at the printed pages through his bifocals. "We need to review this case, determine if there was any deviation from the accepted standard of care, and then we must *brainstorm* for solutions, ferret out any *root cause,* and send our findings off to the Joint Commission." His tone was ironic as he ticked off the buzzwords that fueled this process.

Papers rustled around the table as Garret's chart was reviewed. I glanced through the increasingly familiar pages and focused on my own notes. Earlier, Sonja had reassured me that my documentation had been excellent. It was good to hear coming from the attorney, but I wondered what this group would have to say.

"Who is Dr. Katz?" the chairman asked, looking in the direction of Raj and me.

"I am."

"Good. In a succinct fashion present the patient, please."

And for the second time that morning I recited the facts of the case.

"What about risk factors for violence?" Dr. Miriam Gladstone asked.

"There was no prior account of violent behavior, either toward himself or toward others," I explained.

"I see where you say that in your note," she persisted. "I'm just wondering about the event which brought him in, where he was on the roof. It's not clear from your documentation if he intended to jump or not." She began to pontificate. "Whenever an assessment of dangerousness is made, you need to take into account the closeness between harm to oneself and harm to others . . ."

My cheeks flushed as she went on. I flipped through my handwritten intake, which it was clear she had only scanned. "On page two of my admission note," I said, breaking into her discourse, "I wrote, 'While client's speech is tangential and non-goal-directed he does deny any thoughts of wanting to hurt himself or others. He reported that God was trying to speak to him and that to hear better he had gone onto the roof of his house.'"

"So you didn't feel that his going up on the roof represented a significant risk for self-harm?" she shot back, not at all pleased that I had interrupted her.

"Not intentionally," I countered, "but I did think that it showed poor judgment. He was . . . is profoundly psychotic. I admitted him because of the degree of his disorganization and grave disability."

"Did you feel he was depressed?" Dr. Curtis Lawrence asked, getting in his question before the contentious Dr. Gladstone could raise a further objection.

"If he is, it's difficult to say. Based on observation alone I would say that he's not depressed. He eats well, sleeps well, and does not appear tearful or sad. His delusions, at least those that he expressed before becoming catatonic, were grandiose rather than depressive."

"So no identifiable depressive symptoms?"

I mentally ran the mnemonic for signs and symptoms of clinical depression. "The only one I can see would be he vacillated between agitation and now catatonia."

"Good," he said with a warm smile. "But as we know, in this case that seems much more tied to a psychotic process rather than to a depressive one."

"Exactly," I agreed, glad to have at least one ally in the room.

Then the discussion moved on to Raj and to the events of Saturday night. "I was paged with a double code at around two," he began in tones that carried hints of a British accent. "I arrived on the unit at the same time as the medical resident and security. We found the patient in the hallway holding a knife. Security was able to get the knife, and as we placed the patient in restraints the medical resident initiated a code on Helen Weir." His voice cracked as memories of the night flooded over him. Across the table, Marge Trask, the nurse who had provided chest compressions, began to sob quietly.

The room became silent.

"I guess the real question that must be answered," Dr. Schlessinger said, all traces of irony now gone, "is where did the knife come from?" He looked at Felix.

"That's not yet been determined," the unit chief answered. "All sharps have been accounted for, so it's unclear how the boy got the knife onto the unit. He was searched in the emergency room when he was admitted, and that's documented in the record. According to the police, the knife is compatible with others found in the hospital. So somehow it made its way onto the unit."

As he spoke a sickening thought occurred to me. I fought back the impulse to ask if it was serrated or not—once today had been enough. With a growing certainty I now knew where the knife had come from.

There was a small staff lounge off the main patient corridor. It wasn't much more than a place to have a refrigerator, microwave, small table, three or four chairs, and a bulletin board festooned with schedules and pictures of new children and grandchildren. It was also the major grazing site for the unit staff and the location where impromptu birthday parties were held. The table almost always had a variety of foods that had been left over or donated.

Just last Friday a sheet cake had been delivered for one of the nurse's birthdays. I held the image of the white, butter cream–frosted confection with its red and blue roses. In my mind's eye, next to the cake lay a long, wood-handled stainless steel knife.

I had to know. And there was no way that I could bring myself to share this new hypothesis . . . at least not in this forum. So I sat and listened as people offered up suggestions to tighten security.

"It looks like it wasn't one of the knives from the cooking group," Felix said. "But maybe it is time to rethink that. By and large the patients we have now are much sicker and stay for shorter periods of time. The cooking group was about the milieu, and frankly, with a less-than-one-week length of stay, there's not a whole lot of milieu anymore."

"Good," the chairman said, making a note of Felix's suggestion on the appropriate blank space. "What else?" He looked around the room. "We need at least one or two more suggestions."

Dr. Lawrence spoke up. "I think it's important that we not lose sight of how incredibly difficult it can be to predict violence. The chart is pretty clean in terms of addressing the major risks for both suicide and for dangerousness to others. That said, we might want to consider an inservice seminar on the topic of the prediction and documentation of dangerousness."

"That works for me," Dr. Schlessinger said, glad to be moving down toward the bottom of the form. "Can I count on you to put something together? Maybe we could have it videotaped?"

"My pleasure."

"Any other suggestions?" the chairman asked. "Okay, if the faculty physicians, other than Felix, could stay for the vote, the rest of you are free to go."

Fueled by my suspicion, I left the eighth floor conference room and headed straight for the staff lounge on Hamilton 5. The door was unlocked, and inside a lone nurse sat eating a tortilla-wrapped seafood-salad sandwich—one of the kitchen's latest creations. She looked up from her reading and asked, "Are they all done up there?"

"Just about," I said, while staring at the gray plastic tray that contained the remains of the birthday cake.

The nurse misinterpreted my interest and warned

me, "That's getting pretty old. It should probably be thrown out."

"Right." I checked and rechecked around the cake, on the floor, behind the refrigerator, and under the microwave, looking for the knife; but just as I suspected, it was gone.

CHAPTER SEVEN

This day would never end. It was six o'clock and I still hadn't written notes on all of my patients. My body felt as if lead had been poured into my veins; every movement took effort. My thoughts kept breaking free from my control and would return to the events of Saturday night. How did I miss this? Why didn't I see something? I couldn't stop. Every time I focused on some other task, I'd be reminded of Garret and would once again rehash the entire morning. That I hadn't told anyone about the cake knife was another thing that added to my anxiety and guilt.

I forced myself to pen the last two notes on my inpatients. I looked around the cramped quarters of my office, picked up my coat, and wondered if Josh had sense enough to go ahead and defrost a block of lasagna. The moment I thought of my son my mind swerved and I pictured Sandra Jacobs pleading with me in the hallway. "You've got to help him, he's sick."

I stood there, coat in hand, bag on shoulder, and the last three charts tucked under my arm. "You've got to be kidding," I said out loud into the empty space, hoping that somehow I wasn't about to do the thing that just flashed through my mind. I turned back to my desk, dropped the coat, bag, and charts onto a chair, and began to ferret through my Rolodex. I found the number for Whitestone Forensic Hospital and dialed.

An operator picked up.

"I'm Dr. Katz from Commonwealth Hospital in Boston. I had a patient transferred today and I wanted to see how he was doing."

"One moment, please hold."

Muzak spilled through the receiver and I listened to the soothing strains of an all-string arrangement of "Getting to Know You."

"Hello?" The operator returned.

"Yes, this is Dr. Katz—"

"I'm sorry," she interrupted. "We can't give out information regarding any of the patients without express written permission."

"Could you at least connect me to Garret Jacobs's physician or nurse?"

"I can't even tell you if we have such a patient here."

"He was transferred today."

"That might be," she explained in an officious tone. "Our rules are clear. I can't divulge anything without prior written permission."

"But the patient's catatonic."

"This is a forensic facility. You need permission from the treating physician."

"Is there anyone I can talk to?"

"They've all left for the day. I suggest you call back in the morning."

"Fine," I said, hating myself for giving up so easily. "I'll call back."

"Very good." And she hung up.

I sat there, holding the receiver. What a bitch, I thought. At least you tried. And I reassembled my gear and headed toward the door.

As I returned the charts to the rack behind the nurse's station, I caught sight of Rob coming out of the examination room.

He looked at me and smiled. "What are you doing here so late?"

"I could ask the same of you."

"Wretched call," he moaned. "And your excuse?"

"Bad time management. I can't believe this day. And to add the frosting on the cake"—a statement I regretted the moment it left my lips—"I just got off the phone with one of the most annoying operators I've ever encountered."

"Ours?" he asked.

"No, I wanted to see how Garret was doing. She wouldn't even let me speak to his doctor. Come to think of it, she wouldn't even acknowledge that he was there."

"That's how they do things over there," he explained. "They're very tight-lipped."

"And you know this for a fact, because . . . ?"

"I moonlight there."

"That's right. I forgot."

"You know," he continued, "they're pretty desperate for overnight docs right now. You might want to consider it. Plus, if you really want to see Garret that bad . . ."

"Like I don't have enough to do? But just for the sake of argument, what do they pay?"

"That's the beauty, right there." His eyes

twinkled. "You get forty-five dollars an hour and nine times out of ten you get to sleep the whole night. Weekends are even better. If you take the whole day on both Saturday and Sunday you gross over two thousand bucks. I call it sleeping for dollars. I've been able to sock away about half of it into mutual funds. It's amazing how those things add up."

"Nice. Of course you don't have kids and a house. But isn't it scary?"

"Not really. Security is excellent and most of the time you're not even on the wards. And the truly dangerous patients are kept in locked rooms. It's not a bad gig. Besides, they've been calling me daily trying to see if I'll take some extra call. Even if I wanted to, I've been maxing out on my hours. If anyone were ever to check, they'd probably make me cut down. But until they do . . ." He rubbed his palms together in the universal sign of greed.

"The money's good," I agreed.

"Better than here, and frankly I'm getting real tired of living on what they pay us. Plus I'm trying to keep my school loans under the six-digit mark."

"Amen to that. But I thought your folks were helping out."

His smile fell. "Blood from a stone," he commented. "My father is not the most giving of people."

"Sorry."

"Don't worry about it. You've got your ex and all that. And I've got my father who's worth a small fortune but has a hard time parting with his money."

"Crosses for everybody."

"Ain't that the truth. Anyway, let me give you the number for the medical director at Whitestone." He pulled out a pen and hunted inside his jacket for a small pad of yellow stickums. Bracing the paper square against the wall he jotted down a name and number. "Give him a call."

"I might," I said, as I pocketed the sticky-edged paper.

A pager sounded and we both reached for our beepers.

"Rats," he said, looking at the LED readout, "it's the ER. Wonder what they want?"

"Enjoy your call," I said, stifling the guilty thought that I was glad that it was him and not me.

"Such bliss," he quipped, and as he reached for the phone, I retrieved my charts and my belongings and headed toward home.

CHAPTER EIGHT

The following day I settled into the comfortable overstuffed chair in my supervisor's office. When I began to work with Dr. William Adams I had been miffed at his insistence that we meet in his Beacon Hill office. My other supervisors came to the hospital—it was easier. But I quickly realized that the time away from the wards was precious and that seeing the possibility of private practice was helpful. It was my weekly window into the world that lay outside training.

"How's it going?" he asked as he sipped his coffee.

"The truth?"

"No, lie to me." He chuckled.

"I don't even know where to start. Have you heard anything about what happened at the hospital?"

"No."

"There was a murder on the wards . . . one of my patients killed a nurse." I didn't know how to soften the information and it's what I desperately needed to discuss with him.

He looked across at me. "How horrible. How are you dealing with that?"

"Not well," I admitted. "I don't think fifteen minutes goes by without my wondering what I did wrong, or what I didn't see. The nurse was someone I knew, Helen Weir." I looked across at him as he searched his own memory. "Did you know her?"

"I don't think so."

"I didn't know her well," I admitted. "But still . . . I keep seeing her and I look at the other staff and somehow feel that I let people down."

"How could you have known? Did you forget to do an evaluation? Did you leave something out?"

"No. I don't think so. God knows I've been through the chart enough in the past three days. All day yesterday was spent with police and then there was a peer review. I keep looking to see what I missed . . ."

"Maybe you didn't miss anything," he offered. "I suspect that's closer to the truth. Tell me about the patient."

It had almost become canned, my presentation of Garret. But very quickly, as is his habit, Dr. Adams shifted from the surface and had me dive below. Cupping his chin in his hand he looked at me, his eyes dark and filled with concern. "You have a son about the same age as Garret," he commented.

"I do. And that makes it worse. I keep so many things going in the air at the same time, but what if something were to happen to one of my children? I look at Sandra Jacobs—this is her only child. She has to work full time and she has a kid who's getting worse and worse; what is she supposed to do?

It's not like there are a whole lot of choices. And now this."

"What are the choices?"

"I don't know. She could stay home with Garret, although that's a moot point, because in all likelihood he'll stay at Whitestone or some other forensic hospital for a long time."

"Could she have prevented this?"

"How? He has schizophrenia; I don't see how anything could have stopped this. Unless you think that there's some way that parents can give their children a psychotic disorder?"

He smiled. "No, I think that's been debunked, although that's what we used to think. Psychiatrists and psychologists used to throw a lot of guilt onto parents with theories about the schizophrenogenic mother."

"Can you imagine, to have a child that sick and then be told that it's your fault. It's no wonder people are scared of psychiatry," I commented.

"We've made some wonderful blunders in our brief history. But back to your case . . . the guilt that you're feeling, do you think it's warranted?"

"I don't know." I flashed on an image of Garret tied to his bed. "There I go again. I can't put it out of my mind."

"Molly, in cases like these, whenever something bad happens to one of our patients it is important to review the case with clear eyes; it sounds like you've done that. Between your review of the chart and all the various legalistic proceedings you've been through, any deficiency in your assessment has been ruled out. There is no objective data that you forgot to do something. This then leaves us with the greater and more disturbing truth. We're not great at predicting what people will and will not do, we're not mind readers. I suspect that Garret struck out at the nurse in response to some delusion-driven impulse. I doubt it was premeditated and I suspect that when you were with him he had no thoughts of stabbing anyone."

I let his words wash over my unsettled thoughts. I saw Garret tied down to his bed, staring at the ceiling. "It's so unfair. Why does something like that happen?"

"The killing?"

"The whole thing. I don't get it." I leaned forward in the chair and searched for words. "I believe that schizophrenia is mostly a biologically mediated illness, and at this point I'd say with ninety-five percent certainty that Garret has schizophrenia. It was going to happen that somewhere in his teens or twenties he would develop symptoms. I accept that as a given. What I don't get is how someone with a nonviolent temperament can as a result of his illness, become a murderer."

"It's rare, but it can happen. Typically the person doesn't believe that he's doing wrong. For instance if I had a delusion that you were Satan incarnate, would it be wrong if I tried to kill you? In my delusion, that might make me into a hero or a saint."

"He had religious delusions," I admitted. "Should that have clued me into something else?"

"Not really. How many patients have you seen with religious delusions?"

"A lot."

"Exactly. How many of them have killed?"

"Just Garret."

"Right. There's no way you could have known, Molly. It's beyond your control."

"So what does make someone kill?" I asked.

"Different things," he responded. "Let me be annoying and answer your question with a question. When would you kill?"

I didn't hesitate. "If someone were threatening, I mean really threatening my children."

"That's reason number one, again probably biologically driven. The mother has to protect her young up to and including killing the offending agent. What about your own life?"

"Self-defense?"

"Yes."

"But that's not murder," I argued.

"Sure it is. To kill in self-defense is an excusable homicide, but it's still homicide."

I mulled this over. "But what about people who deliberately set about to kill someone? What drives them?"

"Different things. Think about the newspaper. Look at all the murders of adolescents. Not a mile from my office two teenagers were shot and killed by two other teenagers. What was the motive? Money, drugs, a sense that at sixteen years old the rules that govern the rest of society don't apply. It's a kind of normal developmental narcissism that can go horribly wrong."

"It's true." And I thought about the last two years with Megan before she went to college. "Teenagers don't hold the same concept of death. They take more risks."

"Most killing is a combination of factors," he continued. "Intense emotion, possibly mixed with drugs and/or alcohol. For kids there's often a precipitating event or insult. A girl who turns you down, a group of kids who make fun of you. Then combine that with ready access to a firearm . . . that's what fuels a lot of murders. It's what also leads to a great number of successful suicides. Guns and alcohol are a bad combination."

"But something has to trigger it," I persisted. "Even kids don't just start shooting people for no reason."

"True, but why are the adolescent suicide and homicide rates so high? These are two demographics that have been on the rise for the past four decades. What's causing it?"

I sat back, deep in the arms of the comfortable chair; my mind focused on the subject. "I see two things straight off that might relate. I think about the incredible fights I had with my daughter in her last two years of high school; they were awful." And as so often happens in supervision with Dr. Adams, the line between therapy and instruction blurred.

"What made them awful?" he asked.

"They had a life of their own." I felt heaviness in my body as I recalled the specifics. "She'd shriek at me and tell me how unfair I was, what a hypocrite I was, what a bad job I did raising her. And afterwards she'd sulk, or she'd do stupid things that sometimes I think the sole reason was to annoy me, like going to New York and getting her tongue pierced—I could have killed her."

"And then what happened?"

"I can't quite figure out what happened, but a couple of months before she went away to college, they stopped. For those two years, there were times I didn't recognize her. Not physically, but as a person, if that makes any sense. It was like someone had taken my daughter and replaced her with this angry, obnoxious person."

"You said there were two things?" he prompted.

"Right. I was on call Saturday night and there was a thirteen-year-old girl brought in by the police. Her name was Jennifer, she was a pretty girl, a little more physically developed than either I was or Megan was at that age, but neatly dressed and initially very calm and composed. She just wanted to go home, told me there was some sort of misunderstanding with her mother. But the police report said she attacked her mother, and when I met the woman she had a huge bruise on her cheek. When I finally got the two of them together, it ended up with the girl losing control and the mother running out of the emergency room without even signing a permission-to-treat."

"Not a good night, I take it."

"No, but it made me see that what Megan and I went through was mild by comparison."

"How was it different?" he prompted.

I paused to think it through. "I think the magnitude of the girl's response. She completely lost it. She had the intensity of an infant throwing a tantrum. Once it started she couldn't control it. It took three guards and a nurse to get her into restraints, and she wasn't large. I couldn't imagine what that would be like if I were her mother."

"But you do draw comparisons with your own

daughter. So on some level you're imagining part of it."

"You're probably right. In which case, it's a matter of degree. Once I thought that Megan might actually hit me, but she didn't."

"So despite the surges of adolescent fury, your daughter was able to exercise some degree of self-control and the girl in the emergency room couldn't."

"Is it couldn't or wouldn't?" I asked.

"Again, it may be a matter of degree," he offered. "At least initially the girl in the emergency room was contained, and then something happened between her and her mother and any self-control went out the window. Let me ask you this, if there had been a gun in the emergency room, what would have happened?"

"I'm not sure, but I see where you're going. So if it's a question of degree, what's normal?"

"Probably what you went through with Megan is right in the range. Some of that mother-daughter friction helps with the adult separation process. She's establishing her independence and clearing the way to head off to college. Why it happens with so much Sturm und Drang is unclear. The girl in the emergency room, almost by virtue of being there, has stepped into the realm of the pathologic; her behavior is not adaptive. I also suspect it was not an isolated incident."

"No." I described the case, complete with her history of suicide attempts and past psychiatric hospitalization.

"All by age thirteen." He took a deep breath. "Was there any history of sexual abuse?"

I looked at him. "I couldn't get details, but the mother hinted that a past boyfriend might have molested Jennifer."

"On more than one occasion?"

"She seemed to discount the whole thing."

"I see, and the father?"

"Out of the picture almost from the very beginning."

"And now we have a thirteen-year-old who's sexually precocious and unable to contain these powerful surges of emotion. It's not a good mix," he commented. "Unfortunately, it's quite typical. There are a lot of these kids out there."

"What becomes of them?" I asked.

"Good question. Some of them will learn to handle their emotions, some of them go on to develop full-blown personality disorders, often with episodes of depression, panic, and anxiety. Some of them kill themselves and some kill others and end up in prison. In the latter cases there seems to be a sex differentiation, with boys committing the vast majority of violent crime. But even there, that statistic is changing. It used to be that one in ten violent crimes was committed by a woman. At least with adolescent girls that number has changed to one in four."

"And girls kill themselves more?" I asked.

"No, but they try more. Girls make more attempts, but boys use more lethal means."

"Pills versus guns?"

"Exactly."

"And when you're talking about personality disorders," I continued, "you're saying that these kids with conduct disorder and oppositional defiant disorder go on to develop what . . . ?" My sentence dangled.

"Using the current diagnostic criteria, the girls will likely be diagnosed as having borderline personality disorder and the boys will either be given that diagnosis, or if the majority of their acts are against others, they'll be formulated as antisocial personality disorder."

"Patients and prisoners for life?" I asked.

"Not necessarily, but certainly people who will have a difficult time negotiating adult relationships." At which point he glanced at the clock. "We have to end. Same time next week?"

"Yes," I agreed, not wanting the conversation to end. "But if they're diagnosed as antisocial," I asked, trying to tease out a thought that was struggling toward the surface, "doesn't that imply that they know what they're doing? What we've been talking about has a lot more to do with emotion gone haywire."

"It's an important distinction," he said, as he opened the door. "If you think about it, the question becomes what is uncontrolled—or uncontrollable emotion—and what is evil."

CHAPTER NINE

What am I doing here? I thought, as I surveyed the beat-up chairs and old, framed prints of horses that decorated the walls of Dr. Eric Freeborn's waiting room. In front of me a forty-something-year-old woman with badly dyed henna-red hair fielded the phones while simultaneously inputting data onto a computer spreadsheet. A single grime-smeared window let in the late-afternoon sun; the glass itself was criss-crossed with a grim wire mesh. The floor was old linoleum tile that had been recently waxed, leaving yet one more layer of the yellowish buildup that provided a shiny patina to the dingy, white-speckle pattern.

As for myself, I was in my job interview garb. My suit was charcoal gray, a find at last year's spring sale at Talbot's. My black pumps, courtesy of Nine West, were killing my feet. My briefcase, filled with every piece of documentation that I could think to bring, sat perched on my lap.

But again, what was I doing here? As I had announced myself at the locked gate and then driven up toward the brick and concrete structure, I had felt fear. I shouldn't have come. I was crossing a potentially dangerous boundary. On the one hand

I needed the money. From what Rob had said, moonlighters at Whitestone did quite well. Maybe that's all this was. Yeah right, I reminded myself, knowing full well that if I could have gotten through to Garret's doctor or nurse, I probably wouldn't have come.

The secretary's intercom buzzed. She looked in my direction. "You can go in now."

"Thanks." I stood up and smoothed down the soft wool of my skirt. With briefcase clenched firmly in hand, I went in.

An attractive dark-skinned man with glasses and close-cropped black hair met me at the threshold. "Dr. Katz," he said, taking my hand. "I am so glad you were able to come on such short notice."

"My pleasure." I settled into one of several matching gray upholstered chairs that were arranged around his conference table.

"Coffee?" he asked, refilling his own purple plastic mug, which bore the logo of a new antipsychotic medication.

"I'm fine." And I watched as he replaced the carafe on the burner and then ferreted through the stacks of papers and folders that festooned his desktop. "Here we go," he said, retrieving a bright yellow folder. He flipped it open and then settled into the chair across from me. From where I sat, I caught a glimpse of the familiar cream-colored linen paper that I used for my resumé. He quickly scanned the information and then looked up with a perplexed expression. His gaze darted around the room and then came to rest on the purple mug he had left behind at his desk.

"There it is," he said, and with rabbitlike

movements got up, retrieved his coffee, decided he wanted more, and finally came to rest back in his chair. "Much better." He looked across at me and smiled, his dark eyes sparkled with energy. "Without coffee there is no life. So, you're a third-year resident. And I can see that you've had a pretty broad training experience. You were also a nurse?"

"Yes."

"That must come in handy."

"In what way?" I asked, wondering what sort of conclusions he was drawing from his ten-second scan of my resumé.

"Different perspective, don't you think? I would imagine you have a much different take on certain things than your colleagues. Or am I just getting myself into hot water?"

I caught myself smiling. "You're probably right," I admitted. "I still use some basic nursing paradigms when I formulate treatment plans."

"Level-of-care kinds of stuff?"

"Exactly," I agreed, surprised to find any physician with a grasp of this most basic of nursing principles. "You always want to match your intervention to the patient's functional level. If you overshoot you create dependency, and if you aim too low you don't address the patient's basic needs."

"It's a sound model. At Whitestone, our philosophy of treatment is becoming increasingly more cognitive-behavioral. So that kind of practical framework is useful. Of course with our folks, there's a whole lot of carrot-and-stick work that needs to occur."

"You've lost me."

"In a forensic facility most of our patients are here because of egregious acts they have committed, combined with well-documented psychopathology. We certainly do not want to see those behaviors occur while they are here. Our bottom line is one of safety, both for the patients and for the staff."

"How do you maintain that?"

"I'll show you; let's go for a walk." And before I could comment, he was out of his seat and headed toward the door with his coffee mug grasped firmly in hand.

Realizing that this was not an optional event, I followed.

"Don't be put off by the age of the facility," he explained, and then turned toward his secretary. "Jill, I'm going to take Dr. Katz on a tour. Would you fax a copy of her CV to the staff office and have them begin processing her credentials? Let them know I want her cleared ASAP." He then looked at me and grimaced. "You don't happen to have copies of your license and DEA number on you?"

"I do," I said, retrieving the cards from my briefcase.

"Wonderful. If you could give those to Jill, she can make copies while we take our tour. You might want to leave that here," he said, pointing to my briefcase.

I handed over the cards and caught a glimpse of the secretary's computer screen. It showed an elaborate multicolored bar graph with labels such as *Assault, Homicide, Manslaughter, Arson, and Larceny*. "Nice graph," I commented.

Dr. Freeborn looked over my shoulder at his secretary's handiwork. "It's coming along nicely, Jill." And then he turned and explained. "I'm trying to put together a series of graphs that show the diagnostic and criminal makeup of our population. Kind of like how many schizophrenics are here for starting fires versus assault. I have no idea if it's useful information, but sometimes the numbers generate interesting data."

"Have you found anything so far?"

"Just what you'd expect, but I'm hopeful." He headed toward the door.

I trailed behind, struggling to keep up with his rapid, caffeine-powered gait. "What do you expect to find?" I asked.

"Things like the relationship between drugs, alcohol, and violent crime. People are more able to do stupid things when they're drunk or high. Combine that with a mind that may already be disordered, and you've got the potential for some real mayhem. The other stuff that emerges, particularly as we get pressured to take patients who are younger and younger, is the history. Most of our patients have significant histories prior to their admission here. We do have a facility on the other side of the campus for kids, but it's completely filled. So where we used to not take anyone below the age of eighteen, we're having to revise that policy."

"How young do you go?"

"We definitely take seventeen, and I suspect before the year is out we may need to create an adolescent ward in the main building. Probably flex down to hit the thirteen-to-seventeen range." He veered right down a deserted corridor that dead-ended with a massive gray steel door. We stopped outside the door. Without slowing his rapid-fire speech, he pulled a keycard out of his pocket and swiped it against a magnetic pad. "This is the first in a series of locked units," he explained as he punched in a seven-digit code on the keypad.

The door clicked open and I followed behind, trying to take in the various details. I was eager to catch a glimpse of Garret, but if I was really planning to moonlight here I wanted to know what I was getting into. To make things worse, my head had started to throb with a dull ache that centered in my sinuses. I tried to focus as we passed a variety of padded seclusion rooms designed to contain out-of-control patients.

We then emerged onto an open ward that seemed like many others I had worked on. Patients in blue and gray hospital uniforms milled about the nurse's station. Dr. Freeborn smiled and greeted the patients and staff alike. At several points in the tour he would stop and introduce me to a nurse, a patient, or a burly aide. All the while, I kept waiting to hear the word *inmate,* but apparently that was not the operative term.

As Dr. Freeborn continued through the facility he pointed out the varying degrees of security on each of the units. As we took a stairwell down to the next floor, he commented, "Now we're getting onto the double-locked wards. Typically these individuals remain in their rooms. It's high security and one always has to be on guard. When and if you are requested to evaluate someone here you should always come with a guard."

"Is that hard to do?"

"Shouldn't be, but it might mean waiting a little longer until you have the amount of manpower you need, just in case. A rule of thumb is never get yourself into a position where you feel unsafe."

"I can't help but notice how big some of your aides are."

He smiled. "It's no coincidence. You need people who can handle difficult patients." He then stopped himself. "Not to say that sort of thing happens with any regularity, but this is a forensic facility and you have to be careful. I think for a moonlighter that's the biggest concern. Also, if you ever find yourself in a situation that you can't figure out, there are always attendings on back-up call."

"Good to know."

The next ward contained a single corridor lined on both sides with locked rooms. Each door contained a small window through which we could view the inhabitant. It was like a human zoo.

Our arrival was met with staring eyes and calls from behind a locked door. "Doc, I need to talk to somebody, I'm not feeling good."

"That's Edward Gold," Dr. Freeborn said, under his breath. "He frequently feigns illness. Unfortunately it has to be investigated. This can be a problem. He's gotten into a habit of developing vague and potentially dangerous physical complaints. He's had more tests run, all negative, than I care to mention. Again, if you get called to see him, always have at least two aides with you."

"What is he here for?" I asked.

"Sexual predation and rape. I think there may

be some breaking and entering as well, but that's largely because he was homeless and would break into warehouses for a place to sleep."

"Why is he in the locked rooms?"

"Every time we try to introduce him into a ward, he becomes sexually inappropriate with the other patients. Sometimes I think he's down here more for his protection than for others. He's not very big, and some of the patients he's attacked did not take kindly to his attentions."

"Oh. How long will he be here?"

"I would imagine quite a while. His case is on a six-month review schedule, but he's not going anywhere until he can achieve some lasting resolution of his symptoms."

"Medication?" I asked.

"Pretty much everyone is on something. More often than not, several somethings."

"For him in particular?"

"Long-acting hormone shots."

"Chemical castration?" I asked.

"Basically. We wouldn't do it unless he agreed. I'm not sure if it's helping, though."

"Are the rules different here?" I asked, realizing that I had not once prescribed a long-acting hormone for such a purpose.

"In what way?" he asked, as we passed out of the locked corridor and entered another stairwell.

"Can you medicate people against their will?"

"Only with a court order, and even those are time-limited. If there's an emergency and someone is out of control, you do what you have to do, and that's well within the letter of the law."

"So it's pretty much the same."

"Pretty much. I mean, the biggest difference between a forensic facility and a regular psychiatric facility is the degree of security. No one is here on a voluntary basis. Most of our patients would be in prison if they weren't here." We left one set of stairs and went through a door that came out on yet another staircase. "This place is like a rabbit warren," he explained. "It's a bunch of old buildings all pieced together. It's not that hard to figure out once you've been here a little while. Every so often the state talks about tearing it down and putting up an all-new facility. It'll never happen."

"How come?" I asked, as we emerged onto a brighter corridor lined with wire-mesh windows.

"Not a priority for people. A prison you can get money for, a forensic hospital is a much harder sell. Although the way things are going, prisons are having larger and larger populations of psychiatric patients."

"It's amazing," I agreed. "I get the trade papers, and there are a ton of ads looking for psychiatrists to work in prisons."

"A growth industry," he commented. "One sure way to avoid having to deal with managed care. Now this is our intake ward." He indicated a door on our right. "And probably where you'll spend most of your time. The call room is down here." He fumbled through a ring of keys and unlocked another door to show me a small but tidy room with a bed, desk, phone, and TV set. "There's a bathroom through there, and by and large, the call is pretty light. The grounds are beautiful, and during good weather, as long as you have your pager, you pretty much have the run of the place. Now, when patients first arrive, that's when you'll do the bulk of the work." He closed the door to the call room and went across the hall. He again swiped his card, punched a code, and we were now on the intake unit.

As I followed him, my gaze drifted to a patient's open door. I saw a shock of blond hair sticking up from a pillow and a motionless body hooked up to an IV pole.

Dr. Freeborn followed my gaze. "Sad," he commented. "He may need to go to the prison infirmary if he doesn't start eating soon. We try to avoid feeding tubes with our catatonic patients and anorectic patients, but from time to time we'll do it. It's a big pain, because you have to send them out for X-rays after the tube is in, and invariably the patient gets agitated and pulls it out in the middle of the night. So you have to go through the whole thing all over again. But we tend to get a lot of resistance when we want to admit one of our guys to the infirmary, or God forbid, to a regular hospital. So as much as possible, we try to attend to their medical needs on site. We have a medical consultant who comes at least three times a week, and if there's ever an emergency he can be contacted."

"And if someone is acutely sick?"

"You call an ambulance."

"What if someone's faking it so that they can try and escape?"

"You always transport with the same level of security that the patient requires on the ward. Typically, they'll be manacled to the ambulance stretcher and we generally use the prison infirmary or a correctional facility hospital. I hope this isn't an overwhelming amount of information. I'll give you the pared-down guidelines before you leave. And the nurses know all the rules, so you can leave the details up to them."

"It's a lot," I admitted while trying to get a closer look at Garret.

"Still interested?"

"Sure."

"Oh my goodness," he said, looking at the clock over the nurse's station. "We should head back to my office and get your paperwork underway. I think you'll like it here. There's a lot you can learn working with this population."

Reluctantly, I let myself be led away from the ward and from Garret. Like following the March Hare through the maze of Wonderland, I trailed behind the coffee-toting Dr. Freeborn through the convoluted corridors and cock-eyed stairwells of Whitestone Forensic. By the time we reached his office, Jill had processed my application, and with a handshake and a smile Dr. Freeborn thanked me for coming and bid me farewell.

CHAPTER TEN

I left Hamilton 5 and walked down Huntington Avenue, aka Hospital Row, to the Franklin Clinic and my Thursday outpatients. This whole week on the inpatient unit had focused on the murder—how could it be otherwise? But still, the more time I could get away from it, and from my own guilty recriminations, the better.

I slowed my pace and savored the clear spring day. The maple trees that had been planted years ago along this broad and busy street were filled with fleshy green buds. Splashes of yellow and white daffodils and narcissus peeked out from carefully tended plots that added a softening touch to some of Boston's most austere and venerated hospitals. They were all here, although the names and affiliations were rapidly changing. Not even these once sacred institutions had been spared the ravages of managed care.

The Franklin Clinic, which was around the corner on Brookline Avenue, was part of the public mental health system in Boston. It was a small community-based outpatient facility that catered to the poor and the under-insured. Even here, the signs of spring refused to be dampened by the clinic's uninspired cinder-block construction. As I walked through the front door, the guard waved me past. All others were stopped so that they could have the metal-detector wand waved over their bodies. Some of the more psychotic patients had complained about this. But just like at the hospital, there had been an incident, at least one that I knew of, where a patient had cornered a physician. There were no injuries, but it created a backlash that resulted in heightened security and a metal detector at the front door.

As I headed toward the office I shared with four other residents, I tried to think if the danger came from working with the mentally ill, or from working with people in general. At Josh's school, there was pressure from parents to have a metal detector for the students. Both he and Megan told me how commonplace it had become for the police to show up at the high school to question or to arrest a student.

I stopped by the receptionist's desk to pick up my charts for the afternoon. "How's it going, Dara?" I asked.

"Not bad," she replied. "Your one o'clock canceled and you've got a two o'clock evaluation."

"Thanks." I glanced at the top chart for my canceled patient. It was Gerry Ewell, my man with agoraphobia. For him, half of the therapy was making it out of his house and getting down to the clinic. This was not a good sign.

Balancing the charts between my body and the wall, I let myself into the office. I dropped the stack onto the institutional gray metal desk and opened Gerry's chart to find his home number.

I dialed. The phone rang three times—it always does with Gerry—and then he picked up.

"Hello?" His tenuous voice greeted me.

"Hey, Gerry, it's Dr. Katz. What happened?"

"I'm not feeling good."

"Physically or emotionally?"

"Both. I've got bad diarrhea and I can't leave the house."

"Because?"

"I just can't."

"What do you think will happen if you do?"

"I could have an accident."

"Has that happened before?" I said, honing in on his catastrophic response.

"No . . . but it could," he argued.

"Even if it did, Gerry, which it won't, would it be the end of the world?"

"No," he admitted grudgingly.

"Let me ask you this, is there something going on that might be making your stomach feel bad?"

"I think it's just a bug," he said, not wanting me to ferret around in his pantheon of anxious monsters. I had worked with Gerry since I started at the clinic last year. For him, nine times out of ten, the physical symptoms were generated by his out-of-control fears and anxiety.

"How's your mom?" I asked, taking a clinical stab in the direction of his aging mother.

"She's okay," he said.

"Have you gotten out of the house at all this week?"

He hesitated. "I got the mail."

"Hmmm. Weren't you supposed to be taking a walk twice a day?"

"I can't right now."

And then it came to me. "Did you take care of the phone bill?"

His breath quickened over the line.

"What's happening with the phone bill?" I persisted, remembering how worried he had become over some 900 calls that had been erroneously billed to his number. "Did you call to get it straightened out?"

"I couldn't," he admitted. "I tried. I really did. I just kept thinking what if they were sex calls, they'd think I made them. I couldn't do it."

His breath came in faster and faster gasps. "Gerry, you're starting to hyperventilate. Focus on the bottoms of your feet, let yourself feel your right foot against the sole of your shoe." I coached him into a centering exercise that helped distract him from his anxious demons. "This is what I want you to do. If you come down here now, with your bill, I'll get you through the phone call."

"Could you do it?" he asked, with a spring of hope in his voice.

"I'll help *you* do it," I said. "We'll be here together and we'll get through it. But you've got to come now."

He hesitated and pondered the dilemma between his paralyzing anxiety and panic attacks versus the possible relief at getting over this stressful hurdle. "You'll be there when I make the call?"

"Yes."

"Will you dial for me?"

"You're stalling. Are you all dressed?"

"Yes."

"This is what I want you to do, keep working

on feeling the bottoms of your feet as you walk here. Each time you catch yourself worrying, focus on how your feet move on the sidewalk, and really concentrate. I'm going to hang up now, and I have a two o'clock patient, so if you come right now we can get this taken care of. Okay?"

"Okay." His tone did little to reassure me.

I listened for the click. He did the same. "I'll be waiting. Just focus on the bottoms of your feet." And I hung up.

I had no idea whether he would show up or not. This was his pattern. Whenever his anxiety latched onto some event in his life with a grain of truth to it, the frequency and severity of his panic attacks soared. Even with fairly stiff doses of medication, every trip out of the two-bedroom apartment that he shared with his mother was a struggle.

I reminded myself that there was just so much that I could do. If he managed to get out of his apartment and walk the four blocks to the clinic, it would be a small victory. If he didn't, well . . . it was just one battle.

I centered the stack of charts on my desk and scanned down the billing sheet that listed the names of all the patients I was to see today. Huh, I thought, looking at the last name of my two o'clock intake appointment—Ryan. I pulled the new green chart out from under Gerry's dog-eared navy one and began to read.

It was the girl I had seen in the emergency room on Saturday night. She had finally been admitted to the adolescent unit at Boston General Hospital, BGH. By the time I had finally gotten her cleared for an admission, I discovered that her insurance wouldn't cover her at Commonwealth Hospital. So at four in the morning I had an ambulance take her to Boston General—the facility that managed her psychiatric benefit. Now, supposedly for outpatient sessions, her insurance *would* cover the Franklin Clinic. Every day the insurance craziness worsened. It made life in the emergency room horrendous, because you never knew with any certainty to which facilities you could admit your patients. The days of just sending someone up to the floor had passed. Now if you did that without having the stay approved by the insurance company they could turn around and say that they wouldn't cover it. So either the patient or the hospital would get stuck with a bill for nearly a thousand dollars a day.

As I flipped through Jennifer Ryan's thin chart I came upon a copy of my transfer sheet and paperwork from the ER. Behind those were several pages copied from her inpatient record at BGH. The admission had been written up by a fourth-year resident, probably a moonlighter. The writing was hurried and difficult to read; it sprawled across two pages. I tried to decipher it and met with limited success. I then hunted for a discharge summary—usually these were typed and were the most readable part of the chart. Unfortunately, it was nowhere to be found. Probably it hadn't been done yet. BGH is notorious for being weeks behind in their transcriptions. It was common to get copies of a discharge summary a month after you had already begun seeing the patient in the ambulatory clinic. What I did find was the handwritten interagency transfer form. These were completed by nurses and contained a brief overview of why someone was in the hospital and why they were being transferred. I scanned the page, which talked about a "brief focused admission to address issues of mother-daughter conflict, oppositional behavior, and suicidal ideation." It then stated that two family meetings had occurred during the three-day admission. They had also started Jennifer on an antidepressant, and whoever filled out the form clearly stated, "At the time of discharge client was in good behavioral control and denied all suicidal and homicidal ideation. She was deemed to not be gravely disabled. Client to return home with her mother. Follow up with the Franklin Clinic on an outpatient basis. The recommendation is for individual and family sessions, with ongoing medication management."

As I sat there trying to suck information from the scanty documents, a sharp rapping sounded at my door. Startled, I asked, "Who is it?"

"It's Gerry, Dr. Katz."

I opened the door on the tidy egg-shaped man in his white button-down shirt and well-pressed Dockers pants.

"I made it," he proclaimed with a breathless smile. "Can I come in?" Beads of sweat blossomed on his forehead and his breathing was labored.

"Did you run here?" I asked, trying to imagine his heavy frame running down Brookline Avenue.

"I walked really fast. Can I sit down?"

"Of course." And I watched as he dropped into the tattered armchair that was positioned at a forty-five-degree angle from my desk.

"I did what you said," he stated proudly. "I just thought about the bottoms of my feet. Here . . ." He retrieved a crumbled phone bill from his pant pocket and thrust it in my direction. "Can you call?"

I glanced at the clock; I still had thirty minutes before the next appointment. "Let's think this through, Gerry."

"Okay." He nodded, still trying to get his breath.

"Would you like some water?" I asked.

"I'm fine, I took a Klonopin before I left."

I thought about that as a rejoinder. For Gerry, taking the Valium-like pill before emerging to handle what would be the major stress event of his week was probably a good move. "Let's try this," I began, formulating a strategy that would let him confront his fears in manageable bites. "Pretend that I'm the person at the phone company and you call to try and get your bill corrected. Okay?"

He nodded.

I made a ringing noise. "Hello?" I said, as if answering a phone.

Gerry was silent.

"Your turn," I urged.

"Hi, this is Gerry Ewell."

"Your account number, please," I interrupted him, trying to interject a bit of realism.

He fumbled with his bill and read off his account number.

"What seems to be the problem?" I asked.

"There's all these calls on my bill that I didn't

make, and my mother said she didn't make them either."

"One moment while I call up your account . . . Yes, I can see that you have several 900 calls on your bill. You're telling me that you didn't make these."

His forehead was damp with sweat, but he hung in. "That's right."

"Are you telling me that none of those 900 calls were made by yourself or any other residents at that address?"

"That's right."

"What I will require is a letter stating that none of those calls were made from your house, and then we can have the bill corrected." I had no idea if that's how these things happened, but I couldn't in good conscience prolong his agony.

"Okay," he said. And we hung up our pretend phones.

"How nervous are you right now?" I asked.

"Really bad," he said.

"On a scale of one to ten?"

"About a nine-and-a-half."

"Okay, sit in the chair and take some slow deep breaths. Feel yourself in the chair, feel your weight in the seat and your arms on the armrest. Now, I want you to dial the number on your telephone bill for customer assistance."

And with his pudgy hands shaking, he dialed.

I watched and waited.

"I'm on hold," he said, looking across at me.

"That's okay, just keep breathing."

Finally, an operator came on. In a normal tone

Gerry stated, "I have a problem with my phone bill."

Then apparently the operator asked for his name and number, which he gave in a slow and even manner.

"There are all these 900 numbers on my bill for calls that I never made."

The operator said something back. I almost wished that we had done this using the conference-call feature on the telephone.

"Just me and my mother," he replied, "and she's not well and she told me that she didn't make the calls either."

I watched and listened as Gerry fought to contain his nerves. Somehow he managed to keep his voice calm, but large circles of sweat drenched his underarms and had begun to spread toward the front of his shirt.

Finally, he told the operator, "Thank you."

"Ask for her name," I instructed in a hurried whisper.

"Could I have your name? Thank you." And he hung up.

I looked across at him, with his big relieved smile. "So what did she say?" I asked.

"She said that this has been happening a lot, that people are getting other people's numbers and making toll calls. She said that all I had to do was pay the regular bill, and that she would take care of it."

"How do you feel right now?"

"Much better."

"I'm really proud of you," I told him. "This whole thing, getting out of your apartment when you were so afraid, coming down here, making the phone call. That's great." And for the remaining ten minutes of his session we reviewed the underlying theme of his therapy, which was to consistently confront and challenge his fears in an attempt to get them to lessen.

As I showed him out the door, I instructed him to try to walk slower on his way home. I also offered the suggestion that he stop at the newsstand and reward himself with the latest issue of *Popular Mechanic*—his favorite publication.

After he had gone, I quickly scribbled a note about the session and then called Dara to see if my two o'clock patient had shown.

"She's here, but her mom took off."

"You've got to be kidding. I can't see a thirteen-year-old without her guardian's permission."

"Excuse me," Dara said, with a bit of attitude. "Did you think I would let her out the door without signing a permission form?"

"God bless you, but still . . ."

"I know, she said she had some errands to run and would be back in an hour. I tried to tell her that the kids get seen with their parents at least in the beginning."

"What did she say?" I wondered.

"Next time."

"Oh well, I guess you've got to work with what they give you. I'll be right out."

"That's the spirit."

I had a sense of déjà vu. This was too close to the night in the emergency room when I had turned around to look for Jennifer's mother and she had left.

When I entered the waiting area, with its mismatched chairs and ancient magazines, I began my evaluation of the girl. She looked much as she had on Saturday night. Her glossy red hair was tied back in a ponytail and she wore baggy jeans and a too-small knit shirt that allowed a thin strip of flesh to show around her abdomen. It wasn't particularly slutty, but then again, I don't think I would have allowed Megan to wear that shirt at thirteen. The other thing that struck me was her size. She was a tiny thing, probably around four foot ten, but her body had already developed breasts, and I felt it was unlikely that she would gain much additional height.

She saw me coming and put down the pamphlet she had been reading. She smiled over even white teeth. "I remember you," she said. "You were the doctor who sent me away."

"I'm Dr. Katz, Molly Katz."

"I told you she was going to try and put me away," she declared, almost proudly.

I felt a surge of something akin to anger, and stifled a retort—*If you didn't hit your mother you wouldn't get locked away.* "Let's go to my office," I said, and I led her back in the direction of the receptionist. "Dara, if Mrs. Ryan comes back, could you please buzz my office?"

"That's a big if," Jennifer stated in tones that sounded too old. "I'll be lucky if she remembers to pick me up at all."

"The fighting continues?" I prompted, as I let her into my office.

"I guess. See, but no one ever says anything about her, it's always my fault."

"That must be a drag."

"You have no idea, and now they have me taking all these pills."

"Do you know why?"

"I don't know." She stared out the window that looked out on a garbage-strewn alley. "I don't even know why I should have to come here. She needs this more than I do."

"How long have you been feeling this way?"

"Which way?"

I struggled to put my impressions into words. "Mad, angry, sad. You don't strike me as a happy person. Are there things you like to do, or people it feels good to be with?"

"I guess."

"Like what?"

"I don't know."

"Give me a for instance of something or someone you like."

She looked up at the ceiling, and then across at me. "I like to dance."

"Do you get to do that much?"

She smiled. "It's kind of dorky, but when I'm by myself I'll turn on the stereo and I can dance forever."

"What do you like about it?" I asked, glad for the thread of something that interested her.

"It feels good, like free. I just go and go and go. When I was a little girl I used to take ballet and tap and jazz. I'd go all the time."

"Why did you stop?"

"I just did." Her expression turned sullen.

"Did you want to stop?"

"It doesn't matter."

"Not to argue, but if there's something you like and you have to stop, that's going to make anyone feel bad."

"It was pretty stupid . . . I was good though. I remember when I was seven, Mrs. Grayson told me that I was a natural-born dancer." Her eyes sparkled with the memory. "We had these recitals, and there was one where I got to be in three different pieces, and I was so excited. I was going to have three different outfits—" Abruptly, she became silent.

"What is it?"

"Nothing."

I watched in fascination as she moved from emotion to emotion. Clearly, something had been triggered. I gently pushed. "That must have been nice, to be that good at something."

"It was stupid," she said, leaving little room for discussion. She stared at the floor.

I let a silence grow, wondering what she would do with it.

"So is this all we're going to talk about?" she asked.

"We can talk about anything," I offered.

"Yeah, but then you'll tell my mother. I know how this works."

"It's kind of hard to trust people."

"Tell me about it."

"Is there anyone you trust?"

She answered without hesitation, "No."

"That must be hard."

"Why do you keep saying that? It's just the way things are. Life sucks and then you die."

It was an uphill battle. I thought about Dr.

Adams and what he might do or say. He frequently encouraged me to acknowledge the reality of the situation with my patients. "I was wondering," I began, trying to pull together a few different thoughts. "This must be weird, coming to see me after I was the doctor that helped get you admitted over the weekend. Especially if you're ever going to trust me."

She looked at me. "It doesn't matter. You can't trust anyone, at least with you I know where you're coming from."

"I'll bite. Where am I coming from?"

"This is, like, your job. You're not my friend and you're not my mother—thank God—but you're supposed to try and help. And you get paid for it, so at least I know why you're here. It's not like there's something else—you're paid to be nice to me."

"So everything's on the table?"

"I guess. Just don't try to lock me up again."

"What was that like?" I asked.

"It's stupid. They kept me for three days; I had to go to all these stupid groups. If you ask me, it makes things worse."

"Like how?"

"You're there with all these other kids who are more fucked up than I am. How's that supposed to help?"

"Good point. I think the hospital is mostly to keep people safe."

"Maybe. But if someone really wanted to kill themselves they could do it anywhere."

"True. In the ER you told me that you think about suicide every day. Is that still true?"

CHARLES ATKINS

"Yeah, but don't worry, I'm not going to do anything about it. At least not yet."

"What stops you?"

"I don't know." She picked at the worn upholstery on the arm of her chair. "Aren't we almost done?"

"Soon." And for rest of the session I tried to get even a hairsbreadth below the surface. I was not successful. At the end, I gave her a card for the following week and then walked out with her to the waiting area. Her mother had not yet returned, and my three o'clock appointment was waiting. I made a mental note to try to call Jennifer's mother tomorrow. As I went back with my next patient, Dara handed me a pink phone message slip. It read, "Sandra Jacobs called about Garret. Please call—urgent."

CHAPTER ELEVEN

Six o'clock found me laying out strips of al dente lasagna in preparation for one of my massive cook, wrap, and freeze efforts. Years back I developed a meal system, perhaps more to assuage my guilt than anything else, that kept my freezer stocked with stacks of foil-wrapped single servings. I wasn't an adventurous cook, but those things I made, I made well. The entrée repertoire was fairly fixed, including the following: lasagna, sausage and peppers—Josh's favorite—beef stew, chicken fricassee, and barbecue chicken.

As I poured sauce and then sprinkled ground beef over the first layer of pasta, I thought back to my conversation with Garret's mother, Sandra. No matter how hectic I made my life, there were always these moments where I knew it could be worse. My patients, with their damaged lives, provided a constant reminder. Sandra Jacobs had brought that home; she had been to Whitestone.

"They're killing him," she had sobbed. "You've got to do something."

I wanted to comfort her, but she had a point. If Garret continued in his present state they would have to insert a feeding tube; if not, he would die.

In a weird way her call made me feel better about yesterday's subterfuge with Dr. Freeborn. Maybe I could help. I didn't know how, but I could at least try. I told her none of that; it would only have complicated matters and given her false hope. I listened and let her talk. Afterwards she thanked me in a voice that sounded lost and sad and hollow.

As I laid down the second layer of noodles, being careful to allow no space between them, the phone rang. I picked up and heard a familiar male voice.

"Hello, James," I said, immediately shifting gears for a chat with my ex-husband.

"How are you, Molly?"

"Fine, what's up?" I asked, not wanting to spend a second longer than necessary with him.

"We need to talk," he said.

"About what?"

"Our children," he continued in an ominous voice.

"James, I'm busy. Could you just say what it is that you want."

"We need to revisit the college thing."

"In what way?"

"If you're going to be like that, I'll just come out and say it."

"Yes?"

"I don't think I should be the one paying eighty percent of Megan's tuition. When the settlement was made, you weren't a doctor."

I struggled to keep my voice steady. "James, I make less money now than I did when I was a nurse."

"Yeah, but my attorney says your earning potential is probably the same or better than mine. He says that if we were to go back to court the judge would see things differently."

"James, first off, I don't even want to tell you what your constant griping about money is doing to your kids—especially Josh. Beyond that, I make thirty thousand dollars a year as a resident, and I have another year of this and then I might do a fellowship, which is just about the same salary. So maybe by the time Megan is a senior you might have a case, but until then, I'll fight you all the way."

"It's not fair, Molly, and you know it. I have more obligations to meet than you do."

I held my breath for a moment. "And that was your choice, wasn't it?"

"That's ancient history," he said, wanting to back down before I drove the point home.

"No, James, that is the point. You were the one who went out and had an affair, and now you have a second family. Those were your decisions. If you had asked me about it, I probably would have said, 'Don't do it.' But you didn't. And if you try to worm your way out of the settlement, I will give you *such* a battle, that frankly, if it wiped me out financially I wouldn't care. It's not like I have a whole lot at stake, unlike some people who get twice-yearly bonuses of stock options. I wonder what those are worth, James? If we go to court everything is discoverable; you know, maybe it's not such a bad idea."

He was silent.

"I have to go," I said, "but I'll be sure to let my lawyer know you called."

"Wait," he said, before I could hang up.

"What?"

"How's Josh's basketball going?"

"It's fine. Why don't you go to one of his games? It would mean a lot to him."

"You know I can't."

"I have to go." And before he could say anything else, I hung up.

I stared at the three Pyrex trays of half-assembled lasagna and felt my stomach want to heave. No matter how hard I tried, he still got to me. Waves of anger pulsed through my body. I meant every word I said; if he attempted to get the settlement reworked in his favor, I would fight him tooth and nail. And truthfully, I suspected that if we did go to court, it would probably go in my favor. James was at the VP level of a software firm that was currently doing quite well. If we went to court, I'd be more than a little curious to see what he was making. And like so much with my ex-husband, I suspected that his phone call was more an attempt to bully me than anything else.

I was angrily spooning the next layer of sauce when the phone rang. If it's him, I'm going to hang up. It was my mother.

"Hi, Mom," I said, with a sigh.

"That's a lovely way to greet your mother. What's wrong?"

"I just got off the phone with James."

"Oh. What does he want?"

"Freedom, from his bitch ex-wife."

"Don't talk that way, Molly."

"Sorry. I'm real worked up right now."

"I can tell," she said in a soothing voice. "Maybe you should try and take a hot tub or something to try and calm down."

"I'm making lasagna."

"That's good, too. Did you make your own sauce?"

"You've got to be kidding. I barely have time to boil water for the noodles."

"Canned sauce?"

"Bottled."

"Oh my. I could bring some over." It was clear that she felt I was about to poison my son and myself.

"Josh doesn't even know the difference," I replied.

She grew silent. "It makes a difference."

I braced myself for the inevitable.

She warmed slowly to a favorite chestnut. "Every bit of effort you expend on your family makes a difference. That's what I've always believed. It's what my mother taught me and her mother taught her. Sure sauce is sauce, but it's the caring that goes into it that matters." As she laid out her theory on wives and women in general, I remembered the icy tension that existed between her parents and my father. It amazed me how much she had embraced her mother's philosophy while simultaneously doing the one thing that had put her at total odds with her parents. "I don't like to say this, Molly, but I think this whole doctor thing could have waited until your children were grown."

This was no revelation. "Look, Mom, I don't even want to get into this. If this were Jonathan,"

I said, bringing my sainted older brother into the mix, "we wouldn't be having this discussion."

She didn't budge. "You had a perfectly good job."

"This is what I want, Mom. I love meeting with patients and having more control over how things will go. In truth," and I knew I shouldn't say it, "I never really wanted to be a nurse."

I heard a sharp outrush of breath over the line. "That's not true."

"It is. But I remember in high school that you let me know what the choices were. I think it was something like, 'You need a job until you get married, but be careful not to do something that will make more money than your husband.'"

"I never said that."

"You did. Or something pretty close, because Lord knows it stuck with me."

"I don't care what you say, your nursing certificate gave you something to fall back on."

"Absolutely, and thank God I had it." A clicking sounded over the receiver. "Mom, I've got someone trying to get through, hold on." I depressed the button before she could reply. "Hello?"

"Dr. Katz?" A male voice responded.

"Yes."

"This is Dr. Freeborn, we met yesterday."

"How are you doing?" I asked, having no clue as to why he would be calling me in the evening.

"We have a situation here, and I was wondering if you might be able to help out." He sounded tense.

"If I can."

"Our overnight resident is in the hospital with a

ruptured appendix. And none of the other on-call doctors are available. I was wondering if there was any way you might be able to fill in for the rest of the night." And then he hurriedly added, "Because this is such short notice, I'd throw in a couple hundred dollars extra and I will be very available by telephone if you need help."

I looked out over my counter of fully constructed, yet unbaked lasagna. "It'll probably take me about an hour to get there," I told him, quickly calculating the drive time, plus a few minutes to throw some clothes into an overnight bag for work tomorrow.

"You'll do it?" His voice lightened.

"Sure, why not." I was already reaching for the Saran Wrap.

"I really appreciate this."

"Glad to help."

He thanked me again and hung up. I was about to put down the receiver when my mother reminded me that she was on hold.

"Did you forget me?" she asked.

"No, sorry. I'm going to need to go. They're short an on-call doc." I neglected to tell her that this was a new moonlighting job.

"And your son?" she asked, implying with her tone that my behavior was less than motherly.

"He's at basketball practice and planning to sleep over with friends afterwards."

"On a school night?"

"I've got to go. Give my love to Dad."

"If you ask me," and she fired one last volley, "you have got to slow down."

With the phone crooked between my ear and

my neck, I maneuvered the large plastic-covered dishes into the freezer. "Love you, Mom." And before she could rally any further thoughts, I hung up.

I dialed the home where Josh would be staying tonight and left word with his best friend's mom as to where I would be and the number. Three minutes later I was at my front door with my canvas on-call bag. I ran through a mental checklist of everything I needed to make it through until tomorrow, then I locked the door and headed to my car.

I thought of Garret and wondered if maybe tonight he would be able to talk. I had a delicious sense of doing something almost illicit, a faint echo of the childhood excitement of sneaking downstairs in the middle of the night to raid the cookie jar.

As I backed out of my driveway I saw something large run across the driveway in my rearview mirror. I turned to see what it was, but it had vanished into the darkness. Just to reassure myself, I let my headlights play across the front of my house, but I saw nothing and told myself that it must have been a dog.

CHAPTER TWELVE

What had I done to myself? At 3:00 A.M. on Friday morning I raced through the back stairwells of Whitestone Forensic. A nurse had just paged me to say that one of the patients was having a seizure, of course she couldn't tell if it was real or not. Apparently this particular patient had discovered that seizures were frequently treated with Valium-like drugs.

I emerged on the third floor, checked the wall sign to see if I was on the right ward, and pressed the button to be let onto the unit. Dr. Freeborn had presented me with a large ring of keys for the evening and had apologized that he didn't have time to get me the bar-coded identification tag that would make ninety percent of the keys unnecessary. In retrospect, I should have asked to borrow his. None of the keys was labeled and it was just faster for the staff to look at me through their monitor and then buzz me onto the unit. I waited and tapped my foot; I now understood why Whitestone had such a hard time keeping moonlighters. This place was huge, and as one of the nurses was telling me, "They just wait for the regular docs to leave and then see what drugs they can scam out of the moonlighters."

The door clicked and I pushed it open. I called out as I approached the nursing station, "What's up?"

"George Brisbane," the nurse replied. "And the question is, is he having a fit or pitching a fit?"

"Let's go see. You have the chart?" I asked.

"You got it." And she handed over a thick yellow three-ring notebook.

As we walked I riffled through the pages. In reading his admission note I learned that Mr. Brisbane had a long history of cognitive deficits secondary to some form of traumatic brain injury. I also learned that he was a dangerous pedophile. "It says he does have a seizure disorder," I commented as we approached the room where an aide was monitoring the patient from the doorway.

"That's what it says," she agreed, and then under her breath added, "but you can't believe everything you read."

We both took in the sight of Mr. Brisbane. He flapped his arms and his legs like a fish after it has been pulled from the water. He shouted out, "I'm having a seizure . . . I need something for it."

Without missing a beat, I made the diagnosis of pseudoseizure, i.e., pitching a fit rather than truly having a fit. In a loud voice I told the nurse, "Let's try 325 milligrams of salicylic acid."

She smiled and whispered, "You, I like." Then in tones that could be heard by the patient, "I'll get that right away, Doctor."

"Okay, Mr. Brisbane," I told him. "I'm going to give you something to try and make you calm down."

He looked at me with a hint of suspiciousness

while maintaining a rhythmic jerking of his extremities. "What are you giving me?"

"Salicylic acid."

"They usually give me Valium or Serax," he stated.

"You'll like this, it'll help," I let him know, with a semiconspiratorial tone.

"Whatever you think, Doc."

The nurse returned with a small cup of water and the white tablet.

The patient dutifully swallowed the pill while still trying to maintain his seizure.

Within moments his flailing had stopped.

"Try to get some sleep," I urged as I hurriedly scribbled a note on his chart.

"Thanks, Doc."

"Don't mention it." And still balancing the chart, walking, and writing, I signed my name. The note read—if anyone could actually decipher my early-morning scrawl—

Called to see patient with complaint of seizure. Upon examination, patient was fully alert and oriented and stated, "I'm having a seizure." Based on presentation this most likely represented a feigned seizure. A placebo—aspirin 325mg—was administered with rapid resolution of the symptoms.

The whole night had been like this. I thought back to what Rob had said about Whitestone. This was no "sleeping for dollars." At least tomorrow, actually today come to think of it, was Friday. And God be thanked; I didn't have any on-call responsibilities over the weekend. It was now a quarter to four; the shift ended at seven-thirty. If I allowed for drive time, I would make it to the unit in time for eight-thirty rounds. At least I would be several hundred dollars richer for my suffering. Maybe I could even get Dr. Freeborn to give me the bonus under the table. Hmmm. Other than that, this night had been a bust. My attempts to see Garret were sadly ineffective. As a result of his catatonia they had decided to give him electro-convulsive therapy to try to break him out of it. When I saw him earlier in the evening he was still mute and appeared sedated. He blinked when I called his name, but other than that, there wasn't much to be learned. At least I had the chance to review his chart and to see where things lay. The court-appointed psychiatrists were all in agreement that he was unfit to stand trial. Down the road, that could certainly change.

I reached into the pocket of my lab coat and retrieved the folded copy of the map of the facility that Dr. Freeborn had given me. I looked around for landmarks and began to head in the direction of the intake unit and the on-call room. Whenever I'm on call I have these superstitious patterns of thought that take over. One of them is that I don't like to acknowledge that I'm going to try to get some sleep. Somehow, that comes too close to tempting the fates. So I'll head in the direction of the on-call room and if I happen to lie down and fall asleep, so be it.

I emerged on the right floor and anxiously looked in the direction of the intake suite. My heart lightened as I realized that there were no new late-night admissions. Then I spent a good three minutes fumbling through the keys until I came upon one that unlocked the on-call room. I switched on the light and looked around at the dingy furnishings and single bed covered in a worn and suspiciously stained off-white spread. My overnight bag lay on the desk where I had hurriedly dropped it when I first came in.

I sank down on the bed and was grateful for the layer of clothing between the stained linens and me. Where my lab coat and scrub shirt brushed up against my neck I could feel a sticky layer of grime. I would want a shower before heading onto Hamilton 5. I plumped a couple pillows back onto the bed and turned on the television. Flipping between channels I found nothing to hold my interest so I turned down the set, lay back, and closed my eyes.

As I knew it would, my pager sounded.

I sat up, looked at the number on the display, and dialed.

"Hello? Is this the doctor on call?" a man's voice asked.

"This is Dr. Katz, I was paged."

"We have a patient who's complaining of substernal chest pain."

My ears perked.

"How long has he had it?"

"He says it started after dinner. He thought it was indigestion, but it's been getting worse. We gave him some Maalox about an hour ago and that didn't help."

"How are his vitals?"

"I don't have them right here, but I can get them if you want?"

"Please."

As I waited, I watched the flickering images on the silent television. It was now 4:00 A.M. Any chance I had for sleep had just been eliminated.

When the nurse returned he read off the patient's blood pressure, pulse, and respirations. The pressure was high and the pulse was fast.

"I'll be right there," I told him. "I want you to get a stat EKG and give him a sublingual nitro 1/150. Is he sweating?"

"A little."

"I'm on my way."

With the skirts of my lab coat flapping in and out with every step, I jogged in what I hoped was the right direction. All night long I had been besieged with calls for extra medication. Apparently the word was out that there was a new moonlighter and everyone wanted his shot. As I raced toward the unit I knew that in another setting I would have already called for an ambulance. Why didn't I have the nurse do that here?

I rapped loudly on the door of the unit and pushed the buzzer. The aide let me in and pointed me in the direction of the room where the nurse was now rolling out the EKG machine.

"Here you are," he said, handing me the glossy page. "I gave him the first nitro about a minute ago."

This was not my area of expertise, but even I knew that the depressions I was seeing on the EKG indicated a possible heart attack in progress. I looked at the patient, a middle-aged man with the gaunt look I associated with tuberculosis or AIDs. "How bad is the pain?" I asked.

"It's a little better."

"Still there?"

"Yeah."

I turned to the nurse. "He needs to go to the hospital."

"I'll call an ambulance."

I stayed with the patient and asked the litany of chest pain questions. "On a scale of one to ten how bad is the pain?"

"A six now. It was a ten."

"Okay, when the nurse gets back we'll give you another nitro. Is the pain sharp or stabbing?"

"Like a pressure, like someone's squeezing my chest."

"Does it go anywhere? Up your jaw or down your arm?"

"Not really, maybe a little down my left side."

The ambulance arrived, and soon my man with the heart attack was heading toward the hospital accompanied by the EMTs and an armed police officer.

I scratched a brief note in the chart, indicating what had happened and where the patient was being taken.

The nurse looked over my shoulder. "Thanks," he said.

"For what?"

"For coming so quickly . . . you must be new." He smiled. "My name's Gerry."

"Molly." We shook hands. "So the other doctors wouldn't get down here that fast?"

"Not usually. I think after a while the ratio of real versus malingering gets to wear them down. They don't jump as fast as the new guys."

I thought about my not having called the ambulance earlier. "The hospital that cried wolf?" I offered.

"You never know what's real or not, particularly on the overnight."

I mulled over his comment as I walked back to the on-call room. My body and my thoughts had the curious lightness of too little sleep. I was running on adrenaline and would probably crash sometime around midafternoon.

I glanced at the clock; it was five-thirty. The television was still on with the sound turned down. I grabbed the remote and turned to the local news, which was just coming on with the early morning edition.

A woman reporter was running through the morning headlines. One in particular stopped me cold!

This morning police discovered the body of a local nurse in the fens. The woman's identity is known but has not yet been released, pending notification of the family. This case is being treated as a homicide, although police are not yet willing to comment on the motive.

I stared at the screen wanting more. But she had already moved on to scandals in the White House and to the upcoming campaign against inner-city violence.

Perhaps it was the hour or my lack of sleep, but I had a sickening premonition that the nurse would turn out to be someone I knew.

CHAPTER THIRTEEN

Something was wrong. I felt it in the prickly sensation as my neck scraped against the back of my blouse. I had managed a quick shower in the mildew-stained bathroom at Whitestone, but even so I felt the sticky residue of my night on call. And back on the unit, Hamilton 5 was too quiet. A group of nurses clustered around the station, one of the aides was in tears. This did not look good.

"What's going on?" I asked, approaching Barbara, one of the nurses.

She looked at me with the wide-eyed expression of someone who has just been in a car accident. "Janice Blake was murdered."

I felt numb as my head took in the information. This couldn't be happening. I thought of the woman reporter and the body found in the fens. "When?" was the only response I could muster.

"Last night," she answered. "It must have been last night."

"Right," I said dully. "She was here yesterday." And that was the awful truth. Just twenty-four hours ago she had been in rounds. We had discussed patients; she had asked me for a stat

Ativan for a twelve-year-old who was banging his head against the wall.

Carol Petrullo came over to us. "We have to round," she said softly.

She attempted to gather up the staff; there was work to be done. I found it difficult to move. I stood there with Barbara, unable to focus, thinking about Janice. How could she just be gone?

A fourteen-year-old boy approached us. "I want to play Nintendo," he stated.

"You can't . . ." Barbara started, then changed her mind. "I'll get it."

I followed her to the locked cabinet in the occupational therapy room. "I know they're not supposed to play this early in the morning," she said, apologetically, "but maybe it'll keep them quiet."

"I think it's a good idea," I offered, helping to extricate the box.

We set up the video game and asked one of the aides to supervise. Like lemmings to the cliff, five of the adolescent boys, most of them admitted for out-of-control behaviors with diagnoses like conduct disorder and oppositional defiant disorder, descended on the game. I was a bit concerned that they would fight over the controls, but the biggest and meanest boy claimed it as his own and there was general agreement with that plan. Barbara and I stood back watching the five children. They were between eleven and sixteen and in the bright morning sun flooding the airy room, they looked like a Norman Rockwell painting. Five beautiful boys caught up in the excitement of Death Race 2000. But that was in the sun; I looked around at each of them individually: at the fire-starter, at the boy who learned how to make guns over the Internet, at the fourteen-year-old who had shot holes in his English teacher's new car with his father's handgun, at the boy who was caught dissecting the neighbors' cat, and at the twelve-year-old whose group home was trying to kick him out for being sexually inappropriate with the other children. The one with the joystick, the oldest and biggest and therefore the alpha dog on the unit, would likely go to jail following his stay here. His arms bore a gang tattoo on the right and a home-made banner with the name of an ex-girlfriend on the left. He had several outstanding warrants, and the police checked on his progress daily. He was here for depression, most of it situational and related to his upcoming arraignment. He didn't want to go to prison.

The other children on the unit, those with early psychosis, depression, or anxiety disorders, tended to avoid this group. The bad boys we called them. Each one of whom could break your heart as you got to know him. The stories embedded in their charts were modern nightmares. The twelve-year-old at the group home had been prostituted by his drug-addicted father from the age of three until he was taken away from home at age eight. He was then placed with an aunt who beat him, and again he was removed. Since that time he had bounced in and out of group homes, each one a little more regimented than the last. Now he awaited placement at the end-of-the-line residential home: Brentwood. The behavior that had so disturbed the workers was becoming

harder for him to control. With all of these boys
that seemed to be a unifying factor—poor impulse control and an inability to handle stressful
situations without becoming violent. I watched
the video game they were playing, where all situations were handled with the crashing of cars and
the blowing up of various obstacles; perhaps it
wasn't the right message.

But still, with the sunlight streaming through
the windows catching the dust like glitter in its
rays, they were beautiful.

Carol stuck her head in the door. "Molly, Barbara, we have to round."

The gun-maker looked back at us and smiled.

"John," I said to the oldest boy, "make sure
that everyone gets a chance to play."

He nodded, his attention riveted to the screen
and to the animated racer that zoomed ever faster
around the track.

I could have stayed there watching them. I didn't
want to go into rounds. I didn't want to hear about
Janice, I just wanted her to be alive and at work. I
wanted this to be a normal day with normal children playing Nintendo.

I looked at Barbara. Two tears slowly tracked
down her cheeks. "Come on," I said. "We may as
well get this over with."

We left the boys under the aide's watchful eye
and went into the large group room for morning
report.

I took my usual seat next to Rob, and Barbara
sat down with the row of staff nurses. There was
no assigned seating, but I suspected that as residents and medical students came and went they

always sat in exactly the same places. Everyone knew his or her place at the table.

I looked at Rob, who seemed tired and upset. His eyes had the red-rimmed look of someone who had been crying.

He nodded his head and rubbed his right temple. "It doesn't seem real," he said. "Why is this happening?"

I was about to respond when Felix cleared his throat and began to speak.

I struggled to focus on his words. I looked around the room, and saw that I wasn't alone. I saw shock mirrored in my coworkers' eyes; it was the glassy expression of news that had not quite sunk in. One nurse looked in the direction of the door and began to sob uncontrollably. I followed her gaze and saw the now familiar duo of the hospital attorney and the police lieutenant.

Felix nodded in their direction and they entered. Just as earlier in the week, they took up positions behind the unit chief. Sonja stood back to the left and Lieutenant Harris was her bookend on the right, just as before—a place for everything and everything in its place.

CHAPTER FOURTEEN

It had been thirty hours without sleep and my head buzzed with too much coffee. My thoughts kept pulling me back to Janice's murder. Two nurses from one unit did not seem like a coincidence. Lieutenant Harris had repeatedly stressed that there was no clear connection between the cases. Still, on day one of a murder investigation what was he doing on Hamilton 5 if he didn't think there was some connection?

I forced myself through rounds and through seeing all of my patients. I took a new admission—a twelve-year-old boy with a suicidal depression—and then I tried to catch up on my discharge summaries. It was now four o'clock; I could leave in an hour, but my reserves had been depleted despite hourly cups of coffee. I stared at the hateful Dictaphone and at the pile of undictated charts. I couldn't make myself do it. Other residents had no trouble keeping up with their paperwork. Rob kept telling me to do my discharge summaries right as the patient leaves the hospital; I hated them. I'm forever flipping through the chart while trying to maintain a cogent thought. Some people rattled off discharge summaries barely looking at the chart. In my present mood, the waiting charts just made me crazy.

I pushed back from my desk and the Dictaphone. I looked at the clock—just one hour until the weekend. A tacky song from my youth sprang to mind. "I'm only working for the weekend." I smiled at the thought and at the brief flash of high school memory. I pictured driving around with my girlfriends, the radio blasting and the windows down—how many lifetimes ago was that? This is where we were now, my girlfriends and I, all in our thirties and all of us working to support families. And that was Janice too, just like me. Who would take care of her children? What would this do to them? I thought of my own kids, what would it be like if I were murdered? Who would take Josh to basketball or keep Megan on track? I suppose my mother would step in, and maybe even James would come through if I were out of the picture.

I chewed on the thought that the two deaths may not be a coincidence. What if someone was deliberately killing the nurses on the unit? I'm a nurse—no, I reminded myself, you were a nurse. Still, I'm not one who can let things alone—especially if there is any chance it could hurt my family. Even my divorce was probably more for my kids, Megan in particular, than it was for me. That's what I told myself at the time, but I was damned if I was going to have my daughter grow up thinking that it was okay for her father to cheat on her mother. It was Megan, when she was eight years old, who told me about the pretty woman she had seen with Daddy. That was the start of my most horrible year. Perhaps I had always known about James and his roving eye. I had just thought that like Jimmy Carter he was only lusting in his heart. I was wrong and I couldn't ignore it. I hounded James until I learned the truth, and no amount of pleading or apologizing could sway me from my course. The loathing that grew inside of me was something I had never before experienced. Even looking at him made my stomach turn. Years later I still felt the anger boil. In a weird way, I almost relished the idea of him trying to take me back to court. I had been too timid at the time of our divorce. Since then, just as I advise my patients, I have learned to assert myself.

And that was the missing piece in today's scenario. The entire unit was in a state of near panic. Uncertainty and fear fueled a lot of it. To a psychiatrist, fear is our stock in trade. We encourage our patients to look into the heart of their fears and to challenge them. Sitting with patients and talking with Dr. Adams I had begun to understand how fear grows and how it can be beaten back. The passivity and fatalism that had swept through the nursing staff were making matters worse. There were too many unknowns, and neither the hospital attorney nor Lieutenant Harris was able to supply satisfactory answers.

The pink elephant dancing in the room that no one had spoken about was Garret. Granted they were stressing that these were unrelated crimes—and maybe they were. But what if they weren't? And in that question lay a more important one.

I looked at the phone, picked up the receiver, and asked the hospital operator to get me the number for the Major Crime bureau of the Boston police. I felt a swarm of anxious butterflies in my stomach as I waited to be connected.

A secretary picked up. "Major Crimes Division."

I pushed forward. "Hi, this is Dr. Molly Katz, I want to speak with someone involved with the Janice Blake case."

"One moment, please."

I waited and listened to the radio music that had been piped in over the phone line. About a minute later the operator returned. "Detective Wallace is on another call. I could give him your message or you could hold."

"I'll hold. Thanks." And the music started up again as the call was transferred. Time dragged and I tried to formulate what I was going to say. Finally, he picked up.

"Wallace here," a man's brusque voice answered.

"Hi." And I felt my resolve weaken. "This is Dr. Katz from Commonwealth Hospital, I wanted to talk to somebody about the Janice Blake case."

"There's no one here right now, but I can take your information and get it to them."

"It's not so much information as I'm wondering if they're completely certain that this case and the Helen Weir case are unrelated. If they're not one-hundred-percent sure, then we need to look at the prime suspect in Helen's case, who couldn't have been the killer in Janice's case, because he's been locked up for the past week." I heard myself prattle on and wished the detective would say something. "Do you see what I'm saying?"

"I'll pass on your concerns . . . was there anything else?"

"No."

He thanked me and hung up.

I sat there feeling like an idiot and stared at my clock. I looked at the pile of charts that needed to be dictated. In fifteen minutes I would be free to go, but any anticipation of my weekend off had been destroyed by today's news.

I dragged the top chart off of the stack and picked up the Dictaphone recorder. "This is Dr. Molly Katz dictating a discharge summary on Ludy Duncan, last name spelled D-U-N-C-A-N. Date of admission—" And the phone rang before I had even made it into the chief complaint.

"Hello?"

"Dr. Katz?" a man's voice asked.

"Yes."

"This is Lieutenant Harris, I just got the message that you called."

"Right." I took a deep breath. "I don't want to sound like I'm prying. But I need to know if Janice's murder and Helen Weir's murder are totally unrelated."

He hesitated before responding. "Because of Garret Jacobs?"

"Exactly."

"You were his doctor," he stated. "Let me ask you, do you think he was capable of the killing?"

"At first I wasn't certain," I said, glad for the chance to really discuss the case. "I thought it was possible, and based on what I had been told, I think I assumed like everybody else that he had killed Helen."

"And now?"

"I don't think so. He's too sick. I can't imagine him being able to string together enough linear thought to track down a knife and then carry through with an attack. I mean, maybe if someone put the knife in his hand and maybe if he happened to have been sufficiently frightened or overcome with a powerful enough delusion. But Garret's thoughts vacillate between complete disorganization and whatever the thought process becomes when someone is catatonic."

"Out of curiosity, when did you last see Garret?" he asked.

In for a penny, I thought, knowing that I was about to tread on shaky ground. "Last night."

"You were at Whitestone," he stated.

"Yes."

"May I ask what you were doing there?"

"I moonlight there." Of course he didn't need to know that last night was my very first shift.

"Interesting . . . and you saw Garret?"

"Yes."

"Isn't it possible that he could be faking?"

"I don't think so."

"What do you base that opinion on?" he asked, not in a rude way, but with a tone that made me think he genuinely wanted to understand my reasoning.

I pondered the question. "There are a few things." And I wondered about the ethics of talking to the lieutenant about a patient. But I quickly argued with myself that it was in Garret's best interest that the detective heading up the investigation get a true understanding of the severity of his illness. "First off, he's catatonic. He stays fixed in the same position for hours. He's not eating and they have him hooked up to a feeding tube to keep him from starving to death. If he were faking, I think it would be near impossible to maintain the postures that he freezes in. In talking with his mother you can get a sense of the progression of his illness. Also, if he were malingering, what would be the benefit?"

"No motive," he admitted.

"Exactly."

"What about the delusions you mentioned earlier? I don't deny that he's a sick kid—probably one of the few times I wouldn't be upset with a not guilty by reason of insanity plea. But isn't it possible that he acted out of some delusional belief?"

"It's possible, but again, and I'm not a forensic expert, I don't think he was ever organized enough to carry through on something that would require any planning and steps."

"Steps?"

"Sequence, you know like find a knife, pick up a knife, follow a nurse. That takes the ability to have linear thought. Garret, ever since he was admitted, had almost none of that. He just didn't make sense; one thought would get interrupted by another. It was like there was no filtering mechanism in his brain." The more I talked to the lieutenant, the more convinced I became that Garret couldn't possibly have killed Helen.

"Dr. Katz, would it be possible for you to meet with me and talk about this further?"

"Of course, when?"

"How about tomorrow morning?"

"What time?"

And we made plans to meet.

After he hung up, I had second thoughts about what I had just done. Then I thought of my dad and what he might say about civic duty. In my heart I truly believed that Garret couldn't have killed Helen. That I just now articulated that thought raised several more disturbing concerns. The chief one being, if Garret didn't kill Helen, then who did?

CHAPTER FIFTEEN

It was Saturday morning at the police precinct. I waited outside Lieutenant Harris's office; a uniformed officer who served as his secretary offered me coffee.

"He's on the phone and should be right out," he said before continuing with his stack of filing.

The station was in a rehabbed Back Bay office building. The redbrick facade dated back to the late eighteen hundreds, but the interior had been changed and remodeled to the point where it looked like any other office building—that is of course without taking into account the holding area and the drunk tank on the first floor. There were no magazines and only a few trifold brochures titled "Know your Legal Rights," littering the wood-grain Formica-top coffee tables. I picked one up and started to scan the text that had been carefully written to not exceed a sixth-grade reading level.

Lieutenant Harris emerged from his office. He was dressed down for the weekend in well-pressed khakis and a white button-down shirt with the collar open. "Dr. Katz," he said coming over to me. "It was good of you to come down on your Saturday."

"My pleasure," I said, while appreciating the color of his eyes, which were somewhere between a sapphire blue and something a bit darker. If he had been a woman I might have suspected colored contact lenses.

I followed him into his office; it was a tidy room filled with filing cabinets and dominated by a large oak banker's desk. On top of it a computer displayed a screen saver of animated Batman villains who appeared and then got placed behind prison bars.

"Nice screen saver," I commented, while sitting directly across from his desk.

"My son gave it to me."

My heart skipped a beat, but what did I expect? Hadn't he told me that he had children? Just because he didn't wear a wedding ring was no reason to think he wasn't married. "How many kids do you have?" I asked, trying not to appear too obvious.

"Just the one. And you?"

"Two."

"No wedding ring," he commented.

"No husband . . . not for a long time. And you?"

"No wife . . . for a short time."

"I'm sorry to hear that," I said, feeling nothing of the sort.

"Stuff happens." And a half smile broke beneath his bushy salt-and-pepper mustache. "You want to do this somewhere else? Maybe grab a late breakfast or early lunch?"

"Absolutely."

"Great. I need to get away from the office." He

held the door for me. "Jim, we're going out; I'm on the beeper if you need me," he told the officer/receptionist.

Outside, a cool breeze blew, and the air was scented with perfume from the flowering pear trees that had been planted along the street. He glanced quickly in both directions. "Any preference?" he asked.

"Not really—you probably know what's around here better than I do."

"You up for a bit of a walk?" he asked.

I felt my rubber-soled Timberlands underfoot and was grateful that I had talked myself out of a more dressed-up, feminine choice. Like the lieutenant I had opted for the universal default mode—khakis from the Gap and a button-down shirt. It was kind of scary how similarly we were dressed. "I love to walk and it is a gorgeous day."

"Isn't it?"

We took a right and headed at a companionable clip down Beacon Street. It must have been close to eleven, but the street was still relatively quiet. The trees in the center island park were filled with soft green buds, and carefully tended beds of crocus and daffodil added vivid purple, yellow, and white splotches against the awakening green of spring.

"I love this time of year," he said.

"What's not to love?"

"It must be very hard," he said.

"What?"

"From what little I know about you, you have two kids, are doing a psychiatric residency, and then you moonlight on top of that."

"I keep busy," I said with a chuckle.

"I guess you do."

"And you're at work on a weekend," I countered, "so what does that mean?"

"You don't even want to know."

"The buck stops here?"

"Something like that," he agreed. "It's not like the work goes away just because it's Saturday." His tone was grim.

I wondered if his job dedication might have had something to do with his relatively recent single status. At this point it was just a hypothesis.

"How do you feel about diners?" he asked.

"Love 'em."

"Great, can you take a bit of a longer walk?"

"Sure."

"It's on the other side of the Gardens."

"I'm a hardy woman."

He laughed. "Yes, I can see that. You're like that woman in the old ad where she brought home the bacon and fried it up in a pan."

"Oh yes, that's me. It's more like defrost the bacon and stick it in the microwave. Then fall asleep in my clothes because I'm too exhausted to get undressed."

"The freezer is our friend," he agreed.

I noticed that we had barely mentioned the case. Apparently so had he, as his expression changed.

"You were saying some stuff about Garret," he began. "That you really didn't think he could have killed Helen Weir. Let's suppose that despite a dozen witnesses seeing him on top of the body with a bloody knife, that he hadn't done it. That would mean someone else had," he said, admitting to the possibility that the entire case would need to be reopened.

"I know, and that's why I was asking about Janice's murder. There wasn't a lot to go on from the papers."

"That was deliberate," he said. "Sometimes you keep back bits of information from the press."

"I figured . . . do you think the killings were connected?"

"You are direct, aren't you?"

"So my mother tells me—apparently it's a problem."

"Not with me, but what we talk about can't go any further."

"Understood."

"They might be connected," he conceded.

"So if that's the case," I continued, "then Garret is pretty much off the hook."

"If he acted alone. Dr. Katz, did Garret make friends with any of the other patients on the unit?"

"Call me Molly, but let me think."

"Peter," he offered.

First names—very nice, I mused, as I tried to recall what we were talking about. "Did Garret make friends . . . that's difficult to say. The kids tend to cluster on the unit, and even though he was pretty out of it, for the first few days, he was around the other kids."

"Tell me about the kids on the unit." He steered us toward the Boston Gardens.

"It's a pretty sad lot. They come in a couple basic varieties, maybe three. There's the depressed group, and these are the kids who come in suicidal but otherwise have been doing okay. It's actually the smallest number. Then we've got kids like Garret who are in the early stages of some major psychotic disorder that's probably seventy-five percent or more biologically driven. That's the second-biggest group. But far and away most of the kids we get are there for out-of-control behavior either directed at themselves or at others."

"Sociopaths?" he asked.

"In the making. Even the diagnostic language stays away from calling them that until they're over eighteen. They get diagnoses like oppositional defiant disorder or conduct disorder, the latter being the more ominous."

"So there is a criminal element, albeit juvenile, on the unit."

"Big time. You look at these kids and it's sometimes hard to believe that they've done the horrible things that are written all over their charts."

"What sorts of things?"

"You name it. Torturing animals, beating up other kids, beating up their parents, setting fires, threatening people with guns, shooting people, trying to kill their siblings, threatening their teachers, destroying property. And that's just the stuff that can get them arrested. The other things, like talking back to teachers, getting thrown out of school, sexual promiscuity, drugs, the list goes on and on. Every time I meet with one of these kids the stories are the same, it's just that the events get shifted around."

We stopped in front of the man-made lake in the middle of the Gardens and watched as a group of tourists in one of the swan boats was pedaled around in the shallow water.

"There were seventeen kids on the unit the night that Helen was killed," he said. "Of those, how many would you put in that last category?"

"It's hard to remember the specifics, but in general it's over half the unit."

"How many of them are still on the unit?"

"The ones who were there when Garret was there?"

"From Monday."

"Probably less than half. Our average length of stay is less than a week."

"Really? That seems kind of short."

"It's very short, but that's what you get now. It's very hard to keep them longer on the inpatient unit. The insurance companies stop paying the minute they're no longer acutely suicidal or homicidal. You have to fight for every single day."

"Then where do they go?"

"It depends," I said, as we exited the park and headed onto one of the cobblestone side streets at the base of Beacon Hill. "Typically they go back with a parent or some other relative. Some of them who've been in the system for a while live in group homes. It varies."

"I don't mean to sound disrespectful, but what can you possibly do in a week or under?"

"Not much," I admitted. "We provide a safe environment . . . or at least try to. We look at what caused the most immediate problem and see if there's anything we can do to help. Maybe we do some testing to see if we've missed something diagnostically. We'll probably use some medication to try to get these kids to think before they act on their impulses, but it's a lot of quick fix and then send them out. Most of the work has to take place in an outpatient setting. Sometimes you can get them and their parents to follow through and sometimes you can't."

"Who sees them outpatient?" he asked.

"We refer a lot of them to our day program and clinic. Others have their own treaters that they go back to."

"It must be kind of discouraging," he commented.

"At times. I don't think about that much; I actually like working with them, because most of the time, they're just kids. But when they get upset or frustrated, all hell breaks loose."

By this time he had steered us into the maze of cobblestone streets that comprise Beacon Hill. He stopped. "This is the place," he said, and I looked up at the sign for the ancient storefront restaurant: Caroline's Home Cooking.

"Looks great." I caught the first whiff of bacon and sausage as he held the door for me.

We sat in one of the two window booths, and within thirty seconds the waitress delivered steaming cups of coffee and well-worn menus. I snuck a glance or two over my menu at Peter. All my life I have been attracted to tall, well-built men. As much as I loathed my ex, there was no denying that he had been genetically blessed. Peter Harris, who I guessed to be around my age, fit neatly into my template. And then there were those eyes. As if on cue, he looked up and smiled.

"What were you saying about frustration?" he asked.

It took me a couple seconds to figure out what

he was alluding to. "Right, the kids. If they get upset, they're not able to contain it. Like if you or I get some bad news, we figure out ways of handling it. They don't. The emotion becomes too big and they go off."

"We see that with the criminal element," he stated. "A guy gets drunk, gets pissed off, and does something stupid—at least some of them. And those guys, you can actually feel kind of sorry for them. But with murder, if it wasn't Garret, then there's someone out there who really thought it through and put together a very nice cover-up. That doesn't strike me as an impulsive act."

"No," I agreed. "That's what we could call a planful behavior."

"So these kids aren't 'planful'?"

"No, some of them are. Some of them are very bright, and when there's something they want they can be extremely goal-oriented. Or if they feel that they've been insulted, they can organize around revenge. Unfortunately, the stuff that interests them, especially the boys, has to do with weapons and other things that go bang and blow up. Some of them fantasize about revenge, and some of them, especially as they hit puberty, have violent sexual fantasies."

"Which, because they can't contain the emotion, they're more likely to act out?"

"Exactly. A lot of them have already assaulted others. I've treated thirteen-year-old rapists."

"So what's the treatment?" he asked, with a trace of skepticism.

"By thirteen . . . I think we're mostly looking at damage control." I stopped myself, hating the tone of clinical nihilism that had colored my words. "I shouldn't say that. Some of these kids do pull it together and sometimes we're able to turn things around. One of the big problems is that at thirteen they have no concept of repercussions. They can't make the connection between their impulse, their action, and the resultant chaos or punishment that gets generated. It's a developmental issue that's very hard to get around."

"Like trying to toilet train too early?"

"Right. Teenagers, especially early teens, just can't think things through in the long term. Everything is based on the moment. It's why a lot of antidrug and unprotected-sex campaigns are met with limited success. And then you have the other major teen factor that can undo your best parenting or clinical efforts."

"Which is?"

"Peer pressure. Kids desperately want to fit in. Even when they wear crazy clothes, they're the same crazy clothes their friends are wearing. If you see a kid dressed strangely I'd be willing to bet he's trying to fit in with other kids dressed just as weird. Plus it has the added advantage of ticking off their parents. When my daughter was sixteen she went to New York and had her tongue pierced."

"No kidding. What did you do?"

"What could I do? Aside from ripping it out, which probably would have gotten me reported to DSS. I yelled at her. Then I grounded her. I focused on the fact that she went to New York without my permission and that the piercing could easily become infected. Basically, I played right into her hand. She got what she wanted. Her friends thought she was a hero, and she had successfully pissed off both me and her father."

"So it was deliberate?"

I formulated my answer as the waitress returned with large oval platters of French toast and bacon. "Deliberate is a funny word, because it implies planning. Yes, I think my daughter had some notion of going down to New York with her friends. Beyond that, I don't think she had thought through the piercing, and I doubt she thought about how severe the punishment would be."

"Help me with that one. Colin's not there yet, he's only ten, but this stuff is just around the corner."

"That's a nice name," I said, honing in on the crumb of personal information. "English?"

"Irish. I had an Uncle Colin and my wife liked the name."

I couldn't let that drop. "Who does he stay with?"

He looked at me across the table. The twinkle had left his eyes and there was a grim set to his lips. "My ex. Mostly, at any rate. I'm supposed to have him on the weekends."

"But here you are," I said softly.

"And that was the problem." He took a sip of coffee and looked around for the waitress to refill it.

"You were asking me about the punishment for Megan's tongue-piercing," I offered, wanting to help him shift the conversation away from what was obviously a painful topic. "She got grounded for a month and I only let her drive her car to and from school. And then her tongue got infected and I was sure to drive home my point about how foolish she had been."

"So she had it taken out?"

"Not then. I didn't want to force her to take it out. It's her body and if she's going to make alterations then she has to make some decision about the pros and cons. Two years later she's talking about taking it out, but I just say, 'That's nice, dear, whatever you want.' "

"You have two children?"

"That's right, my son, Josh, is completely absorbed with sports. That's the other thing about teens—they latch onto things."

"What do you mean?"

"Kids embrace things with their entire being. Just as they don't think about tomorrow, they also aren't good at halfway measures. Let me try to find a for instance . . . Okay, morality."

"Excuse me?"

"My son, Josh, looks at things in a very black and white way. Either something is okay to do, or it isn't. He's extremely rigid. When his sister got her tongue pierced, he was completely unsupportive of her. To him, she had broken the rules and should be punished. It's like with basketball, he eats, sleeps, and drinks basketball. If I suggest that he get involved with another activity, he'll shut me down. Megan is active in a pro-choice group, which completely irritates my mother—so I encourage her. But it's the same kind of deal, although the rigidity is leaving Megan as she gets older. That seems to come with age, an ability to see things from more than one side."

"It's like the gangs," he said. "When I was a patrolman I used to get involved with all the gang kids. They honestly didn't seem to care that they were getting arrested or that they'd seriously hurt or even killed somebody. Their allegiance was to the gang—end of story."

"That's the danger of the teen years, these kids can be easily led. Think about Hitler Youth and the skinheads."

"Or the Boy Scouts and basketball," he countered.

"Exactly, that kind of devotion can go in any direction."

We completed our meals and the waitress came by with a last refill and the check. Peter deftly took the tab. "It's on the department." And then he looked at me. "So what is it that makes a kid go in one direction or the other? Why do some kids wind up on the honor roll and others gun down their classmates in the schoolyard?"

"That's a great question," I said. "Which means I don't have a great answer."

As we walked back to the station we discussed risk factors for teen violence. But when we finally separated—he to run down a series of new leads and I to spend a couple hours by myself wandering through the Back Bay—my mind played with his final question. "How does someone grow up to be a killer?"

CHAPTER SIXTEEN

My body eased back into Dr. Adam's tufted chair. "It's been quite a week," I started, "and it's only Tuesday."

"What's happening?" He sipped his tea.

"Where to start? They've reopened Helen Weir's case. I think the police are less certain that Garret is the guilty party. So over the weekend, and then all day yesterday, they've been reinterviewing staff. All of the patient charts from around the time Garret was on the unit have been subpoenaed. They're not just taking the ones for the kids, but because the adult unit is connected they're wanting to look at those as well."

"Kind of disruptive."

"To say the least. And I can't even think what this says about patient confidentiality. The hospital attorney has been having a cow. But that's not really what I want to talk about." I scratched my forehead. "I want to talk about development."

He took my request in stride. "Okay . . . something in particular?"

"The kids on the unit—not the ones like Garret, but all of these kids who are getting into trouble over and over. Or like the kids who go out and kill their parents or gun people down. They're all alike," I stated, deliberately opting for a sweeping statement.

"Why don't you start there?" he prompted.

"I've been on Hamilton Five since September, and by now I've treated dozens of teenagers who were there because they did something awful, or threatened to do something awful. Usually they talk about wanting to kill themselves or somebody else. Or they get completely out of control at home. What's happening that there are so many of these kids? Like the girl I told you about last week who attacked her mother—that's pretty standard. Actually, she might be one of the less violent ones. But it's the same story over and over."

"What does that suggest?"

"Can't you just tell me the answer?" I quipped.

"Assuming that I have one." He smiled, and the small lines around his brown eyes crinkled. "Tell me about some of the common features."

"Violence, anger, rage. It's either directed toward themselves in some type of suicidal thought or behavior or it's focused outward at someone else."

"Like your girl beating up her mother?"

"Exactly."

"What else?"

I looked up at the ceiling and then at the ancient marble bust that stared out from his mahogany bookcase. "The histories . . . a lot of them, maybe all of them come from disrupted families. Or even if the parents are still together, there's something not quite right at home."

"Define 'not quite right.'"

I thought back through the evaluations that I had done over the course of the year. I pictured the databases that got completed on every new admission. "Abuse," I said, "of one kind or another. Most of these kids have either a documented history of abuse or a suspicion of abuse. Like the girl we talked about, the discharge summary from her inpatient admission said that one of her mother's boyfriends may have raped her. And the psychologist's assessment hinted that something was not right with her father. And then looking at how her mother reacted to her . . ."

"Tell me about that last bit," he prompted.

"Well, it just struck me as odd that her mother walked out of the emergency room. And then again when the girl showed up at my outpatient clinic, her mother left despite being told that parents needed to stay—especially for the first visit."

"Let's take that piece of information. What do you make of it?"

"I'm not sure what you're getting at. It seems like lousy parenting."

"Of course, but be more specific. What about her leaving her daughter in the emergency room and in your waiting room is lousy parenting?"

"It's the wrong response. Not that I'm an expert on childrearing, but if you have a kid who's struggling, that's not the time to pull back."

"Exactly. A more normative response would be concern and involvement on the part of the parents. Instead you have the mother pulling away."

"But what about the girl? If my daughter had tried to beat me up—aside from the fact that I would have killed her—I might not want to spend a lot of time with her."

"True. As you look at the kids on the unit, do you ever find yourself thinking that they kind of get what they deserve? That if they behave this poorly, maybe they should be locked away?"

I thought back through conversations with the nurses on the unit—especially those who had children of their own. "Absolutely, because they're like walking time bombs."

"Good. Now back to your earlier question, how did they get that way? And I think part of the answer may be in your observation of the girl and her mother."

"Because the mother backed away when the girl was in distress?"

"Did the girl seem surprised by her mother's behavior?"

"No. In fact she made some comment that she didn't think her mother would return until well after the session was over."

"What does that tell you?" he asked.

"It's not a new pattern."

"Right. What if it's a very old pattern? Let's take this girl . . . what was her name?"

"Jennifer."

"Take Jennifer all the way back to infancy and let's see what happens. Here we have a newborn baby that comes home to . . . was there a father in the picture?"

"Briefly. Again, according to the discharge summary he drank and got abusive toward the mother."

"Physically?"

"I haven't been able to get that level of detail," I admitted.

"Because you've never been able to thoroughly interview the mother. Be that as it may, let's make an assumption, which could be wrong. But the assumption is that the behavior we're seeing from the mother goes all the way back. We know that the mother is capable of withdrawing from her daughter when the girl is in great distress. But is there another side to Mom?"

"She cares about her daughter," I stated, thinking about the worry and concern I had seen in the emergency room.

"Of course she does, and at times she may be able to show that to her daughter. Now go back to the infant. The baby finds itself in a chaotic situation, where if the father is getting drunk and abusive, what effect will that have on the mother?"

"She's probably depressed."

"Agreed. Most women in abusive relationships are not exactly happy people."

"So what will that do to the baby?" I asked, as I tried to picture the home environment for the newborn Jennifer Ryan.

"There are a number of different theoretical frameworks to look at. In this case I'd probably think about things in terms of attachment theory."

I must have given him a blank look. "Bowlby?" I offered, trying to recall anything from my one seminar on the subject as a second-year resident.

He laughed. "You got the name. What do you remember?"

155

"Not much," I admitted.

"What do babies need to survive?" he asked. "Bottom line."

I pictured my own babies—how many years ago that was. "Food, safety, someone to hold them, someone to change them—they need a lot actually."

"Right, and depending on their parents they may or may not get everything that they require. It's not just about food. I don't know if you remember Harry Harlow's work with chimpanzees, where he was able to demonstrate that primate babies needed comforting in addition to food."

It felt like a pop quiz. "Those were the experiments with the wire monkey and the cloth monkey. That the baby chimp would take food from the wire mother but would then preferentially return to the cloth mother. And if stressed, the chimp always went back to the cloth mother."

"Exactly, the baby needs a sense of being protected. It wants to feel safe. It's very primitive stuff, that if a human infant can't get that sense of security it may be the start of something further down the line. Now in the case of your girl's mother, where we can probably say that she was depressed when Jennifer came home, what effect might that have on the baby?"

"She's going to have trouble taking care of the baby."

"Why?"

"God, you're unrelenting . . . because she's probably having trouble holding it together herself. And . . ." My mind clicked with connections. "If the pattern we see with Jennifer's mother is an old one, which it probably is, then when the infant was distressed, the response was inconsistent. Sometimes she'd comfort the baby and sometimes she would be too stressed out to respond."

"Yes, and so what?" He goaded me forward.

"The 'so what' is that children learn by reading off their parents. So if the baby cries and gets told to shut up—repeatedly—then the baby learns not to cry when it's feeling unhappy."

"Right," he agreed. "That's what Bowlby would call the repressed child, the one who learns to mask its feelings in order to get an okay response from the caregiver."

"But Jennifer doesn't mask anything—she's blurting out emotion all over the place."

"But what did you tell me about her mother? Is she consistent in her response?"

"No, she blows hot and cold. Sometimes she's there and other times, literally she's nowhere to be found."

"And that's what compounds the problem," he stated. He leaned forward in his chair. "Think about things from a behavioral standpoint—a good way to go with infants, because the thinking/rational part of their brain hasn't been turned on yet. In a behavioral model we learn based on punishment and reward. If the infant is hungry or wet or frightened it cries. If this behavior is rewarded with mother coming to soothe and feed and change, the baby learns that it can reliably have its needs met by crying. If the mother can't handle the baby crying, she might yell at the baby, or worse. In that case the punishment will likely extinguish the crying behavior and the infant may learn to get its needs met with a smile or a cute gurgle, even when it's distressed. But if the response is inconsistent and sometimes the baby is soothed and sometimes it's yelled at or ignored or slapped, then the infant has no way to find security. This makes for a very anxious baby. Or it creates a baby that trusts neither the spoken word nor the expressed emotion. Because it has learned that both of these can be false. In that case the infant may withdraw altogether and become detached from the caregiver. Or, the baby learns a variety of responses and will use different ones until it gets what it needs."

"All right," I said, following him so far. "But how do we get from an anxious or detached baby to what we see on the unit?"

"Remember that we're working inside a theoretical frame. But let's say that for some reason the infant never is able to attach, or at least to do so in a relatively secure way. We're left with an individual that is never able to bond with another. Some of the things that go along with attachment have to do with the development of character and morality. If you're not able to connect with anyone it's unlikely that you'll develop empathy, which is typically established around age four. On some level, it's our ability to feel for others—to empathize—that prevents us from doing horrible things."

"So children who can't empathize have no constraint to their behavior," I added, struggling to stay with his argument.

"Right. That's why things like torturing animals and destroying property are red flags, because embedded in those type of actions is a callousness to the feelings of others. They just don't care, and in some cases, there may even be an emotional reward from seeing others suffer."

"Reward?"

"A sense of power, or mastery over something or someone. If they come from an abusive upbringing it might also provide an identification with the abuser that feels good."

"I hate to say it, but this theory reeks of some older ones, where the parents get left holding a bag of guilt," I commented.

"True, one has to be very careful of how we look at this. In many cases we are talking about parents who are depressed or alcoholic or undergoing major stress in their own lives. And there are several other factors that play into the whole picture."

"Such as?"

"Well, the role of divorce, of increased access to firearms, of increased usage of drugs and alcohol, all of these things factor into the picture. It's one thing to have an antisocial kid, it's another to give him the means and the opportunity to kill someone."

"What about the media and all of the violence on television and in the movies?"

"Difficult to say, but certainly that's something to consider. The amount of violent imagery on the television has increased dramatically over recent years. The reporting of violence and tragedy outweighs all other news stories. Then you have the big blockbuster movies where violence is glamorous and blowing things up is presented as the solution to many of life's problems—these movies are aimed at twelve-year-old boys. And now there's the Internet, where these kids have ready access to information and to adults, who may themselves be predators. It's a volatile mix."

"So how do you know which ones will do something?" I asked, thinking about all the children on the unit who had significant histories of violent acting out.

"It's hard to predict," he admitted. "Certainly there are risk factors, like a history of oppositional behavior, excessive aggressiveness, cruelty to animals, early arrests, substance abuse. It's tricky because there are so many of these kids out there."

"It wasn't always like this, was it?" I asked. "I don't remember this when I was growing up. There were a couple wild kids in my class, I think one even got arrested for car theft. But both of my own kids are forever bringing home stories from school. How this one or that one got arrested, or just came out of a psychiatric hospital after trying to kill themselves . . . again. Maybe I just have selective memory, but I don't think it used to be this way."

"No," he commented. "Something has changed. While the overall homicide and suicide rates have fallen slightly in recent years, they've increased dramatically in kids. The homicide rate for children has increased five-fold since World War II and the suicide rate of the under eighteens has tripled."

"It's scary stuff," I admitted. "Especially now."

"I can imagine," he agreed, knowing exactly what I alluded to.

"To get back, what no one has said, but we're all thinking, is that someone has a grudge against nurses. If it wasn't Garret then it's possible that Janice was stalked and killed by somebody she had treated on the unit."

"The police are aware of that?"

"Yeah . . . I met with the lieutenant in charge of the case over the weekend."

"Really?" His right eyebrow arched slightly.

"Oh dear," I said, having wanted to steer away from that. "I may have done a little boundary crossing."

"Yes?" He waited for my explanation.

"I wanted to talk to the lieutenant about Garret, that based on his condition I didn't see how it was possible for him to have killed Helen. That he's still catatonic, and I think it is highly unlikely that he is malingering."

"How do you know he's still catatonic?"

"I started moonlighting at Whitestone."

"Because of Garret?"

I looked at Dr. Adams. He was clearly concerned. "Yes," I admitted, opting for the simple truth. "I can't seem to let go of this case."

"Molly," he began, "I don't know what to tell you and our time is up." He hedged. "Clearly you're an adult and have to make your own decisions. But sociopaths, particularly bright ones, have an acute ability to sniff out threats. You don't want to bring attention to yourself. Please be careful."

CHAPTER SEVENTEEN

I headed into my marathon Thursday thinking that tonight might be my last at Whitestone. It was too much, and my motives for taking the job had been less than pure. Over the past couple of days I had given a lot of thought to what Dr. Adams had said. I wondered about Josh and Megan and the effect the divorce had on them. Just like Queen Elizabeth, that had been my annus horriblis. I had been enraged at my husband, and for my kids, who were eight and six at the time, no matter how hard I tried to shield them from my anger, some of it must have leaked through. It was the one point in my life where I had experienced unbidden fantasies of murder.

At James's insistence we had gone to three sessions with a marriage counselor. The poor woman didn't stand a chance; I had always known that if James were unfaithful, I would leave. I could tolerate a lot of things, but not that. The meetings were a catastrophe. James had tried to cajole me into taking him back and the therapist repeatedly stated how angry and betrayed I felt—no shit. The one thing of value she stressed was the importance of shielding the kids from our own intense emotions, to not get them caught between two warring parents. Much as it killed me, I said not one bad word about their father in front of them. To this day, no matter how pissed off I get at him, I never mention it to either Josh or Megan.

I had finished my duties on the unit and was headed over to my afternoon clinic. While I walked I rehashed Tuesday's conversation with Dr. Adams. This notion of attachment was getting a lot of play in the papers. People used it to discuss failure-to-thrive in Romanian orphans, and certain sectors were trying to use the theory to bolster the argument that women should remain at home to care for their children. How nice that would be, to not have to work, although it would probably make me crazy. Still, I had taken things to another extreme. I sometimes felt that my life was lived on a conveyor belt. That even if I were to stop dead in my tracks, some inextricable force would continue to drag me from the unit to my clinic to my on-call duties.

Gerry Ewell, my man with OCD, was in the waiting area looking anxious and expectant. I signaled to him that I would need five minutes and then I picked up my afternoon charts. My heart sank when I saw the telltale green folder that signaled a new admission. I looked at the name—William Keene—it was familiar.

As I let myself into the office I made the connection. He was one of the boys who had been on the unit last week. I also knew that his hospital chart, along with everyone else's, had been subpoenaed by the police. I wondered if that would extend to the clinic record.

The rest of my afternoon was booked with fifteen-minute medication follow-ups and a second session with Jennifer Ryan and her mother.

I looked at the clock; Gerry had come early. Still, I knew that every minute he remained in the waiting area was torture. I picked up the phone. "Dara, I'm ready for my patient."

Gerry's session flew by. It was a rerun of last week and centered on his daily calls to the phone company. Not only had he overcome his fear of getting his bill corrected, he had now started a practice of calling repeatedly to check that it had been taken care of. I could only imagine how thrilled this must have been making the people at the phone company.

I asked him, "What will happen if you don't call?"

"They might forget."

"But the woman told you it was already corrected."

"She could be wrong," he argued. "I just want to be sure."

I was pleased that he had confronted his anxiety and had called in the first place. It was interesting to see how this had generated a new compulsion. On a more perverse level, I was tickled to think of Gerry hounding the phone company. Still, it was causing his anxiety to creep up. "I'm going to want you to resist the urge to call," I instructed him.

"It's too much, huh?"

"Yeah. When you get the bill, that will let you know whether or not it was corrected. I think after a week's worth of daily phone calls you probably got your point across."

He smiled. "You want me to write down how anxious it makes me feel to not call?"

"You got it, and we can review it next week."

After he left, I called to see if the Ryans had arrived.

"Not yet," Dara informed me, and so I settled down to review Billy Keene's record. I immediately flipped to the typed discharge summary from Hamilton 5.

William Keene   Admit Date: 4/12/99
DOB: 9/2/84   Discharge Date: 4/18/99
Medical Record #: 9999453278-01

Identifying Data: Fifteen-year-old Caucasian male. He is currently a high school freshman who lives with his parents and two younger siblings.

Referral Source: Patient brought by police to emergency room for evaluation.

Chief Complaint: "I didn't do anything."

Presenting Problem: Client referred for psychiatric evaluation after confronting his English teacher and threatening to "blow up" her house. Client was subsequently referred to the discipline office where he was reported to have threatened the vice principal and then stated, "You'll be sorry." The police were called, and a spot search of client's locker revealed a small quantity of marijuana, two hunting knives, and a twenty-two-caliber pistol.

As the officers attempted to take Mr. Keene into custody he stated, "You lock me up and I swear I'll kill myself." Patient was brought to juvenile detention and placed on suicide precautions. While under one-to-one supervision he proceeded to bang his head against the wall, at which point a psychiatric evaluation was requested and he was transported to Commonwealth Hospital.

Past Psychiatric History: This is the first inpatient admission. According to client's mother he has been in counseling with the school psychologist. He has never been on medication.

Family Psychiatric History: Significant for a paternal aunt who committed suicide and client's father, who is reportedly alcoholic.

Medical History: Noncontributory.

Allergies: None reported.

Social History/Developmental History: Client is the oldest of three siblings in an intact family. He was born vaginally and achieved all developmental milestones within expected range. He formed short sentences by eighteen months and walked at two years. Mother reports he wet the bed until third grade and that occasionally this problem can return. Early school history is notable for behavioral and discipline problems. Mother reports that she has attended parent-teacher conferences on a regular basis since second grade. Client's grades are in the C to D range although his full-scale IQ is reported to be well above average.

Client's two younger siblings, both girls, ages 5 and 7, have limited interaction with their older brother. There has been a single DSS referral made regarding the seven-year-old, which focused on an episode where client was noted by a neighbor being excessively rough with his sister. At present his mother states that there is no active DSS involvement with the family.

Client describes himself as a loner at school. He is unable to identify people he considers as close friends.

His hobbies center around the computer and spending time on the Internet. He states that when he grows up he would like to work with computers.

He states that he is not sexually active and that his orientation is heterosexual.

Hospital Course: Client was admitted through the emergency room and was initially noted to be belligerent and threatening toward staff. When interviewed his affect was angry and withdrawn; he answered questions monosyllabically and repeatedly asked, "When can I go home?" After it was explained that he was being admitted to the hospital for a period of observation he became angry and at one point attempted to run out of the emergency room. Security was called and client was room-restricted, at which point he proceeded to bang his head violently against the wall. A code was called and he was placed in four-point-restraints to prevent further self-injury. Ativan and Haldol were administered intramuscularly and client was admitted to the inpatient unit.

On the unit, permission was obtained from his mother to medicate with an antidepressant and with sedatives.

Initially client refused to attend unit groups and focused on his desire to leave or at least to be allowed to smoke. Gradually, he agreed to attend groups but was largely silent. In one-to-one interaction he was able to describe a pervasive feeling of frustration and anger, frequently directed toward his father, whom he viewed as being abusive to his mother and to himself. He also felt that his teachers and principal unfairly singled him out at school, and that his unpopularity was due to a long-standing prejudice against him. He reported that he did not work at school and felt that this was unimportant. "I know I'm smart. I don't need them to tell me that." He talked extensively about the Internet and bragged about being able to access information about firearms and explosives. "It's not hard to build a bomb. There's lots of people who can show you how." When questioned about the weapons found in his locker, he denied any active plan to harm any one individual or himself. When asked about his threatening comments to the vice principal he replied, "I was only kidding. People don't get my sense of humor."

Psychological testing was requested and obtained. Pertinent findings included hypervigilance, which at times bordered on paranoia. On the Rorschach, the client gave responses that raised the question of borderline psychotic thought process, especially under more stressful circumstances. His reasoning was concrete and his judgment, especially in interpersonal situations, was highly self-focused. When asked what he would do if he found a wallet that contained money and identification he responded, "I'd take the money and the credit cards and throw away the rest." When asked if he would consider returning the wallet, he replied, "Why?" On tasks related to problem-solving client was two standard deviations above the norm and was able to come up with creative solutions to complex situations.

As the hospitalization progressed, Mr. Keene was able to maintain self-control and attended all scheduled groups, albeit with minimal participation. He did interact with two of his peers on the unit, but their discussions often focused on weaponry and obtaining information about weaponry over the Internet.

Client, along with his mother and attorney, attended court on 4/16/99, at which point he was given a suspended sentence for the drug and weapons charges with the condition that following discharge from the inpatient unit he attends weekly therapy for at least six months.

Upon returning to the unit, client was greatly relieved and requested that he be discharged. He consistently and reliably denied wanting to hurt himself or anyone else. And on 4/18/99 he was discharged with follow-up to be provided by the Franklin Clinic. Both client and his mother were in agreement with this plan.

Discharge Diagnosis: Axis I: Oppositional defiant disorder Rule out conduct disorder

Axis II: Antisocial and borderline traits

Axis III: No active medical problems

Axis IV: Problems related to school and home environments

Axis V: Current global assessment of funtioning: 45 out of 100

Discharge Medication: Paroxitine 20mg daily

Risperidone 0.5mg twice daily

Robert Jeffreys, MD

I glanced at the clock and saw that I was now twenty minutes into Jennifer Ryan's time slot. I called the secretary. "Any sign of the Ryans?"

"Lucky you; it's looking like a no-show."

"Thanks." I pulled Jennifer's chart out of the pile, flipped open to the demographics page, and called her house.

On the third ring a woman answered.

"Mrs. Ryan."

"Yes." She sounded wary.

"This is Dr. Katz at the Franklin Clinic; I was supposed to see you and Jennifer today."

"I told her," she said, "but she didn't want to go. And I can't make her do things she doesn't want to do."

"Is she there?"

"I don't know where she is," Beth Ryan replied. "Probably out getting pregnant somewhere."

"How has she been doing?" I asked, half dreading the answer.

"The same. Nothing ever changes. She does what she wants; she won't listen to anybody, especially her mother. I get calls from her teachers telling me she's not in class. What am I supposed to do?"

"Let her know that I called, and that I'd like her to call me." I gave her my beeper number. "I have her scheduled in for the same time next week. Even if she weren't to make it, if *you* could come that would be helpful."

"I don't see how," she replied, clearly wanting to end our conversation and I suspected the short-lived therapy, as well.

I fought back my defensive impulses and told her, "It's sometimes useful to get an outside eye on problems in the home. A lot of families are going through similar things, and there are strategies to try and improve the situation."

"Right." She didn't sound convinced. "I'll tell her you called." And she hung up.

I ran my hand through my hair and tried to figure out if there was something more I should do. I was getting increasingly confused in working with these kids. It wasn't just them, it was their parents, their life circumstance, the violence on television and in the streets—I didn't have a handle on how I was supposed to deal with these cases. Was Mrs. Ryan a horrible mother or was she doing the best job of raising her daughter that she could? I suspected the latter was closer to the truth.

At five to the hour Dara let me know that the Keenes had arrived. I went out to the waiting room to greet them and immediately recognized Billy Keene as one of the kids who had been on the unit when Helen was murdered. He seemed small for his age, but he was well dressed and clean. His mother sat stiffly in the waiting area; her hair was a silver brown and had recently been permed. I figured her age as somewhere in her midforties.

"I'm Dr. Katz," I said, looking first at Billy in his baggy jeans and buzz cut hair. I extended my hand first to him and then to his mother.

"Gail Keene," she said in reply, and quickly added, "my husband wasn't able to come, I hope that's okay."

Billy snorted and the left side of his lip curled.

"Maybe next time?" I offered, indicating that they should follow me. I glanced back as the duo approached my office. Billy lagged behind his mother by a good ten or fifteen feet. He rapped at the wall with his knuckles. I winced as he came close to hitting the framed picture of the clinic's groundbreaking ceremony. The next thing I noticed was that his mother didn't tell him to cut it out. She walked in front with the resigned expression of someone who didn't want to see or hear.

I opened the door to my office and waited while Billy came down the hall. He hung back outside the entrance and looked inside at the chairs and the clutter of paperwork on my desk.

"It's small," he commented, while banging his hand a bit too hard against the metal doorframe.

"Doesn't that hurt?" I asked.

"Naah, it toughens up your hands," he explained, with the matter-of-fact tone of someone who had researched the subject.

"Interesting, but I'd rather that you not do that here."

He didn't stop, but kept hitting up against the hard gray metal.

I felt the stirrings of a struggle, should I insist or pull back?

His mother spoke up. "Billy, the doctor asked you to stop doing that. Why don't you come in and sit down?"

He didn't look at her.

"At any rate, come in," I said. "There's a wall in here if you absolutely have to keep doing that." I stepped back from an early conflict.

Apparently my offer was acceptable and he allowed himself to flop down into one of the upholstered chairs. He looked around the room, moving his head from side to side. He took in the furniture and took a quick look at me. The only thing he seemed to avoid was his mother.

"So, Billy," I asked, trying to pull his attention, "why are you here?"

"Because I have to," he said, letting me know that I was approaching retarded.

"How did that happen?"

"You have my chart right there." He pointed at my desk and at the green folder.

"True, but I want to hear your side of the story."

"We all want things. It doesn't mean we get them."

His mother tried to back me up. Her voice was tentative. "Billy? Dear, why don't you tell the doctor what she wants to know?"

He proceeded to pick at a frayed edge of the upholstery.

"Please don't do that," I said, as he started to rip back the edges of the ancient fabric. "Those chairs are all we get here."

"They're pretty crappy."

"They are," I agreed.

"Why don't they give you better chairs?" he asked, finally letting go of the material.

"No money."

"They pay you, and you're a doctor. They must have some money," he accused.

"I'm in training. I don't cost them a whole lot," I said, trying to use humor to deflect some of his anger.

His soft brown eyes looked up, and I realized that this was the first eye contact he had made with me. "So you're not a real doctor," he stated.

"This is my third year of training after medical school."

He stuck his tongue in his lower lip and nodded. "Shouldn't you say something? Or does that come in the fourth year?"

There was no denying the insult. His mother looked over at her son and then glanced at me.

"I'm thinking," I told him.

"That's nice." His mouth twisted in a sneer. "How long do we have to stay here?"

"An hour."

"Now is that a real hour or fifty minutes?"

"Fifty minutes."

"Let's make it thirty and call it a day." He forced a smile and rocked forward in his chair. "I won't tell if you won't tell."

"So what do you like to do?" I shot out in a different direction.

"Nothing."

"Nothing at all? There isn't anything you like to do?"

"What about the computer, dear?" his mother asked.

He glanced over the space where she was seated. His gaze never seemed to take her in.

"Whatever."

"You like to go on the Internet?" I asked.

"It's okay," he admitted, which at this point I took to be overwhelming enthusiasm.

"He's on there all the time," his mother stated, chancing a glance in his direction.

"What do you like about the Internet?" I asked.

"Just stuff," he shot back.

His mother fidgeted in her chair.

"You wanted to say something?" I asked, looking in her direction.

She clutched the strap of her pocketbook. "I don't like him being on the computer all the time."

"Have you or your husband ever talked with Billy about what he does on the computer?"

Billy snorted. "Yeah, like either one of them could figure it out."

"I don't know much about computers," his mother admitted. "Neither does my husband."

Billy shook his head and muttered under his breath.

"What was that?" I asked.

"Nothing."

"I noticed earlier that when your mom mentioned that your dad couldn't be here, you made a noise."

He shook his head, and stayed quiet.

Mrs. Keene interceded. "Billy and his dad haven't been getting along."

"He's a fuckin' drunk."

Gail Keene's cheeks flushed. "Billy, don't say that."

Now if Josh had ever said something like that, I would have been hard-pressed not to slap him—even if it were true.

"Whatever." He rocked in tight back-and-forth movements on the chair. "I got to get out of here," he said. "Can I go outside?" He looked at me. "You don't really want to talk to me anyway. Why don't you just get it all from her? She'll tell you everything you want to know. I got to go." He bolted out of his chair and had his hand on the door.

I looked at his mom. Clearly, this behavior did not alarm her.

"Where are you going?" I asked.

"I want a smoke." His hand had depressed the handle, and he bounced on the soles of his sneakers.

"Is that okay with you?" I asked his mother, feeling like I wasn't getting any sort of grip on the evaluation.

"I can't stop him," she admitted.

Without another word he was out the door.

"He'll come back," she said. "He gets like that where he can't keep still. I know I shouldn't let him smoke, but it seems to calm him down . . . at least for a little."

With him gone, the air in the room seemed lighter. I felt the tension between my shoulders and in my jaw start to release. "How long has he been like this?" I asked.

"It's hard to say. I sometimes think he was born like this. He wasn't an easy baby. I keep thinking it's something I did. Or like with his dad . . . maybe I should have left him a long time ago. But I have three kids, and for all of Bill's faults he pays the bills. No matter how bad the drinking gets he's never once missed a day of work and he's never hit me."

"You said he and Billy haven't been getting along," I prompted.

"They can't be in the same room." A tear squeezed from the corner of her eye. She swallowed and bit the inside of her lip. "It's like I'm waiting for something to happen. Why didn't they keep him in the hospital?"

"You didn't feel that he was ready for discharge?"

"I didn't have a choice. The doctor kept telling me that the kids could only stay for a few days and then they had to get outpatient treatment. The only reason he came today was that the judge told him if he doesn't he'll go into the juvenile detention home." She looked up at me. "Do you think that would be better for him?"

I was getting too much information all at once—clearly she was frightened. "You said you were worried, what do you think will happen?"

"I have two other children," she said, skirting the question. "I have to think about them."

"Do you think Billy will hurt them?"

She paused and put her right hand to the space between her eyebrows. She remained frozen for a moment, trying to decide whether to make the statement that lay poised on the tip of her tongue. She exhaled, and on a rush of breath admitted, "He has."

"In what way?" I asked, not letting the moment drop.

She closed her eyes. "I think he's been touching them. Ashley in particular."

"Sexually?" I asked.

Her upper body trembled, and her breathing grew fast. She couldn't speak and could only nod.

The door banged open and Billy reappeared. He had been listening at the door. Mrs. Keene startled and stared open-mouthed at her son.

He glared at his mother with an expression of loathing. "What did you tell her?" he demanded.

She shook her head.

"*What did you tell her?*" he shrieked. His nostrils flared and saliva shot out of his mouth. His hands balled into fists and he sprang at his mother.

As he lunged for her, I pushed the panic button under my desk and prayed that security would not be slow.

Mrs. Keene curled up into the chair and tried to protect her face as Billy rained close-fisted blows down on her head.

I grabbed him and pulled back, amazed at the strength in the fifteen-year-old's sinewy arms. I had managed to pry back one of his hands when a pair of security guards barged into the office.

Billy cursed and spit and kicked at his mother, at the guards, and at me as we maneuvered him into a human envelope created by the two guards standing back to back with Billy wedged in between them. As soon as the screaming boy was somewhat contained I dialed Dara and asked her to call for the ambulance.

"What are you doing?" Billy yelled as I hung up the phone. "You're all dead!" He looked at his mother, who lay shrunken into the cushions of the chair. Her scalp had been lacerated, and blood matted down her hair and dripped down the right side of her face. He coughed up a wad of phlegm and spat it at her. "You're all fucking dead. And don't think I won't do it. Just wait!"

CHAPTER EIGHTEEN

Thursday night at Whitestone was blissfully quiet. At this rate, I thought, I might even get a couple hours' sleep. Reflexively I pushed that concept away, as though God might take notice of my optimism and punish me for it with three new admissions and a patient with chest pain. It was close to midnight and I had completed my preemptive rounds. This is something that I've learned to do over my years on call at various hospitals. I make rounds on all the floors to head off as many of the little emergencies and late-night requests as possible. It doesn't always work, but the nurses like it and are less likely to call for an order of Tylenol at three in the morning.

I walked the halls in my standard white coat, khakis, and Timberland rubber-soled shoes and looked in on the wards. Randomly I flipped through charts. There were over ninety percent male patients at Whitestone; most of them had committed violent acts. As I read through their cases, certain themes recurred. Most of them came from backgrounds that were violent and chaotic. Many had come from impoverished circumstances. The developmental section, while fairly minimal, typically contained mention of abuse, and/or early separation from one or both parents, and/or parents who themselves were criminals, and/or parents who suffered with untreated mental illness. So the question that ran through my mind was one of nature vs. nurture. If Dr. Adams was correct, or at least the theory he was presenting was correct, then nurture won out in the majority of cases—but at a very early age.

I headed toward the call room and the final unit—the one where Garret had been kept since his admission, a week and a half ago. He was now in a regular room, the feeding tube was gone, and he appeared to be asleep. I watched the even rise and fall of his chest from the doorway. He snored lightly. I moved closer and my presence must have disturbed him as his eyes shot open and he stared in my direction.

"I know you," he said.

I was surprised to hear him speak, apparently the ECT had been successful in breaking his catatonia. "How are you, Garret?" I asked.

"How are you?" he parroted.

"I'm okay. Do you remember who I am?"

"Doctor nurse, mother wife."

"I'm Dr. Katz. I treated you at Commonwealth Hospital."

"Massachusetts is a commonwealth, everything else is a state of mind," he commented, as though reciting something memorized in grade school.

His blond hair was getting long, and I fought back an impulse to smooth down some of the more wild strands. "Are you eating?"

"I eat," he stated.

"Are you getting out of bed?"

"I'm lying in it, but not lying to you."

"What I meant . . ." I tried to formulate a sentence that wouldn't be twisted by his concrete thought process. "During the day have you been out of the bed?"

"During the day I've been out of bed. At night I've been out of bed."

"That's great. Has your mom been to visit?"

"She visits me."

"Do you want to sit up?" I asked.

"Do you?"

"Do I what?"

"Want me to sit up?"

"Yes, that would be nice," I directed, cutting his cycle of ambivalence short.

He repositioned himself against the pillows. As I got a closer look at him, I was shocked to see how much weight he had lost. His face had the gaunt appearance I associated with anorexia or with pictures of Holocaust survivors. "You've gotten very thin."

"I wasn't eating. They say that."

"Now you eat?"

He looked around with an expression of confusion, and then back at me. "No."

"Would you like something to eat?"

"Yes."

"I'll be right back." I went behind the nursing station and ferreted through the refrigerator. I came up with a carton of milk and several packages of peanut butter and crackers. I also grabbed Garret's chart and leafed through the progress notes. Since I had last been here, he had had an additional three ECT treatments, which made for a total of five so far. After the third one, which would have been Monday, he had spoken for the first time since being admitted to Whitestone. Later that day the nurse reported that he had taken food by mouth. After Wednesday's treatment they were able to get him out of bed. Clearly, this was not a question of nurture. Garret's schizophrenia had been genetically preordained. But I didn't really think he had much to do with Helen's murder, other than being at the wrong place at the wrong time.

I placed the milk and crackers on Garret's bedside table. He looked at them and then at me. "I want you to eat the crackers and drink the milk," I explained.

He nodded and proceeded to do as instructed.

After he had devoured eight cracker sandwiches and drained the milk, the mother in me was satisfied. I was about to leave, when he stopped me with a question.

"Have they caught the nurse killer?"

My gut tightened as I remembered why I had come here in the first place. "No." I turned back to look at him.

"He kills nurses," he stated.

"Yes. Do you know who it is?" I asked, trying to keep my voice even.

The hallway light danced in his clear cornflower blue eyes. He stared at me, trying to focus on my face. "He kills nurses," he repeated, "and you're a nurse."

Chapter Nineteen

The following day took on the surreal quality provided by too little sleep and too much black coffee. Then again, this was no average Friday— the unit was tense, nurses snapped at Carol, even Dr. Winthrop wasn't spared their anxious demands.

"It's not safe to work here," one of the old-timers commented to an aide. "You didn't use to worry about stuff like this. But do you think any-one in administration cares? Hell, no."

I hid out in my office and tried to force my way through some paperwork before rounds. I had spotted Billy Keene when I came onto the unit; I didn't feel like having to confront him first thing in the morning. That, and a quick look at the pa-tient board let me know that we were filled to ca-pacity and that the main topic for rounds would be, "Who can we move out today?"

I was plowing through the charts, signing my name to yesterday's treatment plans, when the phone rang. "Yes?"

"Molly, it's Carol." She hesitated. "I know I shouldn't do this, but we're heading into a staffing situation for this evening. I was wondering if you might be interested in picking up some per diem work?"

"As a nurse?"

"I remember you said that you had kept up your license and still did some in-home assessments . . ."

"Carol, I was on call last night, and there's no way I can go two nights in a row."

"I understand." Her tone drooped. "I probably shouldn't have asked in the first place, it's just that no one is willing to pick up extra shifts right now, and on top of that I've had two nurses call out sick for evenings."

My internal martyr stirred. That's the voice that tells me I should be able to help people out, regardless of what is in my own best interest. It bears a lot in common with my mother's voice. I pushed it back. "I'm sorry, Carol. I just can't."

"It's okay." She sighed. "I'll just keep plugging away. Any of your patients leaving today?"

"Maybe one. I'll see if I can get Pam pried off the unit and into the day program."

"If you move quick, maybe you can get her to go there on a pass today, and then discharge her this afternoon."

"Will do."

"Thanks. Although sometimes I don't know if it isn't better to leave the unit full. You know . . . the devil you know versus the devil you don't."

"Yeah." I laughed. "But you got to get them out of here sometime."

"True. Now, if we could empty out half the unit, I'd have enough nurses."

After she hung up, I thought about her request.

While I appreciated how difficult her job must be—having to staff the inpatient unit twenty-four hours a day, seven days a week—I was a little miffed that she had even asked. I was still a nurse, at least on paper. Maybe it was time to let go of my license and let it expire. I hadn't given that much thought. Prior to this residency I had continued to pick up work. But now that I could moonlight, there really wasn't much point. The money for working at Whitestone was better than home nursing, and even if I didn't work at Whitestone moonlighting jobs for resident doctors were abundant. But here was the critical point, where after over ten years as a nurse, I was going to make the final break. In fourteen months I would be able to practice independently as a physician.

The phone rang again; it was the clerk. "Dr. Katz?"

"Yes."

"Billy Keene has been asking to meet with you."

I looked at the clock. "Tell him I'll see him after rounds."

"He's pretty upset."

"All right." This was not how I wanted to start my morning. I forced myself out into the hall.

The pajama-clad fifteen-year-old saw me and ran down the hallway. "I want out of here," he demanded, sticking his face a little too close to mine.

His anger was barely contained and a vein in his jaw had started to pulse. "I don't think you'll be leaving today," I told him. "But I just got in and I don't even know which doctor you've been assigned to."

"Shit!" He stamped his foot. "I don't believe this shit."

I edged away from the boy. I looked down the hall at Carol. "Billy, you're going to have to try to calm yourself."

"Fuck you!" he shot back.

I started to move back in the direction of the nursing station, while inwardly I cursed myself for not having worn my clip-on panic button. I vividly recalled his violent attack on his mother. And I had no illusions that if I didn't think fast, the same could happen to me. In as calm a voice as I could muster, I yelled back to the unit clerk to call a code.

"Where the fuck are you going!" he screamed. "When someone's fucking talking to you, you stay put." He advanced on me, banging the wall with his closed fist. "You're all so fucking smart. You're going to have to let me out sometime, aren't you?"

"Billy, you need to go to your room." I now had my back to the nursing station. There was nowhere left to go. Thankfully, reinforcements arrived. From my periphery I saw the flash of blue-uniformed guards as they rushed through the outer locked door.

"Billy," Carol said, from behind him, "you need to go to your room now."

"Or what, bitch?" He pivoted and stared at the head nurse.

"That's it," she said. "When you can't control your language and your behavior, you go to your room."

He looked around at the guards and at the staff who had positioned themselves in a semicircle around him. Down the hall two aides quickly assembled the restraint bed.

And then the strangest thing happened. "You're right," he said, taking us by surprise. "I need to calm down." His body relaxed and he straightened up. He smiled in my direction. "I'll go to my room. You don't need that." He motioned to the restraint bed. He started to walk in the direction of his room. The circle of staff parted to let him pass and to see what would happen.

He stopped and turned. He stared at me. "I was just upset for having to stay here," he said. "As soon as you know when I can leave, I'd appreciate it if someone would tell me. All I want is to go home." His eyes gave nothing away and his voice was calm, but the vein at the corner of his jaw continued to pulse.

"Is he really assigned to me?" I asked Carol under my breath, once the teenager had returned to his room.

"Yes, when he came in yesterday, we saw that you had admitted him and we thought it would be best if you followed him on the unit."

"Well, if that's the case, I'm going to want him with a one-to-one sitter right now."

Carol looked crestfallen.

"I'm sorry," I said, realizing that she barely had enough staff to cover the unit as it was.

"Not your fault." She exhaled heavily. "Some days it doesn't pay to get out of bed. Any chance we could stick him in the common room?"

"If you're sure someone stays with him all the

time . . . come to think of it, better not, I'd rather segregate him out at least to start."

"Do you want to give him something to calm down?" she asked.

"Yeah, give him a milligram of Risperidone."

"You got it."

I looked down the hallway in the direction of Billy's room. A heavyset aide stood watch outside his door, but the teen was hanging on to the door-jamb. He stared back at me. "Can I at least talk to you?" he asked.

"We'll talk after rounds," I said, not wanting to get any closer.

His eyes narrowed and his teeth clenched. "Fine." And his head disappeared into his room.

Carol watched the exchange. "Scary kid," she commented, coming to stand next to me.

"Yeah."

"The cops have already called and want to know if they can interview him on the unit," she informed me. "Apparently they tried to get him at home, but he always managed not to be there."

"That's interesting. He never mentioned that, neither did his mother . . . not that he was the most forthcoming of patients."

"I read your note," she said. "He actually hit his mother in your office?"

The scene replayed itself in my mind. I saw the expression of resignation and fear in Gail Keene's eyes as she curled her body back into the cushions of my chair. It was clear from her rapid response, like a turtle ducking into its shell, that this hadn't been the first time. If the guards hadn't come I seriously doubted if I could have contained him on my own. "He can't go back home," I said.

"Parents won't take him?" she asked with a weary tone.

"No, I think the mom probably would take him back, I just don't think it's safe. Unless we find some magic pill, I can't see it happening."

"Prison bound?" she asked.

"I couldn't even get to that. Last time he was here it was for threatening to kill his vice principal. Mom was able to give me a little bit of information. Apparently his aggressiveness goes all the way back to kindergarten. Playground bully who's gotten worse over time."

"Bad seed?"

"I don't know, but whatever it is he's one scary teenager about to become a scary adult."

As we walked into rounds a red-suited Sonja Aaronsen entered the unit. She saw Carol and waved. "Mind if I join your rounds this morning?" she asked. "It's getting to be quite a habit."

"What's up?" Carol asked, as she made room for the aide to wheel in the stainless steel chart rack.

"More of the same. The police want to review the charts with the physicians, apparently they're having a difficult time deciphering the handwriting . . . imagine that." She smiled.

I wondered if Peter Harris might make an appearance and found that my mood brightened at the prospect.

Sonja looked at me. "You're Dr. Katz?"

"Yes."

"After rounds, I need to talk with you."

"About?"

"We can discuss that after rounds," she said dismissively.

There was no way I could press the matter. I took my regular seat next to Rob and waited to hear what the attorney would say. When she finally spoke, it was basically more of the same. "Cooperate, but don't speculate."

Rounds themselves were tense. One of the old-time nurses interrupted Carol as she was reviewing the patients.

"It doesn't feel safe," she said. "We need more staff on the floor."

"If you know anyone who wants to pick up shifts," Carol offered, "I'm having a hard time rounding up anyone willing to work."

"We should close the unit to new admissions," the nurse said, and her suggestion was met with a murmur of approval.

Carol tensed visibly. She kept her voice level. "It's kind of a moot point, as we're full right now."

"But we're going to discharge patients this morning." The nurse persisted. "I don't think even if we have beds that we should take new patients if we don't have enough staff—it's not safe, especially on nights. Look what just almost happened in the hallway."

"I'll see what I can do," Carol offered.

"Maybe if there'd been enough staff, Helen would still be alive." The nurse glared at Carol.

With an icy expression, Carol stated, "Staffing on the night that Helen was killed was more than adequate."

Sonja, who had been listening to the exchange,

broke in. She looked directly at the nurse, and at those who surrounded her. "We have to be very careful of what we say, because statements like you just made can be twisted."

The nurse was not intimidated. "Look." She stood up with her hands braced on the table. "I don't give a rat's ass about what looks good or what sounds good. We have to deliver patient care to twenty kids who are totally out of control. And if we don't have enough nurses, something bad is going to happen. Not something bad *might* happen, but something bad is *going* to happen. And frankly, I don't want it to happen to me or to any of my friends. So if you all want to sit there and try to keep a lid on things, don't expect everyone to go sweetly along. Because with this kind of BS attitude, I'm filing a grievance." Having delivered her threat of a union action, she left the room.

An uncomfortable silence settled in the room.

Finally, Felix cleared his throat. "I realize that things are tense right now, but we can't forget that we have to take care of our patients. I know it's difficult when you're focused on other things. No one is denying the fact of Helen's murder, but there is still a job to be done. We have never closed the unit to new admissions if we've had a bed. I don't think that is something we should consider lightly."

"Dr. Winthrop is right," Carol said, as she took the opportunity to look at the assembled nurses. "I will do whatever it takes to bring in adequate staff, but we can't start to deny admissions."

There were no further outbursts. I had little

doubt, though, that the nurse who had been so voluble would likely follow through on her threat and file a grievance. I couldn't blame her. With two dead nurses, I'd have to think twice before showing up to work. But morale, which had never been great, was deteriorating by the second. The staff was splitting off into factions. Carol and Felix were on the side of administration and "business as usual" and the aides and nurses were increasingly resistant. The sick calls and refusals to take extra shifts were a direct result of the staff's fears and anxieties. Two of the nurses purportedly had not worked since the murder, and rumor had it that they were looking for new jobs.

Somehow we made it through rounds without further disruption. The social worker assigned to my team, who sat off to my right, grumbled repeatedly at the multiple requests for family meetings. "What do they want from me?" she muttered. "I'm just one person."

Afterward Sonja followed me to my office. "Dr. Katz, I need a couple words with you."

"Yes," I said, closing the door with an apologetic look to Rob who wanted to get to the office he and I shared.

"I got a call this morning from Lieutenant Harris. Apparently Garret Jacobs is talking again and they want to interrogate him." She paused, and I had no idea why she was telling me this.

"Apparently," she continued, watching me closely, "they'd like you to interview the boy."

"Why me?"

"It seems that the boy is refusing to talk to the

facility psychiatrist, at least in any detail . . . and that he asked for you by name. He said that you were there last night." Her tone was accusatory.

"I was," I admitted. "I moonlight there."

"I see. I assume you had that cleared through the proper channels."

I felt trapped. I had not gotten the department chairman's signature for the Whitestone job. I said nothing and hoped that my silence implied compliance with the hospital policy.

"The choice is entirely yours as to whether or not you help the police. All I would ask is that you try to keep your involvement to a minimum. If it's just a coincidence that you moonlight at Whitestone and that the boy was admitted there, I don't think there's anything improper about that . . . just make sure that all of your paperwork is in order, if anyone were to check."

"I will." And as she left, I had the clear impression that the first "anyone" to check on my paperwork would be her.

"What was that all about?" Rob asked as he finally made it into our shared office.

"Don't even ask. I seem to have a real talent for pissing her off."

"Anything I can do to help?"

I looked at my baby-faced office mate. "Seriously?"

"Name it."

"Take Billy Keene onto your service. You had him the last time. I just can't deal with this right now."

"Yeah, that was quite a scene in the hallway. What set him off?"

"Me," I admitted. "I'm not his favorite person right now, and frankly I can't seem to muster the enthusiasm for working with some of these kids."

"He's too far gone," he admitted. "I don't know what we think we're doing with him on a psychiatric ward. It's not like we have any validated treatments for kids with conduct disorder."

"That's true, isn't it?"

"As far as I know. The literature is pretty unanimous that either they grow up to be full-blown sociopaths or just truly disturbed adults that somehow muddle through. So the sixty-four-thousand-dollar question is, why send them here?"

"Where else would someone like Billy go?"

"Jail sounds about right," he commented. "He assaulted his mother. I think last time he was threatening to shoot somebody or blow somebody up. One of these days, I think he'll actually do it. But tell you what, I'll trade you Billy for my demented alcoholic man on the adult side."

"The guy in the posey chair?"

"That's the one."

"Deal," I said, without dwelling on the moral-slippage that trading patients might imply.

"So what's the plan with Billy?" he asked. "I zoned out when you presented him in rounds."

"The police want to interview him about Helen's murder and possibly Janice's. After that, I'm not certain. It could be that he ends up in custody."

"Or at Whitestone. If I were that kid I'd start playing up the insanity angle right about now. What about the family?"

"I think Mom's pretty burned out. She has two little girls and a husband that drinks."

"Lovely combination," he commented. "I'm having trouble keeping them all straight. He has arrests, doesn't he?"

"Several."

"On probation?"

"I don't think so, but it's worth checking with Mom."

"It's strange," he said, pulling over Billy's chart and adding it to his stack.

"What is?"

"I really don't mind working with the bad boys. Granted that we're just pissing in the wind with them, but something about them is interesting."

"Like where do they come from?"

"Yeah, and there's more and more every day. I was talking with an administrator at DSS and she was telling me that all the residential homes are filled with these kids, and that this is something new. Like a form of evolution."

"That's a lovely thought. We're crawling back into the slime."

"I'm not sure." His hazel eyes focused on my admission note; his tone was thoughtful. "There's a strength to these kids. Not the gang ones where they're just exchanging one set of societal rules for another, but these kids who are totally alienated from society, period. Admittedly they're dangerous, but there's also something admirable about how they divorce themselves from the rules. I know that it's not conscious and that they have the moral development of snails, still . . . and it's not just about thought, either. There's something different, even on a biological level. I don't know if you've read any of the studies that look at arousal patterns in kids with conduct disorder and antisocial adults?"

"I haven't," I admitted.

"It's interesting stuff. Because among the findings is a pretty consistent diminished stress response. They don't get as worked up in stressful situations. They don't secrete as much cortisol and adrenaline. Now if I were a criminal that might be an adaptive advantage."

"Staying cool in tense situations," I offered.

"Exactly."

"So is that something they're born with, or is it developmental?" I asked, harking back to my earlier conversation with Dr. Adams.

"Let me fly in the face of all developmental theory and tell you what I really think."

"Yes?"

"I think they're born that way. And more than that, I wonder if what we're seeing isn't some new variant in genetic selection. A child who feels no remorse or societal constraints comes pretty close to Nietzsche's vision of a superman."

"A lovely thought." I shuddered at his bleak vision of mankind's future.

"Just a thought. And now," he said, tucking Billy's chart under his arm, "it's time to meet with my baby sociopath."

CHAPTER TWENTY

After work I hopped the Green Line and went to visit Megan at her dormitory. I was preoccupied as I walked the last couple blocks of Commonwealth Avenue. I had agreed to drive out to Whitestone in the morning to interview Garret and I was having trouble teasing apart my motives. That seemed to be the norm of late. I did want to help Garret, there was no denying that. I didn't believe that he could have killed Helen, and even if he had, his degree of psychosis clearly robbed him of the ability to make rational decisions, or even to understand the generally held consensus of right and wrong. To him, Helen could have been the devil incarnate and he was doing the world a favor by killing her. But nothing was simple, including my motives.

I was increasingly drawn into the dilemma of what was happening with all these kids. Why did one child grow up as a solid citizen and another mature into a killer? Like everything else I would have loved to find a black-and-white answer, but the truth is never so obliging. My daily life, between the unit, the clinic, and Whitestone, had turned into a living textbook of psychopathology.

And for one of the few times in my career as a resident, I didn't have the sense of being worked to death. The hours hadn't changed, but my levels of interest and curiosity were high. I didn't mind the sleepless nights or heavy patient load.

I arrived at Megan's dorm and announced myself to the young woman with the forelock of turquoise hair on her otherwise shaved head who sat behind the front desk. "She'll be right down," she said, after she had called Megan's room. I allowed myself a moment's cynicism, thinking that my daughter probably did not want me to see her room. Frankly, with four teenage girls sharing the cramped two-room suite, I wasn't going to argue.

"Hey, Mom," she called out from behind me, having taken the stairs.

"Hey back," I said as she came over to kiss me. "Don't you look nice."

She wrinkled her nose. "I'm just wearing jeans."

"You look good," I said, wondering if she had gone one step redder in her choice of hair color.

"I think you're biased."

"Probably . . . so how's the studying going?" I asked as we headed through the glass double doors and back out onto the street.

"I can't believe that the year is almost over," she reflected, settling into her long comfortable stride. "I've already had my first final."

"How did it go?" I felt a twinge of guilt for having forgotten.

"I can never tell," she admitted. "I always think I did horribly, but usually I come out okay. I have the weekend to study and then on Monday I have my calculus and biology finals." She groaned. "No one in my calculus class is doing well. I feel bad for the teacher. When he hands back our quizzes the curve is sometimes more than the base score."

"Really? That and physics were my two least favorite courses."

"I think physics is okay, at least it makes sense. I got a twenty-seven on my last calculus exam and that somehow turned into an A minus."

"That is quite a curve." I laughed.

"It was the second-highest grade in the class. The person who got a thirty got an A. You feel like Chinese?" she asked.

"Sounds good."

We veered off Commonwealth Avenue and headed to Madam Woo's. "This is a bit of déjà vu," I commented as I looked at the familiar white, red, and green sign.

"I know, you and Daddy took us here, way back when. I thought it might be nice."

The restaurant was darkly lit and crowded with Friday night diners, mostly students and faculty. We were shown to a table that was being cleared and sat down while a middle-aged Asian woman wiped the Formica top clean. "Sisters?" she asked, looking at the two of us.

Megan laughed. "No, she's my mother."

The woman smiled and straightened up. "You have a very pretty daughter," she told me.

"Thank you," I said, feeling the rush of pride I get whenever one of my children receives a compliment.

After she left, Megan commented, "Yes, but I have a brain, too."

"Of course you do, dear."

"Has Josh told you anything about his new love?" she asked.

"No, but then again I've been very busy. I take it he's been talking with you."

"Sure. The boy is smitten."

"The Gap girl?" I asked.

"One and the same, and wait till you hear her name."

"Yes?"

She paused for effect. "Candi with an *I*."

"You are kidding?"

"Swear to God."

"Now, do we think that's the name her parents gave her? Somehow I can't see putting something like *Candi* down on a birth certificate."

"I know." She crunched down on a pastel-colored shrimp chip. "It's definitely child abuse."

"There's certainly enough around." I looked across at my daughter, whose features were shadowed in the flickering light of the candle. "Do you think much about your own growing up?"

"You mean the divorce and all?"

"Yeah."

"Not so much now, like I've gotten to a place where I sort of understand things. But at the time . . . I was eight, Josh was six, we had no idea what was going on. I know that I kept thinking we had done something wrong. I wasn't sure if it was Josh or me. For the longest time I thought he might have done something really bad."

"Like what?"

"Who knows? It just didn't make sense. And then when Daddy remarried . . . that might have been even worse than the divorce. I know that it sounds like a cliché, but I really thought that you and Daddy would get back together. We never even saw the two of you fight. I know that you weren't very happy with each other, but there were never any drag-down knock-out fights."

"There were," I informed her for the very first time. "We just kept them away from you."

"I wondered."

We pushed back from the table as the waitress returned with our order. I watched as she lifted the covers off the steaming dishes and announced the contents of each.

After she left, Megan leaned forward and whispered, "I know that Daddy had an affair."

"Who told you?" I asked, not terribly surprised that the root cause of my divorce, which I had deliberately shielded from my children, had leaked out.

"Grandma."

"Of course . . . how long ago did she tell you?"

"I think around the time Daddy married Sheila."

"Should I have told you?" I asked.

"I don't know. I think it's kind of neat that you never trashed him to either Josh or me."

"I tried very hard not to."

"I know you did, Mom."

Tears welled up behind my eyes. "Does Josh know?"

"I told him," she admitted.

"Well, it's probably best."

"So that was the real reason?" she asked.

"Yes."

"It makes a lot more sense. Not to get on your case, but for years both you and Daddy had this party line of 'We had too many differences.' Or the equally popular, 'We grew apart.' Talk about confusing. There was a time when I was afraid that if I disagreed with you I'd wind up on the street."

"Seriously?"

"Yeah, but I always knew that Grandma and Grandpa would take me in, so it wasn't critical."

"Yes, my sainted mother."

"Hey, I know the two of you don't agree on a lot of stuff, but she's always there when you need her."

"Can't argue with that," I agreed. "I don't give her enough credit, the both of them. Let me ask you this, while we're on the subject, if we hadn't gotten divorced what would be different?"

"For me or for you?"

"Do you first, and then I'll do me."

She stared into the candle flame. "You sure you want to do this?" she asked.

"If you do."

She started slowly, "I think about before and after the divorce. I know it changed me, but it's hard to figure out exactly how. Do you know what I mean?"

I nodded.

"I don't think I'm a very trusting person. It takes me a long time to warm up to somebody, and even then, I never quite relax . . . with guys in particular. I think it's probably good that you didn't tell me that Daddy had cheated. If I had known at eight, I think that would have been worse. Now it's more like, I just don't trust the guys I go out with."

"Guys? Plural?"

"A girl's got to keep busy." She smiled and

shook her head. "But I always have this feeling that the guy won't stay around. I get this attitude that I'd rather be the one to leave. The dumper versus the dumpee. On the plus side, between the divorce and you going to medical school I got a second set of parents with Grandma and Grandpa. It's not like it was all bad." She pointed her chopstick at me. "Your turn."

"I doubt I would have gone to medical school," I admitted. "If I'd stayed with your father, I doubt it would have happened."

"That was a strange one all right. I think it's pretty cool, actually. It's like you started a whole new life."

"That was the plan . . ." I hesitated, we were skating around topics that were chock-full of guilt and regret. "It took away a lot of my time. I sometimes don't know if I made the right decision."

"We're not perfect people, Mom. You did what you thought was best. It's not like Josh or I ever went without love. We get it from you, from Daddy, and from Grandma and Grandpa. I don't feel deprived. And I don't think Josh does either."

"Wouldn't it have been better if I'd stayed home?"

"I don't know." She looked me straight in the eye. "Thinking back, you were pretty strange after the divorce. It's like we had to walk around you very carefully. Maybe you had to get out and do something entirely different. You would have been close to my age when you married Daddy. I can't imagine, and then a year later you had me. I'm nowhere near ready to start a family . . ."

"You think about having kids?" I asked.

"Sure, but I think I'll wait until I'm thirty, or maybe by then they can do the whole thing in a test tube."

"A charming thought."

"Well, it does eliminate morning sickness and the wear-and-tear on my figure."

"I see you've given this some thought," I commented.

"If you think about it, how far away are we? I mean scientifically? They can do the fertilization in a test tube, what's stopping them from doing the whole thing in a laboratory?"

"What would you use for a uterus?" I asked. "And where would the placenta attach? You need the whole thing, blood, oxygen, nutrients, hormones."

"Details," she said dismissively as she wrapped the thin pancake around her moo-shoo pork.

"And what about a husband?"

"Optional," she stated. "I haven't quite figured that one out. What about you?" she asked, deftly turning the table. "Any prospects?"

Immediately I thought of my meeting tomorrow with Garret and Lieutenant Harris. "You never know."

"Right." Her tone was sarcastic. "You've had what, three dates in the past ten years?"

"It's been more than that," I rebutted, knowing that she was probably right.

"So is there somebody?"

"You never know," I repeated, allowing myself a moment's contemplation of the blueness of Peter Harris's eyes.

Chapter Twenty-one

I had just left Megan back at her dormitory when my pager sounded. Usually I turned it off on the weekends that I wasn't on call. Now the question was, should I ignore it or answer it? The number displayed on the LED readout was the main extension for the inpatient unit. I spotted a pay phone, fished in my pocket for a quarter, and with heavy heart went to see what crisis would cause them to page an off-duty resident.

I dialed and was greeted by the evening clerk.

"This is Dr. Katz, I was paged."

"Hold on."

Over the line, I heard the clerk call out, "Someone page Dr. Katz?"

I held my breath, allowing myself the hope that it was a wrong number, or that someone had mistakenly thought that I was the on-call doc tonight.

"Molly." A familiar male voice picked up the phone.

"Rob?"

"One and the same," my office mate answered. "I hate to call you on your night off, but in the words of Felix, 'We have a situation.'"

"Which is?"

"Billy Keene AWOLed off the unit."

"Shit."

"Exactly."

"He had a sitter," I stated. "How could he possibly have AWOLed?"

"Easy, he was smarter than the sitter. He told her that he had to go to the bathroom."

"But they're supposed to watch them, or at least maintain some visual contact."

"I guess Billy said that he couldn't go with her watching. So she let him close the door."

"And?"

"If it weren't so terrible, you'd actually admire his creativity. He somehow managed to get the vent off the air shaft."

"How long ago?"

"It's been over an hour. Security thinks he came out by the elevators, went down the stairs, and out the door."

I immediately thought of his mother. "Does the family know?"

"Everybody knows. I called Felix, the police, his mother, the attorney, you, Carol. It's a total mess. The kid is a ticking bomb just waiting to go off. If he does anything we are in such deep shit."

"I can't believe that no one saw a kid leaving the hospital in pajamas."

"It's not that hard to believe. Maybe he even stole some clothes on his way out. The kid is pretty bright."

"Shit," I muttered again. "This is not good. So what did the cops say?"

"That they'd look for him and bring him back if they found him."

"Did you speak to Lieutenant Harris?"

"No, I just got whoever was on duty. Why?"

"They wanted to interview Billy about the night Helen was murdered. They were going to do it on the unit."

"I can give him a call if you think I should."

"It's probably a good idea. Maybe he can make them be a little more proactive in tracking him down. Someone should at least check in with his mother."

"You think he'd hurt her?"

"It's like you said, he's got a short fuse and a long list of people he's not happy with."

"Including you . . . and probably me," Rob stated.

"Yeah, this is not a good feeling."

"Sorry, but I figured you'd want to know."

"Thanks. What did Sonja say?"

"Before or after she called our entire unit incompetent?"

"Let's try after."

"She talked me through a cover-your-ass note word by word. And then let me know that she'd be coming down in the morning to review the chart."

"On a Saturday . . . and this is my patient. It just doesn't get any better."

"Yeah, well it was on my shift. And as you recall, we switched him over to my service. Either way you slice it we're both in hot water. That the sitter was a boob is inconsequential."

"True."

"So if the cops think it was Billy who killed Helen, why the hell didn't they just take him into custody?" I heard anger and frustration in his voice. "Besides, I thought they had their man."

"I don't think it's that clear anymore. You've seen Garret," I said, knowing that Rob worked at Whitestone. "Up until yesterday he was catatonic. Even the cops are having a hard time believing that he could have done it. That, and what happened to Janice."

"That maybe the same person killed them both?"

"Yeah."

"And Billy was on the unit when Helen was killed and off the unit when Janice was found."

"Exactly."

Now it was his turn. "Shit."

"You got it. There's no chance he could still be in the hospital?"

"I've been checking with security every five minutes; he's gone. He could be anywhere."

I stood there on the corner of Commonwealth Avenue and looked out at the city. A train filled with students and businessmen moved noisily down the wide street. "Was there anything else?" I asked. "Would it be any use for me to come in?"

"To do what? Unless of course you want to work up the two admissions waiting for me in the ER."

"So they didn't close the unit."

"Are you kidding? You know what the worse thing about this is?"

"What?"

"We were full and now his bed is open," he admitted.

"Don't fill it. Maybe he'll come back on his own."

"Uhhuh. Along with the Tooth Fairy?" He struggled for a shred of humor.

"Yeah, well, thanks for letting me know."

"Any time," he said and we hung up.

Intellectually I knew that this was not my fault. But in my chest, there was a heaviness that contained equal parts of guilt and fear. I tried to concentrate on the street around me, even though this was a relatively safe section of the city. It was never a good idea to lose your focus, especially after dark. I walked to the T kiosk and waited for the next trolley. I thought about giving Gail Keene a call, but if Rob had already done that, I'm not sure what benefit I would add. I felt there should be something that I could do. I was angry with the aide for disregarding unit policies. But more than that, I knew that Billy Keene was capable of great violence. What I had seen in my office with his mother was the tip of the iceberg, and now he was out and filled with a world of fresh hate.

I pictured the out-of-control teen threatening me on the unit. I knew that he had the ability to make his words flesh. The question was, how far would he take things? Maybe I should have moved quicker or been more stringent. Maybe I shouldn't have hospitalized him at all and had the police take him into custody after he assaulted his mother. Maybe Rob was right; he never belonged on a psychiatric ward.

A Green Line trolley trundled slowly in my direction and stopped. I boarded and moved to the very back seat. I checked out the other passengers and wished that the lights inside the car weren't quite so bright and that I didn't feel quite so exposed.

I stared out the window as we headed back into the hub of the city. I still had to make a connection at the Park Street Station and then return to the commuter parking lot where I had left my car.

I thought about what Dr. Adams might say. I didn't think that psychiatry had a lot to offer Billy right now. In terms of moral development, the ship sailed a long time ago and Billy was left with no ability to feel for others or to acknowledge that society had rules. On top of that, he was smart. His escape tonight could probably be used as some form of IQ test. I tried to picture what he was doing at that moment. But what I saw were the faces of Helen and Janice, and I knew without a doubt that something evil had been freed upon the city.

CHAPTER TWENTY-TWO

Peter was all business as he explained what needed to be done.

"We're going to videotape the entire interview. I hope that's okay."

"That's fine," I said, relieved that I had successfully talked myself into wearing my go-to-court navy suit.

"Have you seen Garret yet?" I asked, as I watched the lieutenant arrange the chairs in the Whitestone conference room that he had commandeered.

"Briefly, he looks like a different kid. They've been giving him shock treatments. I didn't think people still did that, but it seems to be helping."

"For certain conditions it's probably the best treatment," I stated, sounding a bit schoolmarmish.

He shuddered. "It's a little too *Cuckoo's Nest* for me."

"I can see that you need some education on the matter, Lieutenant Harris."

He smiled, and stepped back from the chairs, having finally achieved the desired configuration. "Is that an offer, Doctor?"

My cheeks tingled. "Yes," I stated simply, not trusting myself to elaborate.

"It's a date then." But before we could nail down the specifics, Garret entered the room escorted by a burly aide, a male nurse, Dr. Freeborn and a dark-suited man carrying a briefcase.

Immediately I understood what Peter was talking about. The changes in Garret were dramatic. The hollows in his face had filled out, his eyes seemed clearer, and someone had shaved him and combed his shiny blond hair. If it weren't for the hospital's dull green pajamas and stained blue robe he would have looked like any other healthy teenager.

"Do you need us to stay here?" the nurse asked Dr. Freeborn.

"No," he said, "but we could be a while. Just make sure that if there's a shift change people know that we have Garret."

Satisfied that his charge was in reliable hands, the nurse turned to Garret. "You'll be fine."

As they left, the man in the blue suit stuck his hand in my direction. "Gregg Osborne," he stated. "I'm Garret's attorney." He nodded in Peter's direction. "Good morning, Lieutenant."

"Morning," Peter replied in a careful monotone. "We should get started. Garret, I want you to sit there, Dr. Katz, if you could be across from him, Dr. Freeborn to her right, and Attorney Osborne, if you wouldn't mind sitting at the opposite end of the table."

Once we were seated, Peter stood behind the videocamera and adjusted the lens, while checking the monitor to see that both Garret and I were in the frame.

"Budget cuts?" the attorney asked.

"Weekend," Peter shot back. "Somehow, everything seems to shut down if it's not nine to five, Monday to Friday. Which makes no sense as most crimes occur in the evening . . . It looks like I've got it, but I'm going to audiotape it as well, just to make sure. Are we ready?"

I nodded, not at all certain of how to proceed. Peter had told me just to interview Garret as I would normally and to focus on his last hospitalization and anything he recalled about the night of Helen Weir's murder.

I heard the click of the videotape, and in my periphery saw that the red light was on. Peter spoke and announced the date, the location, and who was present in the room. He then nodded in my direction.

I took the cue, looked at Garret, and smiled. "How are you doing?" I asked.

"Okay, I guess." The rhythm of his speech seemed fuller and more near normal.

I pressed on. "Do you remember who I am?" I asked.

"Dr. Katz. You were my doctor before I came here, and now sometimes you're here."

"That's right," I said, wondering what Garret's attorney would make of my involvement with his client.

"I asked for you," he stated simply. "I don't like the other doctor, the one in the daytime."

"How come?" I asked, not certain if I should head down this road with the videotape playing and with the boss of the doctor in question in the room.

"I hardly see him, he doesn't talk to me. He just talks about the number of treatments I need to have. I'm glad it's Saturday, because that way I don't have to have another one until Monday."

"You're talking about the ECT?"

"Yeah." He looked up and quickly hazarded a glance at his attorney and then at Peter, who was mostly obscured in the shadows behind the camera. He appeared scared and very young. I could see his thin chest rise and fall through the fabric of his pajamas. He brushed a stray lock of hair back off his face. "I don't really remember much about the treatments, and everyone tells me that I'm getting better. I just don't know. I don't really know why I'm here, or what this is all about."

"Tell me what you do remember. Why don't you start before you came into the hospital."

"It's all confused, what happened when. I think part of that's from the treatments, but I don't know. I remember something happened at school and I had to go to the nurse's office and then I got really scared and left and went home. And my mom got called and she came from work, and I don't remember, but someone said something and I ended up on the roof. And there were police cars and my mom was crying . . . it's all mixed up."

His expression was pained and confused, but his words had lost the mechanical and reflexive cadence of Thursday night. I had been taught about the near-miraculous results that could be had with ECT on conditions like catatonia—I had never witnessed it, like this. When I was on the geriatric unit last year I had seen some fairly wondrous results with electroconvulsive therapy on depression, but this was far and away something else. If I hadn't seen it myself, I would never have believed how completely nonfunctional he had been. "It sounds like things were pretty confused. Do you remember anything else?"

He looked at his hands, trying to hide two crystal drops of water that slowly tracked down his cheeks. "I was hearing voices."

"Do you still?"

He looked up and wiped his tears with the sleeve of his robe. His eyes darted around the room, as though waiting and listening. "I don't hear anything, just that," he said, drawing our attention to the soft whir of the camcorder and the tape player.

"Would you like some water?" Peter asked, from behind the camcorder.

"No, I'm okay. What else do you want to know?" he asked, trying to see Peter hidden in the shadows of the room.

"What do you remember about the voices?" I asked.

His attorney stiffened and leaned forward on the table.

"I've had them on and off for a long time. But I never said anything, 'cause I didn't know if that was weird or not. Like I thought maybe everyone had them."

"What kind of things would they say?"

"Stupid stuff, mostly. Like commenting on what I was doing. You know, 'Garret, brush your teeth,' or 'Garret, your teacher thinks you're stupid, just shut up.' Sometimes they could get pretty mean. I think that's what was happening at school."

"Were they telling you to do stuff?"

The attorney cleared his throat. "Leading question," he stated.

I reworded. "Do you remember any other specific things that the voices were saying, especially around the time you went into the hospital?"

"Some. They were all the time. I couldn't even sleep, and they just kept going one on top of the other. A lot of it was just, like, noise, but there were, like, phrases. 'I am God,' 'I am the word,' stuff like that."

"How did that feel?" I asked.

"Scary, like losing control."

"Did you lose control?"

"Leading," the attorney interrupted.

"Try to rephrase it," Peter suggested.

"When you said that you were afraid of losing control, what did you think might happen?"

The attorney snorted, but refrained from further comment.

"There was a voice that would yell at me. It called me bad names . . . it told me to kill myself. It told me to climb a tall building and jump."

"Were you afraid that you might do that?"

"Leading, but go ahead and answer," the attorney commented.

"I wanted to die. I think that's why I was on the roof, but that wouldn't have killed me, would it? It wasn't high enough."

"Do you still feel like that, like you want to die?"

"No. I just want to go home and see my mom. Do you think I'll be able to?"

"I hope so," I offered, "but I don't know when. I need to ask you some questions about when you were on the inpatient unit at Commonwealth Hospital. Start by telling me everything that you do remember."

He looked at the floor, and then back at me.

"I've been trying, because I knew you were going to be here. I can't remember. There are pieces, but they're just bits. I can't see the whole thing. I see you in the emergency room the day I was admitted. You reminded me of my mother. Then there was stuff upstairs. I remember that the ward had lots of kids and I thought that they were devils and that I'd been thrown into hell, because that's where devils live. And I was scared and then there was blood and it was sticky and nothing else, no matter how hard I try . . . nothing else." His eyes seemed to change their focus as he tried to recollect.

"Where was the blood?" I asked.

"Everywhere. I was anointed in the blood of the sacrifice. The Easter lamb was slaughtered." His voice tightened and his breath came in shallow gasps.

"Do you need to take a break?" I asked, afraid that the stress of the interview might worsen his condition.

He shook his head. "No, it's just sometimes hard to stay focused, it's like my thoughts get away from me." He met my gaze. "I sometimes think it might have been best if I had found a higher building."

"So you do think about suicide," I commented, realizing that as he became less psychotic he was at significant risk for depression.

"I don't know. It might just be easier."

"To be dead?"

"Yes." He looked in the direction of Peter and the camera. "I can't remember anything more about the hospital or the woman who died. Was it her blood I see? That's why people think I killed her . . . I don't know. I don't know. I don't know." His words stuck on the phrase.

"There was a knife," I said, trying to pull his focus back. "Do you recall how you got the knife?" After I said that I was uncomfortably aware that I never shared my suspicions about the cake knife— an omission that needed to be corrected.

"It was a sacrifice," he repeated. "An Easter lamb to bathe the earth, to nourish corn, to feed children. We grow out of blood, a mother's blood, the nurse's milk . . ."

He unraveled before our eyes. We had lost him. His body stiffened and his eyes turned distant with a glazed, fevered look. His monologue grew looser and looser.

"We all drink the nurse's blood milk. But the devil comes." His eyes opened wide. "There are devils all around; they suckle at the nurse's breast, looking for milk, wanting blood, eating souls." He stared at me and raised a stiffening hand. He pointed his finger. "He wants to suckle at your breast and drink your blood. He wants to taste your soul."

My stomach rolled, and salt water rushed into my mouth on a mounting tide of nausea. "Who, Garret? Who wants to drink my blood?" I was torn between wanting the information and fighting down the guilt of pushing him back into madness. "Do no harm," I reminded myself. But it was too late.

"The devil does." And like a phonograph record caught in a groove he repeated, "The devil does, the devil does, the devil does, the devil does . . ."

CHAPTER TWENTY-THREE

How did I let this happen? It was Sunday morning, and I was on Hamilton 5 pouring medication for the patients. I was the one who needed a psychiatrist. But when Carol had called this morning, I wasn't awake enough to fend off her pleas.

"I'm desperate," she had moaned. "Joanne didn't show for work; I can't get her on the phone and I can't get anyone else to come in."

"What about travelers?" I asked, referring to temporary help that could be flown in on short notice.

"I'll have to, but I can't get anyone on a Sunday. Just one shift, please." And then she got me. "I'd do it myself, but I've been on since yesterday afternoon. I wouldn't do this, Molly, if I had any other options."

"How long?" I asked, hating myself for giving in.

"If you could do days, I swear you can get off at five."

I had planned to go to Josh's AAU tournament. I'm sure he would say that it was fine, but still.

"Please, Molly," she begged. "I'll bonus you,

whatever you make an hour plus a hundred dollars for the shift."

"Okay," I relented. "I'll be there in an hour."

In some respects, it wasn't that bad. I easily slipped back into the nurse's routine. Although, in the few years since I had done this full time, things had changed. Increasingly nurses just handled medications and took off orders; there was less of the other stuff, the direct patient care and teaching. All of that had been deemed not cost effective. It was now handled by the aides or not at all.

So here it was, late on a Sunday morning, me, Alice Meadows, the other nurse, two aides, a clerk, a half-time social worker, and nineteen severely disturbed adolescents. The kids were presently in an activities group with the social worker and an aide. The other aide was posted outside the rooms of two restricted adolescents who had gotten into a fight earlier in the morning.

I worked in the medication room, with the door open so that I could hear if any problems were developing while Alice sat a couple feet away, taking off orders and writing out treatment plans for the doctors and social workers to sign on Monday.

Alice muttered as she worked on her forms. "You expect a certain amount of professionalism."

"What are you talking about?" I asked.

"Joanne, she didn't even have the courtesy to call out and fake being sick. It's one thing to be mad at administration, it's another to be insubordinate. But worse than that"—and she turned back from the counter to look at me—"it's dumping on us. I mean look at you; it's not like you wanted to be here on a Sunday. She better have a really good reason."

"Maybe she forgot?" I offered.

"Yeah, right. I've known Joanne for years; she doesn't forget shifts."

"Maybe something came up and—" We had the same thought simultaneously. "Shit." I immediately pictured Joanne and then I saw an image of Billy Keene. "Do you have her number?" I asked.

"It should be in the Rolodex." She abandoned her paperwork and flipped through the cards. "Here it is." She stared at it, and then quickly punched in the numbers.

I held my breath and waited.

"Hello, Joanne?" She nodded in my direction. "It's Alice. You were supposed to be here this morning . . . uh-huh . . . right." Her tone was terse. "Well someone had to do it . . . great . . . bye." She hung up the receiver a hair short of slamming it down. Alice tapped her fingers on the stack of paperwork. "She didn't feel safe. What sort of an excuse is that? She didn't even have the courtesy to call."

"At least she's okay." I returned to the task of filling my white plastic pill cups.

The rest of the shift went by in a blur. The problem with keeping kids on an impatient unit is that there's nowhere for them to burn off energy. After the group let out, they were freed upon the unit like a herd of dervishes.

I watched as Alice, who was a good ten years older than I, took on the role of den mother. There was pathos as the teenagers lobbied for her attention, some by pleading, others by starting trouble either alone or in pairs. "Break it up," she bellowed at a pair of boys, who were playing Nerf football in the hallway. Their game had deteriorated into a demonstration of applying suffocating headlocks to each other.

At one point, when I was rounding them up to watch an action-adventure video, I caught Freddie, a fourteen-year-old boy, with thirteen-year-old Melissa, in her bathroom. Taking my cue from Alice, "Break it up," I told them, holding the door for the boy to leave. "Your zipper," I reminded him as he went.

He grinned at me with a cock-eyed smile and then went to brag to his unit buddies about how close he had come to scoring. Melissa, who had a history of being prostituted since the age of nine, couldn't understand my concern.

"It's no big deal," she informed me. "It's just sex. Everyone does it."

"True, but you're both too young."

"That's such bullshit," she said. "I've had my period since I was ten. It's the only thing people want," the pretty dark-haired girl told me.

"It's not," I reassured her, sitting on the edge of her bed. "It's just a part of things—an important part of things—but still there's a lot more out there than having sex in bathrooms."

"Easy for you to say; there's nothing else to do up here. Just these stupid groups, and I'm *so* bored. At least sex in the bathroom is kind of fun." She grinned. "It's something to do. You can't get high, you can't have sex, what else is there?"

She wasn't joking. I thought about Josh with his basketball obsession, about all of Megan's after-school activities. At thirteen, Megan would have still been in Girl Scouts. That was the thing about working with these kids, no matter how crazy and time-constricted my life became, in the global scheme of things I had nothing to complain about. "Any idea how much longer you'll be here?" I asked, knowing just a few of the details about this girl.

"Sometime this week." Her expression grew serious. "I'm supposed to meet my new foster parents here Monday and then go with them, maybe on Tuesday or Wednesday."

"Is that what you want?"

"It sucks. They won't let me go back with my grandmother, and my mother's a junkie. You never know with these people. When you first meet them they seem nice, but you never know. And then they make all these rules; like, I'm supposed to follow them. Who are they?"

"How many foster homes have you been in?"

She counted on her fingers. "At least six, no make that seven, and this will be eight."

"Did you like any of them?"

"The first one . . . I was there for a long time, but then my mother went to court and promised that she'd take better care of me. That lasted two weeks and then they wouldn't let me go back to the same family. After that I don't even try, what's the point?"

"Because you never know when you'll get yanked out?"

"Something like that. So they try to be nice and I wind up being a brat and before you know it I'm back in here waiting for the next one."

It was an old story that I knew by heart. So many of these children passed through the unit, the faces were different, but with minor variations their lives shared much in common. All of them bounced from house to house and in the process became more wild, disconnected, and out of control. "Isn't there anything that you'd like for yourself?"

"For people to leave me alone. That would be great."

"Present company included?" I asked, wondering how she viewed this interruption in her afternoon tryst.

"You're okay. What did you say your name was?"

"Molly," I said.

"But aren't you like Dr. Jeffreys?"

"Yeah, I'm just helping out today."

"Do you have kids?" she asked.

"Two, a boy and a girl."

"They're a lot different, aren't they?"

I wasn't sure how to answer. "They do okay."

"But not like me, huh?"

"You've had a much different life, much harder."

"That's for sure. I didn't ask for it, none of it. I really wonder why my mother had me at all. She didn't want a kid, she can't even take care of herself."

"What about you? Do you want kids?"

"Oh yeah, and the sooner the better. I've been trying to get pregnant since I was twelve."

My heart froze, and I stared at her not certain that I had heard correctly. "You're kidding."

"I'm serious. I really want a baby."

"Why?" I asked, pulling my jaw up off the floor.

"Lots of reasons." Her face lit up as she imagined the joys of motherhood. "It would be someone who really belonged to me. Like I'd finally have something of my own, and I'd take care of it and not let any of the crappy things that happened to me happen to her. I could dress her up and I don't know . . . I just want one."

"Would you still go to school?"

"Yeah, they have these classes now where the girls can bring their babies. I want to finish high school and maybe even go to college."

"Melissa, I think it's great you want to have kids, but where you've been bounced around so much, do you really want your baby to be a part of that?"

"It'll be different." Her mouth tightened.

"You asked me about my kids, and if they were like you or not. I think the biggest difference . . ." I don't know why I felt compelled to tell her this, but it was the only way I could think of illustrating the point without completely attacking her. "I made real certain that my kids had as stable a home as I could make. And it wasn't perfect. I got divorced in the middle of their growing up, but they always had a home, actually the same home. Kids need stability. I bet that's what you liked about the first foster home. It started to feel safe and then it got yanked away. It gets hard to trust anything or anyone if that kind of stuff happens. After a while it changes people."

"But didn't you love your babies?"

"I still do."

"But that's what I want," she pleaded, "to have someone to really love."

I was about to bring up the issue of feedings and diapers when the panic alarm sounded. "I got to go," I said, hearing the start of a familiar school-ground chant coming from the dayroom.

"Fight, fight, fight, fight, fight."

CHAPTER TWENTY-FOUR

The ringing phone intruded into my first moment of quiet on this harried Monday.

"Dr. Katz?" A woman's tentative voice came over the telephone receiver.

"Yes."

"This is Sandra Jacobs . . . Garret's mother."

"How are you?" I asked.

"Not great," she admitted. "They're probably going to discharge Garret tomorrow and they asked me if I had an outside doctor. I was wondering if you might be able to see him."

"They're releasing him? Already?"

"That's what I thought," she said. "I don't think he's ready. He's much better, but as soon as the police said that he was no longer a suspect, it's like they just wanted to get him out of there."

"What about another hospital?"

"I don't understand." Her voice was weary. "He's doing much better after the treatments and they're telling me that no other hospital will take him right now. If he was worse off they might, but now that he's getting better . . . I just don't understand it."

Unfortunately, I did. At this point, if Garret

were no longer under suspicion of a major crime, the forensic facility was not the right place for him. However, that now meant that he had to revert to his mother's health insurance, which was a heavily managed HMO that scrutinized his every day of inpatient treatment. If he was no longer floridly psychotic or at imminent risk of hurting himself or someone else, they would not pay for the hospital and his mother would get stuck with an impossible bill.

"They don't give you much time, do they?" I commented.

"No. But I know that if I can't get him in to see someone right away, he's going to slip back. They also said I should try to find someone who can do the treatments on an outpatient basis, because the medications didn't really work for him. But then I'm not supposed to let him be alone the day after the treatment because of the anesthesia; I have no one to help out and if I miss work, that's it; I'll lose my job. I've already taken off more days then I was supposed to."

"Let me think." She was near the breaking point, but I didn't know if I could take on someone who needed the close monitoring that Garret did into my outpatient clinic. Then there was the issue of the ECT. "We could probably get your insurance company to swing for a few days of a day program. Then we could have him get the treatments at the hospital in the morning and you could drive him to the day program and leave him there. That way you can go to work. They can drive him home after the program and unless he's still confused, it might work out. Let me give you the number for the day program. When you call, tell them I told you to contact them and if you run into any problems, just get back to me."

"Thank you," she said. "A nurse from White-stone called me at work today and just dropped this on me. I'm glad that they're not pursuing charges, but don't they realize . . . I'm sorry for dumping on you like this, but I didn't know who else to turn to."

"That's fine." I glanced up at my office clock, it was getting close to five. "You better call the day program soon."

"Right, everyone goes home, don't they?"

"Not everyone," I confided, probably overstepping some unwritten boundary. "I'm in the ER tonight."

"And you do nights at Whitestone too?"

"A few."

"No kids?" she asked.

"Two, but they're used to it by now and one is off at college."

"Lucky you," she said. "Can I ask you one thing, and then I know you have to go and I have to call this program?"

"Sure."

"Will Garret be able to go to college? I mean I can accept that he's going to have some problems. But he's sounding pretty normal now and he used to be a good student. What are the chances of him having a regular life?"

"That's a hard question," I said. "He might. A lot of people with psychotic episodes go on to have normal lives, or he might have recurrent episodes. But even then if he has a good response to treatment, he could still lead a relatively normal life. There's also the chance that this could get worse . . . It's difficult to predict. I think it's great that he's been having as positive a response to the treatment as he has. That's a real good sign."

"So you really can't say. What about college?"

"If that's what he wants, it's possible."

"I guess I've got to go with that, at least it's not a definite 'no.' "

"You might want to consider going to a support group," I told her. "I can't imagine how hard this must be for you. But there's a wonderful group that really helps out parents and gives you all the information that you'll need, as well as meeting people who've been through similar circumstances. They can give you some perspective on how to handle things."

She listened and agreed to try and attend a meeting of the local NAMI—National Alliance for the Mentally Ill—chapter.

After she hung up I found myself with mixed feelings. I was glad that the charges had been dropped. But like his mother, I wondered if this were too soon for Garret to be released. What a burden had just been dropped into her lap. Again, other than for a few childhood illnesses—mumps and chicken pox—Josh and Megan had been blessedly free of problems. More and more I saw life as a house of cards, where one or two wavers in the status quo could send the whole thing crashing down.

I made a quick call to the day program and let their administrator know about Garret. I told her that when Garret was finished with their end of things that I would clear out a space for him in my Thursday afternoon clinic. I would book him into Jennifer Ryan's slot; I didn't think she was ever going to show. I'd give her another couple weeks and after that I'd empty out her time slot and save it for Garret.

It was now five o'clock, and the mounting acid in my stomach let me know that it was time to head to the emergency room. I grabbed my overnight bag, put a lab coat on over my day clothes, and started my mental timer on the next fifteen-hour shift.

CHAPTER TWENTY-FIVE

Lightning streaked across the night sky of my dream. I was in a darkened field running for cover. Storm clouds swirled overhead, and thunder rumbled, letting me know that there was little time before . . . before what? I stopped in the middle of the meadow, where down around my calves weeds gently tickled my bare skin. I thought about ticks and that deer had been through here. "I don't want Lyme Disease," I said, and the field and the stormy sky vanished. As I looked up there was a door to a pharmacy. I opened it and entered. It was a scene from a 1940's Norman Rockwell painting. There were teens and preteens seated on bar stools; behind the counter was Felix Winthrop in a soda jerk's cap.

He smiled as I entered. "Dr. Katz, we've been holding rounds for you. Your patients were worried."

I turned around slowly, looking at the teens; some were familiar. I saw Jennifer Ryan and Garret and Melissa, who was holding a stuffed cow wrapped in swaddling clothes. Each time I looked, there were new patients. How am I going to take care of all of them? I fretted. But they looked content sipping away at their milkshakes. I didn't want to say anything, not in front of the kids—there certainly were more of them than I could reasonably care for. I would talk with Felix later. Clearly they had exceeded the cap on a resident physician's patient load mandated by the training program's accreditation body.

Felix called out to me, "Are you thirsty? Would you like a soda?"

I didn't want one, but not to be rude, I replied, "Make it a black and white." I walked up to the counter and looked at the boy next to me; it was Josh.

"Hey, Mom." He slurped at his soda.

"Why are you here?" I asked, not knowing what my son would be doing on a psychiatric ward/pharmacy/soda fountain.

"I was thirsty."

"What are you drinking?"

He tipped the frosted glass in my direction; it was filled with pills.

"Your soda," Felix said, as he handed me my own tumbler of medication.

He watched as I stared into the multicolored swirl. "I'm not psychotic," I commented, noticing that several of the tablets were medications like Haldol and Thorazine.

Josh piped up, "It's a protocol, Mom. Like an experiment. We're all doing it."

"Oh," was all I could manage. There was no way I could take the pills, and more than that, I had to get Josh out of there. "We need to go." I grabbed my son's hand.

"Don't forget the discharge summary," Felix called out.

"I won't," I answered, while searching for the door. The floor shifted beneath our feet, and when I looked at the walls they wavered and pushed further and further back, like a box that was extending outward from its center. The faster we moved, the farther away the walls became. "It's the pills," I said, knowing that if we could just make it to the door, things would be okay.

"There is no door," Josh stated. "And I'm still thirsty."

"There's always a door," I replied as we ran. "And I'll make you something when we get to the house."

Trees and grass sprang up beneath our feet; we were lost. "Did you speak to your sister?" I asked.

"She's pregnant," he said.

I stopped. "She is not, that was Melissa . . . where are we?"

"I thought you knew," he said.

I turned to look at him, but something wasn't right, his features were different, his smile was lopsided and had turned into a twisted sneer. "You're not my son," I stated.

"Surprise." He pulled out an axe, and cradling it in his arms, began to advance.

I edged back, frightened and angry. "What did you do with my son?"

"He's gone away."

"Bring him back." I was not going to be intimidated. I raced at the boy and pushed at his chest. I grabbed the handle of the axe. "Give it to me."

We struggled and he laughed. He mimicked me, "Give it to me. Give it to me." The tone of his voice changed as he chanted, "Give it to me. Give it to me." It became huskier and deeper. He stared into my eyes—his were a deep blue. "If you really want it; I'll give it to you." His body began to thrust upward underneath mine.

With a start, I woke up. My heart pounded and my mind skittered over fragments from the dream. I looked at the alarm clock; it was two o'clock. My mouth was dry and I wanted to go to the bathroom. More than that, the dream had left me with an unsettled feeling. I pictured the boy, who was Josh and then wasn't Josh. Thank God I'm not a Freudian. I mulled over the sexual over-tones. But the boy's other comment was haunting, "I'm thirsty." What did that mean?

As I maneuvered out of bed, I thought back to dinner with Josh—the first time we had eaten to-gether in days. I had been dead tired after more than thirty hours straight at work between Mon-day, my on-call shift, and yesterday. His team had won the tournament, and thank God my par-ents and Megan had been there to see him play. I thought about James, and how I criticized him for not being involved with his son—I was a fine one to talk.

On impulse, I padded on bare feet down the hallway. I pressed my hand up against the door of his room, twisted the handle, and looked in at the sleeping form of my son. A full moon shed a silver glow through the windows and I watched the slow steady rise and fall of Josh's breath. One more year, I thought, and he'll be gone too.

Suddenly the house felt very cold. What would it be like to come home and to have no one here? Did I even want to keep the house? I closed Josh's door and headed toward the kitchen. As I walked through the dining room, I glanced out the window, struck by how light the night was.

And then I froze.

There, standing motionless in the moonlight at the edge of my front lawn, was the dark outline of a man.

Chapter Twenty-six

I guess she was right, I thought, as I watched the rhythmic pulsing of the blue and red lights on top of the police cruiser. He wasn't ready to leave the hospital.

A uniformed officer escorted a pliant Garret Jacobs up the sidewalk and into my kitchen. The boy's eyes had regained the wild look he had before first coming into the hospital. His shirt was torn and a steady stream of verbiage poured from his lips.

"Bloody breast, bloody nurse, bloody breast, bloody nurse."

"I hope you don't mind us coming in," the officer said, "but with you being his doctor and all . . ."

"That's fine." I had already put the pot on for coffee, more for my sake than for theirs. "Garret," I said softly, approaching the handcuffed youth.

He stared at me, his mouth never stopping. "Bloody nurse, bloody breast, bloody nurse, bloody breast."

"Garret, it's Dr. Katz, try to listen to my voice. Try to take nice slow breaths, in and out, in and out."

Raw panic, like the eyes of a doe being hunted to ground, shone in his face.

"It's going to be okay," I said. "Just breathe and try to calm yourself."

He gulped in a breath of air and started to hiccough.

"It's okay, just relax."

His head rocked up and down and he continued to rant, "Bloody breast, bloody nurse, bloody breast . . ."

A second officer entered. "Okay if we use your phone?" he asked and then looked at the freshly brewed coffee.

"Help yourself," I offered. I could tell that Garret was trying to calm himself. But his chanting wouldn't stop and a thousand questions tumbled through my head. Why is he here? led the avalanche, followed by, Where the hell is his mother? "Garret, how did you get here?" I asked.

"Bloody breast, bloody nurse . . ."

I tried again. "Where is your mother?"

He stopped his rocking, and with visible force squeezed out, "At home, bloody breast, bloody nurse."

There was something strange about his attachment to the chanted phrases; they had a driven quality, almost as if he were afraid to give them up. "I need her number, Garret, we have to let her know where you are."

"Bloody breast, bloody nurse, bloody breast." He looked up in the direction of the officer who was on the telephone. The policeman looked at the boy.

"We have his wallet," he said, "maybe it's in there."

Garret nodded, without ever losing the train of his chant.

"And we also found this," the officer said, pulling a plastic evidence bag out of his parka pocket.

"What is it?" I asked, not able to get a clear view of the black and chrome object.

"Switchblade," he answered, still holding the receiver to his ear. "It's Officer Johnson," he said into the mouthpiece. "We've apprehended a seventeen-year-old Caucasian male, name of Garret Jacobs . . ."

I listened while he summarized the events of the last fifteen minutes. Garret continued to chant and I wondered if the knife had been for me. The little plastic bag knocked the wind right out of me. What had I done? Had I had been completely wrong? There were certain individuals who, when psychotic, could become violent and kill— it did happen. If Garret was paranoid enough and his delusions were violent enough, it could happen. "I have to go check on something," I said, suddenly needing to see my son.

"Bloody breast, bloody nurse."

"No problem," the seated officer said.

I raced up the stairs, and being as quiet as I could, for the second time that night I peeked into the room of my sleeping son, who, barring a loud explosion, would probably sleep through the sad scene playing out in the kitchen. I stood motionless in the doorway, needing to see the movement in his chest, before I could fully calm myself and allow that we might just have averted total catastrophe.

As I came back downstairs, the officer on the phone spoke to me. "Dr. Katz, were you aware that your patient was just released from Whitestone this morning?"

"Yes, his mother called me yesterday afternoon."

He shook his head. "You'd think they would have kept this one."

I nodded in agreement. "He was no longer a suspect."

"What a difference a day makes," his partner remarked, never once taking his eyes off Garret.

"Do you think there's any point in taking him to the police station?" the policeman on the phone asked me.

"As opposed to?"

"Straight to a hospital."

Garret continued to nod and to chant. "I don't think we're going to get him to stop doing that. A few days back he was completely catatonic. I think he's headed in that direction. What I want to know is how did he get here?"

Another plastic baggy appeared from the policeman's pocket. He jingled its contents. "Drove," he said.

"You've got to be kidding." I was incredulous.

"Beat-up old Buick at the foot of your driveway."

"Did you drive?" I asked the boy.

His head shifted direction, going from an up-and-down motion to wide erratic circles. He was trying to answer; I just wasn't catching the language. "Bloody breast, bloody nurse . . ."

"Yes or no, Garret, did you drive, just one word," I pleaded.

"You may want to see this too," the officer said, producing yet another zipper-locked plastic bag. I recognized the contents immediately. It was one of the computer-generated pay stubs I got weekly from the hospital—that's how he got my address. But before I could react I felt another presence in the room. "What's going on?" Josh asked, rubbing the sleep from his eyes while taking in the unexpected presence of the officers and the chanting youth.

My son had to be one of the soundest sleepers on the planet. "It looks like one of my patients followed me home," I explained, trying to make it sound as commonplace an occurrence as running out of dishwasher detergent. "It's all taken care of."

"Can I stay?" he asked.

"I'd rather you didn't. I'll tell you about it in the morning."

"Can I get a drink?"

"Sure."

The officers watched while my gangly sweats-clad son poured himself a glass of juice.

After he left, the officer who was still on hold asked, "Basketball player?"

"Yeah, AAU."

"My kid too."

"What division?"

He held up his finger and began to speak into the phone. "Yeah, I've got his doctor here. She doesn't think it would do much good bringing him down to the station. I agree. He's totally out of it. Any chance we could get him back into White-stone tonight?"

His eyes rolled as he listened to the response. "Yes, I'll hold." He shook his head and gave an exasperated smile. "So how's he doing?" he asked me.

I looked at Garret.

"No, I meant with the basketball. They winning their tournaments?"

CHAPTER TWENTY-SEVEN

It was three in the morning by the time Garret and the police had left. Whitestone refused to take him back as there were no charges pending. And they weren't willing to accept loitering as a reason to readmit to the facility that cost the taxpayers over $100,000 per year, per patient.

We got hold of his mother. She was frantic.

"Thank God," she said. And then guiltily admitted, "I started waitressing nights. I had to leave him alone. He said he was going to be all right."

"He was talking?" I asked.

"Yes, almost normal. Why, what's happened?"

I spelled out his bizarre and scary presentation. Maybe because I was scared and angry I told her about the knife. "He's not making much sense. He needs to go back into a hospital."

She asked me if I could take him back to Commonwealth. I wasn't certain if that was such a good idea, but at three in the morning, I would have done anything to get him out of my house.

Fortunately Raj was the on-call doc in the ER at Commonwealth. I called him and let him know what had happened.

"You lead a very interesting life, Molly Katz,"

he remarked. "By all means I would be delighted to admit your patient to *your* service."

I wasn't certain that I wanted Garret on *my* service, but there again, it was not the time to argue.

Then we called for an ambulance, and while I had requested no lights or sirens, the two young EMTs who transported Garret felt obliged to flood the suburban night sky with both. The neighbors would not be pleased. More than that, I wondered what sort of rumors this would birth.

Now I was thankful to have them all gone from my house. I checked the front door and looked out the dining room window at the moonlit lawn. I stared into the distance and my mind drifted. I knew there was something I was missing. But without being able to live inside Garret's head, there would be no knowing the truth of what had brought him here this evening. "Bloody nurse, bloody breast." I thought about what Raj had told me about being on call the night that Helen had been murdered. He was haunted by the image of Garret with the knife poised over the dead and bloody nurse. "I've been getting flashbacks," my colleague had admitted in an unguarded moment. After that night, Garret had deteriorated into catatonia—which seemed to be where he was headed now.

I wandered through the house checking the windows and making sure that all the doors were locked. I armed the security system, something I rarely do when I'm in the house, as more often than not I forget that it's on when I go to retrieve the morning paper from the front step.

I wasn't especially tired anymore; it didn't help that I had been drinking cup after cup of black coffee with the officers. Still, I knew that if I could get even two more hours sleep it would help me make it through tomorrow.

I wondered if I was developing a little obsessive compulsive disorder myself as I checked on Josh for the third time. I felt guilty, nothing like this had ever happened before. I knew how to maintain distance between myself and my patients. Invariably that's what gets treaters, psychiatrists in particular, into trouble with their patients—they get too close. Never had I imagined that a patient might come to my home and . . . he came with a knife. One of the officers thought there was dried blood on the blade. I thought about my sleeping son and felt a surge of panic. It's okay, I reminded myself, he's gone, and the danger is passed. It's okay. It helped a little. But only a little.

I brushed my teeth and got back into bed. It was now three-thirty. I usually got up around six; even two hours of sleep would be better than nothing. But my mind wouldn't oblige. An image of Billy Keene flashed through my thoughts. Where was he now? I had little doubt that he would reappear and that the circumstance could be tragic. I saw his mother cowering beneath his blows in my office. I hoped that she and her little girls were secure behind locked doors. In the morning I would call Peter Harris to check and see if they were having any progress in tracking him down.

Were Garret and Billy together? I thought back to a couple weeks ago, before Helen's murder. Both Garret and Billy were on the unit; I couldn't recall if they had spent much time together. There was that one episode in the dayroom where Garret had gotten out of control and another one of the patients had started to attack him. It was a futile exercise trying to remember, as I wasn't there at the time. Although something had been mentioned about it in morning report, it might have been Billy who had gone off and started punching Garret. But what would that mean? And my pay stub, that wasn't something that Garret would take, but Billy would—in a heartbeat.

I tried to distract myself and began to do some slow, measured yoga breaths to relax. The tension eased from my body as I counted out the long inhalation, letting my belly rise, and then counted out the even slower exhalation, letting my weight sink deeper into the mattress. Each time my thoughts started to chatter, I would focus back on the counting of my breath.

Gradually, sleep overtook me and I drifted deeper and deeper.

From downstairs a single sharp tap of broken glass entered my ears and pierced its way into my consciousness.

My heart skipped and my eyes shot open.

CHAPTER TWENTY-EIGHT

Time froze. I grabbed the bedside phone and punched in 911. When I put the receiver to my ear, I heard a recording that told me, "Please hang up the receiver and try again." My thoughts raced. The downstairs phone had been taken off the hook. I heard the distant beep of the alarm system as it counted down the thirty seconds it needed to be disarmed. After less than twenty evenly spaced beeps, it stopped. No siren wailed, the porch lights didn't go on, nothing.

I thought of Josh asleep in his room; I knew that there was little chance of him waking and being able to defend himself from whatever evil had just entered our home. In that instant, a plan formed. Whatever horror awaited us had come for me and I needed to lead it away from my son.

I threw back the bedcovers and landed on bare feet. I heard the wooden floors creak beneath me, and I was glad for the noise. I wanted there to be no mistake as to which room was occupied. I ran to the window, undid the latch, and jammed it open with the palm of my hand, letting it scrape and bang. I glanced quickly around my bedroom, threw one leg over the sill, fully prepared to propel myself out and down onto the lawn.

I listened as padded footsteps advanced down the hall; I held my breath and was thankful that mine was the first bedroom after the landing. I braced myself against the window frame. He must see me, and then I'll jump.

I waited and tried to pierce the darkness as the brass knob slowly turned. A sliver of deeper black blossomed in the doorframe.

I braced for my jump.

A deep male voice stopped me. "Your son will be dead before you hit the ground."

I couldn't move.

"Get back in the room," he commanded in soft, intimate tones.

I looked out once across the silvered lawn and felt a crushing helplessness as my body turned from its escape and fell under the thrall of a beast.

"Come on, Molly," he cooed, "that's right."

I knew that voice. My mind fought against the connection. It wasn't possible.

"That's right." He drew me away from the window and back into the privacy of my bedroom.

A glimmer of moonlight caught on something dark and shiny in his hand.

"It's time to come to Daddy." He moved forward out of the shadows and into the lifeless glow of the moon.

And in that moment, I saw the face of my killer.

CHAPTER TWENTY-NINE

"Get on the bed," he commanded, drawing me away from the open window. "And don't think that's what I want; you're a little too old and a little too stringy." His voice was soft and cruel and low.

I couldn't focus; it was like some sickly syrup had been poured into my veins. My thoughts clogged. This can't be happening.

"Surprised?" he asked.

I allowed myself the smallest flicker of hope. Perhaps this was a joke, albeit a sick and scary one. "Why?" was all I squeezed out.

"Ever the shrink, aren't you?" He motioned with his gun. "Onto the bed."

I followed his command, unwilling to give my height advantage as I sat on the edge of my bed.

"Now lie back."

How had I missed this? I had known Rob for three years. We had interned together, and on more rotations than not we had been on the same unit. I had considered him a friend. "Is this a joke?"

"No joke, Molly. This is real." He reached into the pocket of his black jacket and retrieved a rattling vial. With a gloved hand he tossed it to me. "Open it."

"What are they?"

"Barbs. I should have thought about that with the others. But like with everything else in life, practice, practice, practice."

My fingers fumbled. The bottle tumbled beside me on the bed.

"Pick them up." The round-cheeked face of Dr. Robert Jeffreys glowed in the light and his eyes sparkled; it was the face of a predatory clown drawn in thick charcoal lines of black and gray and white.

"Why are you doing this?" I persisted, trying to slow him down.

"What good will it do? You won't stop me. You might even make it worse . . . in case you're wondering I have no intention of harming your son. In fact, the thought of his waking to find his mother butchered in her bed is, well, delicious. I suspect he'll need some therapy after that one. Maybe I'll suggest it at the funeral. Wouldn't that be something?" A breathy excitement fueled his words.

A silent scream gathered in my belly, the pictures he painted were like fists to my gut. I couldn't let this happen and I had no idea how to stop him. More than anything, I feared for Josh. If he woke I had no doubt that Rob would gun him down without a second thought.

"Why did you kill Helen?"

"That's so cute. You're trying to stall me. Tell you what, why don't you open those pills and take out five, that's a nice round number. Then after you take them, I'll tell you a story. That will be nice, a bedtime story. Come on, just pick up the bottle and don't do anything silly. Because I will kill him if I have to, it doesn't make any difference to me."

My hand searched in the bedding and came up with the plastic vial. I held it in front of me, trying to read the label in the moonlight.

"They're from the hospital pharmacy," he informed me. "Just imagine the scandal. Not only was she murdered in her own bed, but she had been stealing narcotics from the hospital—it's shocking." A high-pitched giggle squeezed from his throat. "Forgive me, I just amuse myself sometimes. Open the bottle."

I pressed down on the safety cap and twisted.

"Take out five."

I held the small dry pills in the palm of my hand.

He moved closer and checked to see that I had taken out the prescribed number. "Good, now open wide and swallow." He placed the tip of the gun against my head. His eyes focused on mine. "Do as I say, don't try to toss them or cheek them. One fuck-up and I kill you and then I kill your son, and maybe for good measure, I take a trip into Boston and hunt down that pretty daughter of yours and kill her, too."

I put the pills into my mouth. My tongue was dry with fear and I felt his scrutiny as he watched the muscles of my jaw. He was too close to try to let the pills drop into the shadows of the bed, but as I worked up saliva into my mouth I tucked two of the five sedatives back behind my tongue.

He watched as I swallowed. He placed the cold tip of the steel gun barrel against my temple.

"Let me see." He eased back from the bed. "Open your mouth. Now stick out your tongue. Let me see the underside. Very good."

The two unswallowed pills tickled the back of my throat, threatening to make me gag. After he was satisfied that I had done as instructed, I pushed them back down into my cheek.

"Now lay back." His tone was soothing. "I'll tell you a story. Once upon a time, there was a brilliant little boy, much smarter than all the other little boys, and much, much brighter than all the little girls. He had a daddy and mommy, she was a little crazy, but that's jumping the gun—or in her case—the rope." He gave a single wheezy laugh. "It was a normal sort of life, filled with the petty woes and worries of the petty bourgeois. Kind of boring, in a bland and lifeless sort of way. And the little boy, who I know you know is I—you're such a smart girl—kept thinking there has to be something more. It was too dull, people were sheep just following behind each other, doing this or doing that. So many rules: this fork, that fork, be polite, don't shoplift, don't cut the cat open to see what's inside. Don't set Granny's nighty on fire. Way too too many rules. And do you know what the little boy discovered?"

"What?" I responded dully.

"Rules don't matter. When I was six years old I figured that out. It might have been earlier, but I knew in my heart of hearts that the rules weren't for me. I also knew that people got upset when they caught you breaking the rules. So that became the only rule: Don't get caught. It's amazingly simple, a philosophy, and a way of life. You might even say it's my religion."

"But why kill? What did Helen or Janice ever do to you? What about me? I thought we were friends."

"You don't get it," he said in a pitying voice. "None of that matters. It's irrelevant. They were irrelevant." He pulled something dark and shiny from his left jacket pocket. He brandished it in front of my face. A loud click startled me back further into the pillows and I found myself staring into the cold-polished steel of a six-inch switchblade. He gave a soft, excited gasp of breath as he watched my expression. "People are sheep, Molly." He switched the gun to his left hand and took up the knife with his right; he ran the tip of the knife through my hair. He leaned across my body, pressing me back and holding himself up on the elbow of his gun hand. I felt the heat and weight of his body against mine. "And where there are sheep, you need wolves to thin down the flock."

I cringed. I would not let go of my thoughts. Perhaps it was the barbiturates that were slowly leaching into my bloodstream that kept me from dissolving into the pool of panic that swirled in my chest. "Why sheep? And what happened to the little boy?" I thought of Scheherezade, the stories that my father read to me as a little girl. For a thousand and one nights that clever woman kept her head from being chopped off through the use of story; I was just looking for the next minute. I didn't move as the blade tip scraped down the side of my neck.

"You really want to know?"

I swallowed and nodded. "Yes, at least let me understand."

"We are surrounded by rules," he began. "Day by day a cage grows around the child and starts to make his movements smaller and smaller. 'Don't do this, it's bad. Don't do that. Mustn't touch.' People grow weak and filled with fear. I have none of that—I never did. But no one knows, except you, of course. I have the most perfect sort of freedom. Wonderful, flowing rivers of bloody freedom."

A sticky wetness trickled down my cheek. He had illustrated his point by breaking the surface of my skin; I hadn't felt it. "But what about the boy in the story?" I persisted, acknowledging a soft pressure of sedation that started to descend like a curtain across my thoughts.

"He feels no fear. He has no regrets. He . . . I am truly strong. I bathe in rivers of blood and I feast upon the herds of sheep and grow stronger, while all the bleating white beasts clamor and scream and try to hide. As I grow, as you die . . . as your son dies, as your daughter is hunted to the ground, they will huddle for shelter. They won't find it and the blood will flow sweet and thick."

A nerve in my cheek shrieked white-hot pain, he was going deeper. I focused my thoughts and my entire being on his last statement; he had no intention of letting my children go. I balled my consciousness into a single thought: I had to stop him.

Sprawled backward into the bed as I was, my routes for escape were limited. Just keep him talking, I thought, Go for his ego. "What about laws? There'd be no society without them."

"Nietzsche was right," he countered. "Laws are just a way that the weak try to band together against the strong. Starting to feel a little sleepy?"

I nodded and let my right hand snake slowly back under the pillows. I aimed for the hard plastic telephone receiver, but my fingers tickled up against something better. They found the three-foot length of two-by-four that I used to bang up against the radiator wrench when I did the yearly bleeding of the system. It was wedged behind the headboard. "We need rules," I said, grabbing at any words that would pass my lips.

"Soon, you won't need anything." The knife passed from my cheek and he backed his weight off me. His dark form rose over me. "What was it Garret said? 'Bloody nurse, bloody breast.'" He brandished the knife in his right hand and the gun in his left. He brought the blade down to the hollow of my throat and proceeded to slice away at the ties of my cotton nightgown.

"What did you do to Garret?" My fingers struggled to free the board from behind the bed.

"Crazy boy? He's papa's little darling. Although I think his time may be at an end. I suspect he's about to succumb to a most unfortunate complication of anesthesia at his next ECT treatment. Tragic, really." His voice mocked. "He was getting so much better. But we've got the next one lined up, and he's even better than Garret."

Clarity struck, with my hand now firmly on the board, I knew what he was talking about. "Billy Keene," I whispered while silently trying to maneuver the board through the four-inch space between the mattress and the headboard.

"Clever girl. Observe." He flicked back the material of my nightgown, exposing my right breast. "Billy's knife." I felt the cold tip of something hard against my bare skin. "And Billy's gun. Naughty boy; I wonder if they'll catch him before he kills again."

"You helped him escape off the unit."

"Of course, how else would he have figured it out? We're talking maybe an IQ of 120 or 125, not bad, probably a little less than yours, certainly less than mine."

"Where is he?" I asked.

But before he could answer, I summoned every ounce of my strength in my body and twisted up hard beneath him. My legs tangled in the bedclothes, but I forced my knees up into his middle while bringing down my makeshift club in a roundhouse motion to where I thought his head would be.

The wood connected with something hard and I heard him gasp in surprise. He was momentarily thrown off balance and I scrambled off the bed while he stumbled over to the other side.

There was too much light in the room for me to hide. I looked once at the door and then at the window. I couldn't wait to see where he was. I raced for the open window, and with my nightgown falling around me in tatters, I vaulted out into the chill night. I pictured Josh as a bullet shot rang out and I landed hard on the lawn, jamming my ankle. I didn't think; I ran and I screamed and I screamed and I screamed.

CHAPTER THIRTY

"Help me! Somebody help me!" How long was it that I ran screaming? I banged on the Carvers' door, my immediate neighbors, but they were too slow or too scared. I heard or sensed or felt Rob chasing me into the night.

A shot rang out and a bullet ripped into the flesh of my right shoulder. I ran. All the houses were dark on my street, why was no one waking up? I screamed out, *"I'm being killed. Help me!"*

At least he had followed me, and I knew there hadn't been enough time for him to harm Josh. My eyes darted up and down the street. My legs pumped under my body; I was a fast runner, was he faster? *"Help me. Help me. It's Molly Katz. I'm your neighbor!"*

A porch light clicked on at the Raymond house down the road and across the street. Kevin Raymond played basketball with Josh. I sprinted across the street and heard my pursuer's feet as they landed fast and heavy on the dew-soaked lawns of my neighbors. Two more shots were fired.

I didn't break my pace and I didn't look back. *"It's Molly. Help, Help, Help!"* I heard Rob's heavy breathing in the distance. I was torn. If I headed for the Raymonds' door and it was locked, I knew that I would die in the well-lit theater of their front stoop. The carefully tended hedges would bar my escape, but still it was the only visible response to my pleas.

A deep male voice boomed out from the Raymond house. "Whoever you are, I've called the police. Leave her alone!" I glimpsed a sliver of shadow around the doorframe; someone was standing there.

I raced toward my salvation and prayed that it wasn't an illusion or a trick of the light. A burst of bullets rang out, and still this was the only light that I saw. My bare feet landed hard on the Raymonds' bluestone walk. *"Help, Help, Help!"* For a split second I wondered if they would let me in.

I cleared the stoop in a single bound and landed hard against the wooden door. It gave way and I fell hard into the carefully decorated foyer of my neighbor's house. John Raymond took one look at me and slammed the door closed.

"Lock it!" I yelled, fighting back against the blinding pain and panic that tore through my mind. "Lock the door."

John's face let me know how bad I looked. "What happened?"

His wife, Betsy, yelled down from the stairway. "I called the police again," she shouted.

"The windows. Close the drapes!" I rambled. "Don't let him see you!"

Before they could respond, their picture window exploded under the force of Rob's semiautomatic weapon. I looked at John and felt such incredible horror that I had brought this into their home. But I heard something else too, the wail of sirens.

"Upstairs," John urged. "Can you get upstairs?"

I tried to move, and the pain in my shoulder broke through the adrenaline. Their hallway wall where I had landed was covered in blood and I was mostly naked. I got to my feet and wondered what would happen if Rob made it into the house. Would I be able to jump out another window? Had I just taken the horror out of my house and visited it upon my neighbors?

For the second time that night, I saw the pulsing blue and red lights of the police as they seeped through the gaping front window. John and I froze and waited. I heard the crush of tires on the gravel drive as the first cruiser screeched to a halt. A powerful beam shot obliquely across the front lawn. It played around the jagged edges of the picture window.

There were heavy footsteps and then a knock came at the door. "Police."

John yelled up to his wife. "Betsy, get a blanket for Molly." He pulled off his pajama top and handed it to me. "Here." He averted his eyes while I tried to cover my breasts. The thin cotton fabric of his pajamas was grabbed by my blood and plastered down to my skin.

He unbolted the door and let in the first uniformed officer. I heard another siren and then another. The officer looked at my bare-chested neighbor and then at me.

Betsy Raymond appeared with a brown wool

blanket. "Oh my God, Molly." Tears flowed down her face.

"Mom!" My son's panicked voice shouted from beyond the door.

He's okay, I thought, with a rush of relief, and I sank back to the floor. "Josh. I'm in here."

He pushed past the officer as I tried to hide my injuries beneath the blanket. He looked so young and frightened. How had I let this happen? At least he wasn't hurt.

The air filled with sirens, but my thoughts were slowing down. I remembered the pills that I had swallowed and I felt the sticky blood that pooled beneath my blanket, between my legs.

As a second officer appeared in the doorway, I asked, "Did you catch him?" My voice was weak and hoarse.

"Not yet, ma'am. Do you know who it was?"

"His name is Robert Jeffreys. He's a resident at Commonwealth Hospital." I looked at my neighbor, who had since put a button-down work shirt on over his pajama bottoms. "I work with him," I tried to explain. "He wanted to kill me. He was going to kill my children. Oh my God! Someone has to get to my daughter. He'll go for her next."

The police tried to reassure me. I insisted they call Megan right then and there. I told them they had to bring her to the police station. They handed me the phone and I heard my baby's voice over the receiver. "I'm okay," I managed to rasp out. "Josh is okay. But just do as I tell you. Don't open the door for anyone but the police, make them show you their identification, and then go with them."

My eyes struggled to focus. I had this funny

floaty feeling as the ambulance attendants banged through the Raymonds' front door. My last words before the EMTs pulled away my blanket and I went down screaming with the pain and the blood loss and the barbiturates were to Betsy: "Don't let Josh see. Don't let my baby see."

CHAPTER THIRTY-ONE

I knew that I shouldn't feel this way, but sitting up in my hospital bed looking at the concern on Peter Harris's face was very reinforcing. Also, the soft fuzzy buzz from the morphine didn't hurt things. I now understood how people became addicted to narcotics. Sure, my life had just gone to hell in a handbasket, but at present I felt no pain.

"We think he's still in the city," Peter said, bringing his six-foot-three frame to rest in a bedside chair. The lieutenant came armed with a bouquet of pink, red, and white tulips and a stack of women's magazines bought in the hospital giftshop. I might have wanted something more personal, but it showed breeding and perhaps something more.

"And my kids?"

"Twenty-four-hour supervision for the entire Katz clan."

"An endangered breed, apparently."

"How's the shoulder?" he asked, pointing at the bulky dressing and sling that encased a good portion of my back and left arm.

"Mommy's on dope," I commented. "Can't

feel a thing. And that's the way I like it. I wonder if I should go on methadone after this."

He looked at me with a serious expression and I felt my stomach turn to adolescent mush. I lost myself in the blue-green of his eyes; they seemed to change color, I noted, and I began to look for things in my room that might be offering the greenish tint.

"We'll catch him," he said in a reassuring tone.

"Good. He won't stop until you do. He's very smart, maybe brilliant, and I don't think he wants to be caught. He's very angry at me, which makes him even more dangerous." I remembered too much from last night. Vivid scenes broke through my opium haze and played with a fierce accuracy. They jumbled through my mind, and I tried to focus on the good parts, seeing Josh and hearing Megan's voice on the telephone. "His anger could make him careless," I added. "But careless in the way a wounded animal will fight tooth and nail until the last breath is gone from its body."

"Any idea what motivates him?" Peter asked.

"Sure, lots of ideas, lots of theories." I remembered Rob's rambling speech about power. "He's a sociopath with principles. If that makes any sense. Somehow he figured out that he really doesn't care for other people or their feelings or their lives and worked that into a life's philosophy. Beyond that, he derives pleasure out of watching people suffer. And then there's the game. I think he's done something with one of the kids who was on the unit . . . you wanted to interview him."

"Billy Keene."

"Exactly. Rob helped him escape. But there

was something else. I'm having trouble remembering, but Rob gave the impression of manipulating events with both Garret and Billy. Where is Garret?"

"He's on the psych floor."

"Any idea why he regressed so fast?" I asked.

"Not yet."

"Poor Felix," I muttered.

"Who?"

"Dr. Winthrop. You met him."

"What are you talking about?" he asked, having no idea where my thoughts had wandered.

"He has no residents on the unit. I've been shot up and Rob is a sociopathic killer. Who's taking care of the patients?"

"I see, poor Felix," he concurred.

"Exactly." I tried to reposition my pillow and felt a dull grabbing pain squeeze around my right side. I let out a slow breath, and with my good hand punched twice on the self-administered morphine pump.

"You okay?"

"I will be in a second." I smiled as the narcotic worked its way through my veins. "I think Billy Keene is in a lot of jeopardy. I don't know if Rob'll let him live. Any usefulness he might have had as a fall guy is gone." I looked at Peter. "He will come back for me," I stated. "It's not a question of if but when."

"You're pretty sure of that."

"Yeah. Over and over I got all these narcissistic hits from Rob. He has to come out on top. He'll be back. But will he be smart and wait till things die down and there's no longer police protection, or will . . . I don't know, maybe he'll come and try to put a pillow over my face or shoot some potassium chloride or insulin into a vein? Hospitals are great places to kill somebody. Look at me. I can barely move, I'm doped to the gills, and I've got easy access."

"There's an armed patrolman outside the door. No one will be getting in."

"That's nice . . ." I felt the scratching of my cheek dressing. I had not yet hazarded a mirror. "How bad do I look?" I asked.

"You look beautiful, stoned but beautiful."

There was that flutter again. "You lie," I said with a yawn. The last double hit of morphine had fully dulled the pain from my injuries. Unfortunately, it was also sending me off to sleep. "I'm sorry," I said as my vision clouded and my lids drooped.

"Don't worry." But already his voice was drifting away, and the last thing I saw as I floated off were the clear twin seas of Lieutenant Harris's eyes.

Chapter Thirty-two

I swam in and out of the drug-filled sleep and the floaty dreams of morphine. I should have know better, but I have never been one for pain. Natural childbirth held little sway for me. Indeed, I had not forgotten the pain of those two most memorable events. When I delivered Josh, I lied about how close together my contractions were, to ensure that the anesthesiologist would give me the subdural. Once that poor man began trying to insert the catheter into my back, it became obvious that I was already moving into active labor. Fortunately he was able to hit a moving target.

But here, in these circumstances, I should have known better. I lost track of day and night, up and down, light and dark. Occasionally a physician or a nurse would come to check my intravenous or to take a set of vitals. It was hard to tell who was real and who wasn't as they all got incorporated into my waking/sleeping dreams. At one point I imagined myself on top of a parade float. As the nurse took my blood pressure, my cupped hand started to wave in slow controlled twists like the queen of England passing in her motorcade. I smiled at the nurse and at all the thousands of well-wishers who had come to see me pass. At the time it made perfect sense that I should be in a hospital bed hooked to an intravenous while simultaneously heading up the Rose Bowl festivities. It also went without question that Robert Jeffreys should find me in my weakened state and complete what he had started.

A shower of tiny fragments of ceiling tile landed on my nose. My eyes batted open, was I awake or was I asleep? I passively watched as a square of white acoustic tile moved back to reveal a gaping hole filled with blackness and pipes and a pair of legs that descended quickly into the room and then dropped silently to the floor on rubber-soled shoes.

Where was my voice? I tried to speak, but all I heard was a throaty mumble.

Then it was too late. Rob was on me in an instant, his face inches from mine. The switchblade that I recalled full well was back at my throat. "Oh, Molly, Molly, Molly," he purred into my ear. "You really fucked things up, didn't you? How could you even imagine that I would let you live?"

"Don't," I said, trying to fight through the drugs, not knowing if the blade had already pierced flesh.

"So sorry. But tell you what, you've been such a good contestant that maybe I'll just have you overdose and stop breathing. Then, for good measure, I'll leave a knife in your chest, just so they don't get confused." He pressed down on the drug-delivery button and watched as the red LED readout confirmed that I had gotten my next dose of painkiller. "That's not much at all," he commented. "Let's see if we can't turn this baby up? It's just like the dog lab, isn't it?"

"I never did it," I mumbled.

"That figures. Too bloody? Too cruel? They would have been killed anyway. Just like you, they were a means to an end. How can physicians ever learn unless they have someone live to experiment upon?" he whispered while starting to reprogram the intravenous pump.

I searched for access back to my body; he was moving faster and time was fleeting. My left hand searched beneath the blanket for my right. It found the tape and the tubing that anchored the intravenous line into the back of my wrist. I grabbed and pulled and kept pulling. Like a strand of taffy it came free from my wrist. Sticky fluid dripped from the intravenous and from my open vein. I had the tube in my hand, and now that I had made contact with my neural network I remembered what movement felt like. I started to roll across the bed and away from Robert, still hanging onto the intravenous tubing.

He turned back toward me. "What are you doing?"

And then I found my voice, and like a child on a swing I started to shriek "Wheeeeeeeeeeeeeeeeeee" as I rolled off the bed and fell to the floor, wrapping the plastic tubing around my body as I went. A loud crash followed my descent as the intravenous pole, pump and all, smashed onto the floor. Rob leaped across the bed, knife in hand. He landed straddling my head. His eyes were filled with rage and the knife was raised for the final stab into my breast. Then his head snapped away as the door to my room banged open.

The officer on guard outside my room entered. "Freeze," he shouted. I couldn't see the policeman's face from the floor, just his heavy-soled black shoes from under the bed.

I looked back up at Rob, wondering in a disconnected way if I would live. Had he killed me yet? An odd smile played around my office mate's lips, and then a drop of blood dripped from his forehead and landed on my cheek. There had been a loud noise that preceded that first drip, and certainly it had come before the second droplet and the third and the steady trickle of blood that fell like a warm April rain onto my face. And then he crumpled to the floor, all in slow motion. His knees buckled, he twisted, and then he fell. His head, with the single bullet hole in the middle of his forehead, finally came to rest across my breast. The blood from the tiny network of veins and arteries laced across his scalp continued to flow. His hazel-rimmed eyes were open, but no longer alive. My final conscious thought was, He was someone's baby and now he's dead.

CHAPTER THIRTY-THREE

It had been two weeks since Robert Jeffreys was shot. Life had sealed itself over that bit of strangeness and the conveyor belt of my existence had resumed. Daffodils and crocus had given way to iris and azalea. Otherwise the walk to supervision was unchanged. My right arm was cradled in a sling and my cheek itched and pulled from where the tiny sutures used by the plastic surgeon had been removed. I would always have scars, he had told me, there and on my shoulder. Every time I looked in a mirror I would be reminded of Rob. Those scars would fade. I tried to joke about my dueling injuries, but overall I wasn't laughing very hard.

I cleared the Boston Gardens and quickened my pace. There was much I needed to discuss with Dr. Adams. Not the least of which was this unsettled sense that followed me around. It greeted me in the morning and at times could swell to where I wanted to run away and hide in some dark closet.

Dr. Adams was still in session when I landed in his waiting room. Soft and complicated strains of a Vivaldi quartet were quietly piped into the screened-off room. I fidgeted with his stack of magazines and thought back to my morning on the unit. Everyone was going out of his or her way to be nice. Even Felix had asked me if I was *really* ready to return. What was I supposed to say? That this whole thing had been a huge mistake and that all I wanted to do was stay in bed and wait . . . for what I didn't know. My appetite had shrunk, and while I always had wanted to lose ten or fifteen pounds, I had now achieved that without even trying.

Finally, the door to Adams's office opened. I tried to listen to the conversation with his patient. Apparently, the music was for more than ambiance; it effectively blocked out the words. I sat and waited and pretended to read an issue of *Smithsonian.*

"Welcome back." His voice startled me and I looked up.

"Hi," I said, rising to my feet and watching his expression as he took in my scar and my sling.

"Come on in." He moved aside and I nestled into the familiar chair. It was still warm from his last patient. "Would you like some coffee or tea?"

"No, but is it okay if we talk about the murders and Rob Jeffreys?" I blurted out.

"Good, we should do that."

"You realize that if I talk about it with you, there's a chance that it could wind up in court."

He looked at me with his dark and empathic eyes. "Molly, these days there is precious little that couldn't wind up in court. The important thing is to not let fear of lawsuits and depositions hold us back from doing the work that needs to be done."

"I've never been this frightened before," I stated. "Which is odd, when you realize that I wasn't frightened while Rob was threatening to kill me. It was something other than fear. But now . . . this isn't me."

"Describe it."

"My mind is playing tricks. It won't let me alone. I know Rob is dead, but I keep looking to see if maybe he's following me, like in those horror movies where the killer keeps getting up and going after the heroine. I've been trying to hide from Josh how many times I check the doors and windows at night to make sure they're locked. I'm having my security system changed because Rob was able to bypass it too easily. I'm not sleeping well, I have to force food down, and if someone comes up behind me and I don't hear them, I lose it."

"Like you're jumping out of your skin?"

"That's the one. Even now, just sitting here, I have this awful feeling in my belly." I let out a slow breath of air and tried to sink into the chair. "The strangest thing, and I have to tell you that I have no thoughts of acting on such an idea, but I've even had momentary flashes of crashing my car. In all my life I have never had a suicidal thought, not even during the mess of my divorce. If anything I wanted to kill him, not me. But a couple times now when I've been driving in to work, I've had these awful flashes of crashing the car over a guardrail."

"What about nightmares?"

"Yes. Awful ones where I'm running or falling or being murdered. Last night, after I finally managed to fall asleep, I dreamed that someone was trying to rape my daughter, and the harder I tried to save her the farther away she was. My whole body seems to pump adrenaline. I need it to stop."

Dr. Adams took in the information. I knew that I had crossed well over the established boundaries of supervision, but right now I needed help and some academic discussion about this patient or that patient wasn't going to cut it.

"You're having a post-traumatic reaction," he stated simply.

"I know. That's the strangest thing about it. I know what the symptoms are, I've read about them, I've had many patients tell me about them. But it's like, now I really know, and frankly I'd rather not. My thoughts aren't under my control. It's a struggle to keep on track; if I relax for half a minute I'll be seeing his face and listening to his craziness."

"Tell me what you know about the treatment of post-traumatic stress."

"Well, there's medication, which I don't want to be taking right now. And there's therapy."

"What type of therapy, especially for someone like yourself where the trauma is quite recent?"

"Exposure."

"That's right. You need to go into the heart of the memories that are causing you so much pain. By going over them ad nauseam they will lose their power."

"This is crazy, I sound like my patients. I can't believe what I'm about to say."

"Which is?" he prompted.

"I don't have the time to do therapy. I really

don't." I looked him dead on; Dr. Adams was without doubt one of the most well-respected psychiatrists in Boston. I was asking him a question, albeit in an oblique way, and I wondered if he would pick up on it.

"We can talk about it," he said. "I think you need to."

"I know you're right, it's just there's no one around. I mean bits and pieces of it, sure. But I'm trying to keep the bulk of it from my kids; they're freaked out enough as it is. I actually thought Josh could benefit from seeing somebody, but he's back to basketball and has little interest in rehashing the night he and his mother almost got killed. I can't talk to my mother, because while she'll probably be sympathetic, I suspect the whole thing would get twisted into an if-I'd-only-stayed-married diatribe. I'm sure she would stress how these sorts of things don't happen to married ladies."

"Keep going," he urged.

"It's strange. I'll be sitting here and suddenly my thoughts get pulled back and I start wondering what if? What if I hadn't been able to get out of the house? Or what if he had followed through on his threat and rather than chase me, he could have gone into Josh's room and murdered him, or stalked Megan at school."

"But those things didn't happen."

"I know, but I can't stop thinking about it. And then there's the other stuff. I see Rob, over and over. He was my friend. How can somebody mask themselves like that? I'd known him since we were interns together. What does that say about my powers of observation? Here I'm supposed to help people who are emotionally distraught or damaged to try to heal and I can't even recognize a homicidal killer when he's working next to me. So now I try to think back. What did I miss? There should have been some sign and all I can recall is that occasionally he'd get an angry look around his eyes if I got a question right, or somehow did something better than he did. But he never said anything, and it just struck me as a sort of professional sibling rivalry. And then what about all the patients who died over the years? Now I begin to question some of the on-unit deaths. Were they all from natural causes? I remember Rob said something about the dog lab . . . did you have to do that?"

He nodded.

"I refused. I couldn't see the point of bringing in dogs from the pound for a bunch of medical students to experiment on and eventually kill. It seemed the wrong message to convey to a group of young doctors. The administration was very upset with me. They had all sorts of arguments about needing to toughen us up and how else could we gain first-hand knowledge of living systems? It was barbaric and I refused. But then I think about Rob with all of his patients, most of them did well with him as their doctor, but was he doing other things? Like with Garret and Billy Keene, he was using them to cover his tracks."

"How is Garret?"

"He's slowly pulling it back together. We're not sure but it looks as if Rob had been injecting him with something to worsen his psychosis, possibly

Atropine. Peter . . . Lieutenant Harris told me that they found a wide array of pharmaceuticals in Rob's apartment."

"And that's where they found the other boy?"

"Right, apparently Billy Keene had lost his usefulness. The coroner said that he had been pretty heavily drugged, so maybe he didn't suffer. And even there part of me is thinking, and this is awful . . . maybe that wasn't so bad. Billy was not a good kid, and he was already heading into the prison system. In a lot of ways he and Rob were alike. Except Rob managed to mask his nature and Billy's rage was right on the surface. That's the problem in a nutshell."

"What is?"

"Our predictive abilities. We can look at someone like Billy Keene, who already has a long arrest history and has committed many acts of violence and we can say with some authority that this is a kid who will likely continue to be violent. If someone like Billy said that he wanted to kill you, I'd listen. But with Rob, how could anyone have known? And then the bigger issue, if there is one of him, there is likely to be more." I stared at the floor, trying to select from the tumble of my thoughts. "I went to the funeral," I stated.

"Which one?"

"Rob's."

"Interesting."

"To say the least. I was still doped up on Percocet and I knew that his parents didn't want me there, but I had to go. I needed to see where he came from."

"What did you learn?"

"Not much. They were clearly mortified that their son had done such a thing. His stepmother and father were stone-faced through the entire ceremony. I knew that he was a judge and she was a homemaker. Rob never said much about them, then again I never asked. I think his real mother may have committed suicide."

"Really?"

"He mentioned something about her being crazy and about a rope. I'd actually like to know for certain. Anyway, they cremated his body, so there was no graveside ceremony. The funeral director gave the eulogy, which was short and said little. I even shook his parents' hands in the receiving line. I said 'I'm sorry for your loss,' and they said, 'Thank you for coming.' That was it. Granted it wasn't the time and the place for more, but there weren't that many mourners, maybe a dozen. And there was no mistaking who I was."

"Maybe that's part of your answer," he offered.

"What is?"

"His parents gave nothing away through their faces or actions. Beyond that, one can't say much. That's what is most striking about Rob, no one saw it coming. It could be that he learned early on to present a neutral or pleasant face to the world, regardless of what he felt inside."

I considered his comment. "The first time he tried to kill me he said stuff about growing up. He seemed to have a well-defined code of conduct. Everything he did was thoughtful and premeditated. As opposed to someone like Billy, who just went off and started lashing out at people.

Although even with Billy, I got a sense that he could let things stew. Rob didn't think there was anything wrong with killing people. That may be the scariest piece. He was completely detached from a sense of morality, that it's wrong to hurt people."

"Are we born moral?" Dr. Adams asked, "or is that something we learn?"

"I think the latter."

"Right. What you describe is that Rob had some code of behavior, but that it was very different from yours or mine. The question becomes how did it evolve? What part of it came programmed in his genes and how much came about through circumstance, environment, and training?"

"I'm so tired of nature versus nurture. It seems like we keep coming back to a circular argument."

"Maybe not. Let's make some hypothesis from the information you have—as with any hypothesis we can be wrong. And with Rob being dead, this may never be provable. But children learn in a variety of ways, and much of it is in response to their parents or other caregivers. Let's work backward. We know that Rob ended up with a personality structure that was incapable of feeling true empathy for others. More than that he derived pleasure from seeing others suffer and die by his hand. We see narcissism, sadism, and a great deal of creativity—he nearly got away with it. From everything you've told me, he might well have set up Billy Keene to take the blame for your murder. The other key factor was his overall success and accomplishment. He was a resident who had gone to a prestigious medical school, but what is so fascinating is this gaping discrepancy between his social exterior and what he revealed to you about his internal life. What if that internal life were an accurate mirror of his home environment growing up?"

"I'm not following."

"Like I said, this is just a hypothesis, but it is based on my experience in working with people and seeing the difference between the social masks that we all wear and the internal world of our thoughts and emotions. You said that Rob's father was a judge. From the outside that has got to be one of the most moral and responsible roles one could imagine. He is a dispenser of the law."

"And?"

"What if the father were not a moral person? But instead wore the mask of respectability to advance his career, while revealing another side of himself at home? How is a child supposed to reconcile such a discrepancy? And if his mother did commit suicide, depending on how old he was at the time, you can pretty much assume that his emotional development suffered."

"But how can you make such an assumption? We know nothing about the father. I could see the truth about having a parent commit suicide. That strikes me as the ultimate betrayal."

"Correct, again we can only work with hypothesis. But looking backward, if it is a question of learning and nurture, Rob had to get it from somewhere. People with strong narcissistic tendencies migrate to professions like medicine, business, politics, and the law. Now, most of us manage to keep our more self-important impulses tied to a greater good. But for some, and this is where the notion of malignant narcissism comes into play, this never happens. What is a child to make of a father whose job it is to dispense justice and morality, but then comes home and talks and behaves toward his family in a manner that is totally opposite to his position at work? Not to be funny, but we see this with politicians all the time. That in front of an audience they present believable personas with empathy and fiery charisma, but then we learn from their behavior that the image doesn't always match the reality. Children are observant, and Rob must have been a very bright kid. If my hypothesis were a correct one, what effect might this have on the growing child?"

"He'd have a hard time developing a clear sense of right and wrong."

"Exactly."

"And if it's not a question of nurture?" I asked.

"Personally, I think it is. But if not, then we're back to the bad seed and a child born missing a key component of his humanity."

"No heart."

"No soul." He smiled.

"It feels good to talk about this," I said. "I think I'll see his face and hear his voice for the rest of my life. I've never been that close to dying before. But if I can somehow get a handle on things, it'll be okay. And then there's the other part . . ." My voice trailed off.

"What other part?" he asked.

"Now this is embarrassing. It hasn't been all

bad. In fact, aside from almost getting killed, I don't think I have ever been as invested in a case. And I can't quite figure out what the attraction was." Instantly I imagined Lieutenant Harris, but that wasn't the whole story or even the biggest part of it.

"Are you disappointed that it's over?"

"Part of me is. I wouldn't want to go through being attacked again, but before that . . . the investigation was exhilarating."

"More so than working at the hospital or at the clinic?"

"I feel guilty saying this, but yes. I've been looking after people for a very long time. I've been a single mother for most of my adult life. I was a nurse and now I'm a doctor. All of which are fine things to be, but even with going into medicine I did it because it seemed the logical choice. As I look back, a lot of my reasons for going into nursing had to do with my mother. After my divorce I threw myself into medical school as a sort of now-or-never option. But in a lot of ways things have changed in medicine. There's not a huge amount of autonomy left to doctors. In a year I'll be finished with my residency and will probably go right into a hospital-based job."

"You don't sound thrilled at the prospect," he commented.

"I'll make more money," I admitted, trying to tease apart my internal uneasiness. "But I look at what the physicians are doing and it's a lot of doc-in-the-box jobs."

"What about private practice?"

"Possibly." I stared at the floor. "I have always

been a practical person. I've had to out of a variety of necessities. But for the first time I found myself doing something that truly fascinated me. Like even today talking about Rob and trying to look back and think of how someone turns out like him. That's interesting. Or going to Whitestone and seeing how minds get formed into a variety of patterns and personalities. Maybe I'm twisted, but it's fascinating."

"Then what about going into forensics?"

It was a simple statement; it made me pause. "That's another two years, isn't it?"

"You can do it in one if you start during your last year of residency."

I pictured my mother. She was already confused as to my decision to become a psychiatrist; I couldn't imagine what impact this would have on her. "I'm almost forty," I admitted.

"What does that have to do with it?"

"Shouldn't I be finished with school by now?" I chuckled and shook my head. "Sometimes I think I have more in common with my teenage daughter than I do with people my own age."

"That might not be such a bad thing. At least you're able to be genuinely interested in learning. Most people shut down and get smaller and smaller lives as they hit middle age. What you're contemplating is moving toward an interest. I can't see the fault in that. What you describe with a hospital-based job will pay well, but it could also reduce you to a fast-paced prescription pad who sees patients one right after the other every ten or fifteen minutes. That kind of work gets real old real fast."

I shuddered at the image and knew he was right. "But is it practical?"

"In what sense?"

"I don't know much about it. Do people make a living at it?"

"Absolutely. In fact forensic psychiatrists bill at a much higher rate. But there's a whole different set of issues. You have to be willing to travel, to go to court, to deal with lawyers on a daily basis. It's much different work. You're not treating patients, but evaluating suspects and defendants. I do a certain amount of it, and you're right, it is fascinating."

My ears perked. "How much of it do you do?"

"A few cases a year and I supervise the forensic fellows."

"So that and a private practice?"

"Right. We need to stop," he said reluctantly. "I hear my next patient outside. But we can talk more about this next week."

I looked at the clock and saw that we had gone ten minutes past the hour. I thanked him and headed out.

My head swam with possibilities. I looked at my watch and knew that I was going to be late getting back to the wards. Plus I had to respond to an angry voice mail from Mrs. Ryan. She was insisting that I see her and Jennifer at my clinic tomorrow; she told me that Jennifer was pregnant. From the tone of her voice, it sounded as if she blamed me.

I quickened my pace and reasoned that it wouldn't make a huge amount of difference if I were another five minutes late. My path veered and I headed toward the administrative offices for the department of psychiatry. If what Dr. Adams had said was correct, then I needed to make a decision fast. Another year wasn't bad. And what would it hurt to at least pick up an application?

The scars on my cheek tingled and my shoulder throbbed as I bounded up the marble steps two at a time. I felt the excitement of possibility and with a clarity that I have felt few times in my life, I knew that I had turned a corner and was headed in the right direction.

CHAPTER THIRTY-FOUR

As I sat with the Ryans, it was almost as if things were back to the status quo. Indeed, Jennifer was pregnant and it was no accident. Her mother was enraged and insisted that she have an abortion. Jennifer accused her mother of wanting to murder her unborn child. It was almost normal. If it hadn't been for the fact that Dara had intercepted me with a small brown hand-delivered envelope I might have been more fully present with the Ryans—or with any of my other patients who came and left like clockwork.

"One of the patients brought this for you," Dara informed me. "He said it was from his doctor and that it was very important."

I thanked her, stared at it, and then dropped it into the outer pocket of my briefcase.

At five o'clock I cleared a space on the desk and slit open the tape-encrusted envelope that read: "To be delivered to Dr. Molly Katz in the event of my death." I thought about Peter Harris and how he would be upset with me for not contacting him first. I couldn't deny recognizing the handwriting, but why bother. The letter was addressed to me, and therefore I would open it and I would read it.

I wondered if perhaps Rob's final gesture was to send me a mail bomb, but I didn't think they could come that thin. My heart pounded as I pulled out the sheets of lined paper and looked at the pages of his obsessively neat print.

I laid the pages across my desk, and stared at the printed words. Do you really want to do this? I felt fear, but I read the letter.

Dear Molly,

I am dead. I enjoyed our evening together and was sorry that it ended as it did. True, I was angry with you: after all you should be dead. More to the point, I must rethink my career goals. The cat is now out of the bag and I suspect Felix will not want me returning to the unit. Suffice it to say that tomorrow is another day.

So why the letter? Why entertain the possibility that I will fail? Shit happens, and last night brought that home. If I am dead you will need to be clear on several points.

There will be much speculation as to why I did what I did. In death, I can at least set the record straight. Last night you wanted to hear my story—it was not the time nor the place. I realize that it was a ploy to buy time, clever girl. It was while I was disemboweling Billy Keene that I thought to write this down. First, let's talk about blood. Even Garret understood, in his own crazy way, that blood is special. I've known this ever since I was a small child. Here again, be careful with the psychological autopsies. It's so easy to go astray when you let the Freudians into the house, and we both know that the department is filled with the desiccated old farts.

As I removed Billy's spleen and squished down on that thick cushion of blood, I tried to articulate the magic of bringing death. What makes this feel so good? And yes, I thought of my mother. Don't think me sick, but there's a womblike feel to crawling around in someone's gut. It's a similar warmth and steamy comfort, but that's not it.

I am certain that my father has effectively shut down any possibility of finding out about my early life. He's quite a self-important fellow who will see no advantage to sharing family secrets with the police. Perhaps that is my greatest motivation for writing this. Father and I have never seen eye to eye and the last thing I want is for him to control my death. I realize that if I am dead you will want to know how I got to be who I am. I enjoyed our conversations on this subject. Let me be clear, I am a creature of nature, but would like you to have enough of the facts to make your own determination.

Did you ever wonder why after three years together you knew nothing about me? I always thought that women were the more perceptive sex. But I'm quite accomplished at being Rob, just Rob. It's amazingly simple to adopt an attitude of the invisible man. Most people, you included, are too self-absorbed to notice all the lives that swim around them.

So let me give you the salient points of my life. In the words of David Copperfield, "I was born." Not to head for the melodramatic highlands, but my first memory is from the age of three when I found my mother dangling, quite dead, from the rafters of our six-car garage. Father has a thing for Mercedes, and I think she was trying to get his attention. I hold a few random images of her but nothing that compares to her one-shoe-on-and-one-shoe-off final pose. Don't imagine that this makes me sad or unhappy. Perhaps it did at the time, but I don't think so—it just was.

Father remarried and I grew. There were no sibling rivalries—there were no siblings. There were no horrible traumas or acts of abuse. So when you review my case, please do not try to tag me as some awful victim of this or that lecherous aunt or uncle. There were no strangers in raincoats asking me to play with their bunny. I was not beaten; I went to private schools. I dated and I had sex with girls. I was normal and looked like all of the other sheep. How strange to write about myself in the past tense—kind of like ghostwriting, don't you think?

But I digress, and we need to hit the meat and potatoes. Why kill? Are you ready for the heady truth?

Why not?

Few things in life give pleasure. As a child in the woods behind my house, I learned about blood. It's that simple. The joy of watching a life pulse out on a thick river of blood, of staring into a pair of eyes as the lights go out. It's better than sex. But the images and the feel only last so long, as with men who become addicted to pornography and constantly need fresh images to fuel their fantasies. The feel of blood dissipates. Whether it's a squirrel or a cat or a person. Even now, where bits of Billy still cling to my fingernails, I feel his death slipping from me. He's the first man I've killed—a boy really, but the thrill is just as good. Another point to keep straight after the fact, nurses were just a theme. I'm sorry that I can't offer a more insight-oriented explanation. It was a first run. I can't even begin to tell you how many years went into the planning of Helen's death—my first human kill. That it was Helen is unimportant. I figured that I would start with nurses, simply because of availability. I enjoyed watching the unit unravel as I started to pick off the staff. I know you're not supposed to shit where you eat, but it was fun. I think that my next series will be lawyers. I've been watching that Sonja woman and I find myself wondering what it would be like to see myself in her eyes as she bleeds to death. It makes me tingle.

Well, I hope you never get this letter, but it

has been fun to write. One last point, which is an important one. Invariably you will want to know whether or not I felt remorse. That would be a no.

Think about me often.
Your friend and colleague,
Rob

✂

☐ **YES!**

Sign me up for the Leisure Thriller Book Club and send
my FREE BOOKS! If I choose to stay in the club, I will
pay only $8.50* each month, a savings of $7.48!

NAME: _____

ADDRESS: _____

TELEPHONE: _____

EMAIL: _____

☐ I want to pay by credit card.

☐ **VISA**   ☐ **MasterCard.**   ☐ **DISCOVER**

ACCOUNT #: _____

EXPIRATION DATE: _____

SIGNATURE: _____

Mail this page along with $2.00 shipping and handling to:
Leisure Thriller Book Club
PO Box 6640
Wayne, PA 19087
Or fax (must include credit card information) to:
610-995-9274

You can also sign up online at **www.dorchesterpub.com**.
*Plus $2.00 for shipping. Offer open to residents of the U.S. and Canada only.
Canadian residents please call 1-800-481-9191 for pricing information.
If under 18, a parent or guardian must sign. Terms, prices and conditions subject to
change. Subscription subject to acceptance. Dorchester Publishing reserves the right
to reject any order or cancel any subscription.

GET FREE BOOKS!

You can have the best fiction delivered to your door for less than what you'd pay in a bookstore or online. Sign up for one of our book clubs today, and we'll send you *FREE* BOOKS* just for trying it out...**with no obligation to buy, ever!**

If you love fast-paced page turners, you won't want to miss any of the books in Leisure's thriller line. Filled with gripping tension and edge-of-your-seat excitement, these titles feature everything from psychological suspense to legal thrillers to police procedurals and more!

As a book club member you also receive the following special benefits:

- **30% off all orders!**
- **Exclusive access to special discounts!**
- **Convenient home delivery and 10 days to return any books you don't want to keep.**

Visit **www.dorchesterpub.com** or call **1-800-481-9191**

There is no minimum number of books to buy, and you may cancel membership at any time.
*Please include $2.00 for shipping and handling.